Kathryn Adams

Summer Shadows
in Grondère

An Alpine tale of mountains and mysteries

THE GONDÈRE SERIES SO FAR
Death in Grondère
Summer Shadows in Grondère

Ski4All Wales is a genuine charity and you are warmly encouraged to get to know it better on http://www.ski4allwales.cymru and www.facebook.com/ski4allwales

Cover design: Kirstie Swinnerton

This book is dedicated to my family. Thank you for your unflinching love and support.

This book is also dedicated with love to Tanya who has worked so hard on it. Everyone should have a Tanya in their life: I am extremely lucky to have had mine since the age of seven.

My thanks to Bethan Drinkall and the team at Ski4All Wales for allowing me to use their real names, Lindsay Reuss for inspiring the character of Poppy, Lee Hammond (and Jack) for inspiring the character of Johnny (and Louie), Tommy for inspiring the character of Tommy and Chris Jones for kindly agreeing to let me do what I liked with him and call him Humphrey.

Whilst these wonderful people provided a starting point for my characters, no one should mistake the originals for the creations they inspired: my characters have minds of their own and I cannot always control them.

Wayne Hills reads maps the way you and I read novels and his own writing sparked the idea for Lucy and Poppy's hike in the Bernese Alps. My thanks to him for allowing me to pirate his article, for helping me adapt his route to fit my story and accompanying me through the Gemmi Pass.

My gratitude also to Marcus Bratter, who continues to allow me to use him as the inspiration for Malcolm McDonaghue and his son Sebastian. Marcus' monthly articles on wine can be found in Verbier Life Magazine. www.verbierlife.com

One

What are men to rocks and mountains?
                    Jane Austen, *Pride and Prejudice*

'Nope, can't see any action.' Poppy squinted back towards the waterfall ledge they had stood upon earlier that morning.

'Oh, hang on, something coming.'

'Yes?' asked Lucy eagerly.

'Flock of tourists, unidentified Asian variety,' grinned Poppy.

'Oh.' Lucy was crestfallen.

'They must have finished filming. Probably some of those Russians we saw with big cameras at the hostel last night messing around,' Poppy offered consolingly. 'Sorry I missed the excitement.'

'Thank goodness we got there early anyway, we'd have just been in their way,' Lucy laughed. 'The funicular hasn't even opened yet. I was warned it could get a bit busy up here.'

'Agreed. It looks like we just missed rush hour.'

They donned their rucksacks and started their hike.

Poppy and Lucy, as they had planned following their harrowing winter season, had ventured beyond Grondère and were starting to explore other parts of Switzerland. That morning they had left their hostel early and hiked up to the ledge at the side of the famous Reichenbach Falls down which Sherlock Holmes and his arch enemy Moriarty had plunged to their deaths. It had been lovely to have the place to themselves and see the scene which had inspired Sir Arthur Conan Doyle to use it as the setting for killing off his sleuthing hero.

They were now on the opposite side of the falls, having climbed above them, crossed over the narrow bridge

1

spanning the highest point where the waters tumbled over the edge and clambered down to the arrival station of the rickety little funicular which would soon be bringing the sightseers up the easy way. Poppy had stopped to look at a rare fern and missed the dramatic re-enactment scene that Lucy had seen taking place on the very spot where she and Poppy had been standing just half an hour earlier: two men grappling on the ledge in front of a big camcorder on a tripod. Lucy had turned back up the path and called Poppy to come and look, but by the time Poppy had appeared from the undergrowth and focused on the right spot, the filming had stopped and the men and camera had gone.

'Still, shame you missed the excitement.'

'Personally, I'm quite happy to be away from the action for a change.'

Lucy laughed.

'Point taken.'

It was true: Poppy had been under a cloud for so long and, for the first time in forty years, she was seeing the world afresh, under a new glow, and part of that renewal was her growing friendship with Lucy Wilson. Despite an age difference of over thirty years, the two women had so much in common: their love of hiking, wildlife, botany; that they could wander through the Alps together for hours and not give a thought to anything else. Having lived in Switzerland most of her adult life, Poppy was a fount of knowledge – from the smallest gentian flower to the largest bird of prey; she was happy to have such a willing and enthusiastic pupil with whom she could share her store of learning.

Lucy Wilson was an athletic young woman in her late twenties with long auburn hair, big green eyes and golden skin. She had come to the ski resort of Grondère in Switzerland for one winter season and found she had more good reasons to stay than to leave at the end of that first season. One of those reasons was the friendships she had made: not just with Poppy but her housemates, Tommy and Eddie and her ski buddies, Sally and Jodie. She had fallen in love with Switzerland, the mountains, the lifestyle and, the following season, she had also fallen *in* love. Her natural beauty and spirited personality had caused the Swiss detective leading the investigation into the murder in which she had briefly been implicated, to realise she was exactly the woman for him and Lucy had decided she rather liked him too. Having now completed two winter seasons in Grondère, she was at the beginning of her second summer.

Following the murder enquiry which had somewhat tarnished their winter, Lucy and Poppy had resolved to go exploring together and see some of the glories Switzerland had to offer beyond the canton of Valais where they lived. And so here they were, in the Bernese Alps.

They planned to hike from their starting point of the Reichenbach Falls at Meiringen to Kandersteg, finishing at the Gemmi Pass. This walk would take them below the north faces of the majestic peaks of the Eiger, Mönch and Jungfrau.

'I have to confess though, I thought there would be more water.'

The Reichenbach waterfall was in the centre of a V-shaped rocky gorge with inward-tilting layers of limestone cliffs either side and lush vegetation above. The water twisted its way down the corkscrewed funnels it had carved over the centuries, but the ledge from which the famous two were reported to have tumbled, seemed a long way from the spray.

'From all the illustrations I've seen, I imagined it would be thundering down from all sides, especially with the late melt,' Lucy continued.

'I read somewhere that they had diverted some of the water to a hydro-electricity plant. You're disappointed?'

'No. The place definitely has atmosphere: the drop is so steep. Crossing the footbridge above I felt quite nervous. I was just surprised that the ledge was not that close to the waterfall, but, if some of the water has been re-routed, that would explain it.'

It was mid-June and Lucy and Poppy's first hike of the summer: it was doing them both good to distance themselves from the scene of their misfortunes for a while, and put things into perspective. They had a big trial coming up at the end of the summer where they would both be witnesses. Neither of them was looking forward to it. They had agreed to go 'unconnected' for a week so they could escape completely and told everyone likely to call them, not to. Alain, Lucy's boyfriend, had managed to extract a promise for her to switch on her phone at the end of each day in case of emergencies.

'I can't believe how liberating being offline is,' Lucy asserted.

'It is,' Poppy agreed, 'but I'm staggered at how many times a day I reach for my phone. I'll have a lot of posting to do when we get home.'

A talented photographer, Poppy posted pictures of the natural treasures she found in the mountains most days on social media. She had developed quite a following and was always getting requests to identify various flowers from friends and strangers alike. She was finding it harder than her younger friend to disconnect.

'I think I might start leaving my phone at home more.'

'I don't think your young detective would like that. He wouldn't be able to track you down.'

'Yikes! Don't! What an awful thought.'

'Just joking. I think you have to switch it on to allow yourself to be tracked.'

'Well, that's one option I won't be investigating.'

'Nevertheless, I still think it's worth keeping your phone on you, just in case you get into trouble.'

'I guess. But I think I've had enough trouble now for a lifetime. What else could happen?'

As they walked, they merrily chatted about the various Sherlock Holmes mysteries they had enjoyed and compared them to the real-life murder cases they had been involved in.

'I used to think the Sherlock Holmes *and* Agatha Christie stories were very clever but contrived and unrealistic,' continued Lucy. 'But now I know the evil that ordinary people can do without anyone ever guessing, I see that they're not so far off.'

Poppy laughed.

'I'm not sure I would class Carla Sturridge as "ordinary". But you won't let it distort your view of the world will you Lucy? I would hate to see you make the same mistake I did and get all hurt and resentful.'

One of the things Poppy loved about Lucy was her determination to always believe the best of someone unless proved otherwise. It was an attitude which had nearly cost Lucy her freedom when she was duped into becoming the main suspect in a nasty murder case.

'Don't worry,' Lucy reassured her. 'That warped woman isn't going to stop me seeing the world through rose-tinted specs, if that's what you mean.'

'It is, and I'm glad to hear it.'

'Do you really need those walking poles, Popps?'

Poppy had come equipped with very professional-looking retractable walking poles attached to her backpack. Lucy had never seen her use them in Grondère.

'They just give me a bit of extra stability when the going's a bit slippery.'

'Oh.' Lucy felt a bit sorry that Poppy should have reached the age where she needed propping up and felt thankful that she herself could scale the hills like an ibex.

They had a long day ahead of them: another reason for their early start. From Meiringen, home to the Reichenbach Falls, they planned to head beyond the usual halt for this trail at Grindelwald and overnight instead at the Alpiglen mountain refuge. They were determined to have their supper up on the mountain prairie in the shadow of that great giant, the Eiger, beneath whose north face they would walk the following day.

From the Reichenbach Falls, they headed up an ancient cobbled path through shady woodland. The going was very slow: Poppy, thrilled to be in a new microclimate, was finding numerous botanical rarities in the shoulder-high, fern-covered bank to their left and Lucy began to worry about them already being behind schedule.

It was a damp, dull start to the day and, as the woodlands opened out, there, framed in a classic postcard shot, dark green forest slopes either side, stood the Wellhorn and white-capped Rosenlaui Glacier, rising above the lifting clouds. The climb levelled and continued winding through the narrow valley where every half hour the distinctive three-note horn of the postbus could be heard sounding as it cornered the blind bends of the narrow, twisting road below. Cows lifted their heads briefly from the long grass as Poppy and Lucy passed, looked at them dismissively and returned to their grazing. By midday, the sun had battled its way through the clouds and now shone upon the long, straight stream which rippled towards them. It sparkled gaily at them as they headed upstream to Rosenlaui, a crossing of ways, where they stopped for a picnic lunch. Lucy looked at her watch and ascertained that they were already two hours behind schedule. She was worried because she had booked all their overnight stops and it was very bad form to not show up at a mountain refuge. They were small and popular and it was mean to waste a slot. But then she looked across at Poppy, happily munching on her bun and some cheese she'd bought at a farm they'd just passed.

Who are you to impose your timetable on Poppy and the mountain? Lucy told herself. We will get there when we get there and if we don't, we have a tent. We can phone the refuge: they'll understand that we underestimated our walking time.

As they lunched, they admired the beautiful belle époque Rosenlaui Hotel in front of them with its curious architecture; it seemed to be composed of three different houses joined together. After lunch they popped inside to have a nose around the ancient interior and use the loos. The Polish waitress, who had seen them picnicking as she served the swanky tables outside, grinned at them and looked the other way.

Over lunch, a sign had puzzled them.

'What do you think the *Rosenlauigletscherschlucht* is?' Poppy asked.

'I'm not sure, *gletcsher* is glacier isn't it, but I've no idea what a *schlucht* is. It could be the "mystical gorge" mentioned in my hiking guide.'

'Mystical, that's an interesting choice of adjective.'

'Probably a translation blip. Yes, it didn't say anything else and I have to confess, I didn't factor it in to the hike.'

And so, having spent a penny in the hotel without spending a centime there, Poppy suggested they go and have a look at the *schlucht*.

'It says it's only five minutes' walk.'

'Okay.'

In fact, it lay directly on their route. They wandered up to a little cabin where a man handed them a flyer in German. 'It looks worth investigating. Look here, it says it's a World Heritage site.'

The man told them that the visitors' circuit took about 45 minutes.

Lucy shrugged inwardly; spending their first night in a tent was beginning to look inevitable. But, Poppy was right, it did look intriguing. They handed over their entrance fee and went through the little wooden gate.

Within five minutes it was clear that they had stumbled across something extraordinary: *schlucht* clearly meant canyon. Water was hurtling through a cleft in the mountain with a force that made the Reichenbach Falls look like a trickle.

A metal footpath led them into a series of dark, man-made tunnels cut through the rock, the force of the water throbbed through the rocky floor and spray filled the air. Entirely alone, the women clung tightly to the metal handrails in utter amazement. They could not hear each other speak: the roar of water was deafening. On and on, they progressed through narrow, glistening walls of limestone which twisted and turned above them as water gushed from pools and ledges through the natural cathedral it had sculpted deep in the rock. It was spell-binding and they took their time, eventually surfacing at the top in a state of awe.

'Well, I get the "mystical" bit,' laughed Poppy, 'that water was giving off one hell of a charge.'

Lucy agreed.

'How close did we come to missing that?'

'Too close.'

'So how come we've never heard of it?'

'The Swiss probably don't think it's anything special. After all, the whole flipping country's one huge World Heritage site.'

'If I was Arthur Conan Doyle, I'd have killed off Holmes and Moriarty there. Wow!'

'Yes, staggering!'

Back at the little cabin, they rejoined their path. Passing the spiky Engelhorn range to their left, and then the sleeping figure of the Klein Wellhorn, the women hiked through deep, green woodland where dark moss carpeted the ground, dead stumps and rocks interrupted only by occasional drifts of ferns. As they climbed, the landscape opened out to views over verdant meadows. Waterfalls splashed down the dark walls of the mountains and ephemeral streams, dispersing the waters of the late melt, glittered down the sides of the valley.

The mountains looked so benign it was hard to believe the dangers they held, but, with the retreat of the glaciers and melting of the permafrost, it was becoming harder and harder for geologists to predict when entire slabs were likely to splinter off. There had been some spectacular film footage taken of entire mountainsides cascading like an avalanche and it was only a matter of time before someone was caught by surprise. The geologists couldn't supervise every rock face in the Alps but they kept the main thoroughfares under careful watch.

They continued their ascent when suddenly the peace was broken by a loud sound from above: startled, they looked up, hoping the mountain wasn't about to come crashing down upon them. At first they could see nothing then suddenly, far above them, a hole burst through a block of ice perched high on the Wellhorn and started spouting water like a whale. It was the strangest sight, an impressive demonstration of the power of melting water and yet slightly comical at the same time.

'Wow! The noise must have been the water breaking through the ice wall,' Lucy surmised.

Poppy didn't reply, she was busy with her camera, already wondering which magazine she might be able to sell it to. Eventually the waterspout dwindled to a gentle waterfall and they carried on, excited to see what other treats nature had in store for them on this trip.

It was a gentle climb to the top of the Grosse Scheidegg pass and as they arrived on the crest they had their first view of the sombre north face of the Eiger: dark and forbidding, the sheer wall that had, for centuries, offered an irresistible and often fatal challenge to alpinists from across the globe. Mesmerising, it dominated the green bowl of the valley beneath it where Grindelwald sat basking in sunshine – just out of reach of its great shadow. The afternoon was drawing to a close as they looked down at the steep path criss-crossing the road down to Grindelwald. The sun, though it turned golden everything it touched, was starting to cool and, beyond its reach, long shadows formed.

'I think I was over-ambitious on the timing. We're never going to make Alpiglen tonight. Maybe we should look for a bed in Grindelwald.'

'Don't be ridiculous,' laughed Poppy. 'We can't afford it and we've walked quite long enough: we'll walk along the road and hop on the mountain bus; then there's a little train goes to Kleine Scheidegg. It'll take us almost to the door of the Alpiglen mountain hut. Last one's just after 5pm. It's not cheating, you know!'

Sure enough, at the next bus stop the timetable told them that they had only ten minutes to wait before the bus arrived.

Grindelwald was chocolate-box pretty: ancient wooden chalets with panelled windows, nestling amongst green hills, surrounded by steep mountains with snowy peaks. It was everything the tourist expected of Switzerland – which is probably why it was full of them.

'Thank goodness we're not staying here,' Lucy exclaimed, horrified at what to her seemed like a heaving mass of humanity but which was in fact just a recent coach arrival.

'No,' Poppy laughed. 'It's a good job this lot all need en-suite bathrooms.'

Fortunately, the wonders of the Swiss public transport system had them back up in the mountains where they belonged and at their destination in plenty of time for supper.

Lucy laughed out loud as they sat on the little train.

'Did you know all along that we would be ending the day resorting to the train?'

'No, but your timing did seem a little tight and it's always good to have a Plan B!' Poppy winked.

Lucy grinned. She still had so much to learn from Poppy.

Exhausted but happy, they sat outside until sundown, admiring the mountains and airing their feet and boots. Tucking into a generous portion of macaroni cheese and a glass of white wine, Grondère seemed a world away, even though it was only a few valleys beyond. Here, everyone spoke Swiss German and neither Lucy nor Poppy could make head nor tail of it.

'It took us three and a half hours to get to Meiringen by train and yet in a helicopter it would just be a short hop,' Poppy speculated.

'No wonder the Swiss do everything by helicopter!' Lucy added. 'Once, on the way to the airport, I even saw them trimming the trees by the motorway with this huge saw dangling from a helicopter.'

'You made that up!'

'Did not.'

'Well, I've never been in one. I'd love to for the experience but not as part of a rescue. I've seen plenty of injured skiers being loaded and that's one helicopter trip I can live without.'

'I agree. I know one guy, got stuck on a ridge without his skis and had to be airlifted.'

'Lucy, we *all* know a guy who got stuck on a ridge without his skis. Grondère is full of them!'

'I guess.' Lucy grinned. She quickly checked her phone. Alain had just dared to send her an emoji kiss to which she replied with an emoji sticking out its tongue and quickly switched off. No communication, that was the deal and she was going to stick to it.

Alain saw the text and smiled as he headed for an early night.

Poppy and Lucy sat out under the stars on the terrace of the mountain refuge and reflected on and digested the events of that winter.

———————————

The first affair had involved a murder at a charity function at La Grande Cour hotel where Lucy had been a waitress for the table of hotelier, Malcolm McDonaghue, the murder victim. For a couple of weeks, Lucy had mistakenly been suspected of having served the poisoned soup. She had, in fact, been deliberately framed by Malcolm's ex-wife, Carla Sturridge and his daughter, Genna McDonaghue, who were now in prison awaiting trial for his murder.

The second matter concerned an older mystery which had resurfaced in the spring. Genna Hobbs-Davison, a close friend of Poppy's, had gone missing in the 70s. The discovery of her body the previous autumn had removed a cloud of suspicion and doubt that had hung over Poppy for almost forty years: it had put her in the clear. The police had concluded that the death had been a tragic climbing accident until Lucy had sown the seed of doubt in her detective boyfriend's mind by asking if, in light of what they had since discovered about the ruthless killer streak in Carla Sturridge, she could also have been connected to Genna's death. Particularly as Carla had subsequently married Genna's boyfriend of the time, Malcolm McDonaghue. In May, Lucy's questions had led to an unexpected turn of events and now a second murder trial was being prepared at which Poppy would be a major witness.

Two

Every murderer is probably somebody's old friend.
                    Agatha Christie, The Mysterious Affair at Styles

That May had been a dreary one and Grondère had been shrouded in mist for most of it. On the first clear day after the snows had melted, Capitaine Alain Dupertuis of the *Police judiciaire* had sent a team of climbers and a drone to the site in the Col des Fantômes where Genna had been discovered, trapped in a deep rock crevice.

A team of climbers slowly lowered themselves into the crevice where Genna's body had been found by Lucy's housemates, Tommy and Eddie, and their climbing guide, Danny, the previous autumn. Another team ascended the cliff face from which Genna must have fallen whilst a technical team measured angles, heights and distances of impact. A drone hovered above, guiding the search teams. Capitaine Dupertuis watched on, determined that this time no stone would be left unturned. He knew it would be a slow, painstaking process as forty years of mud lay on the crevice floor and conditions were cramped for using the metal detector and spades. He had taken a risk employing so many resources on a hunch but when a man who believes in justice feels he may have been instrumental in its denial, his belief in himself can only be redeemed by its restoration.

He stood at the foot of the cliff and looked around him. The Col des Fantômes was a truly beautiful spot; a narrow gorge, hemmed in by cliffs on two sides and a floor covered with thickets which hid deep fractures in the rock floor. At one end of the gorge was a treacherous cliff drop and it was over the edge of this cliff that Genna had fallen to her death and rolled into a crevice just beneath where her body had remained wedged for four decades. A dry spell the previous autumn had caused the soil and vegetation covering the crevice to lose their grip and expose Genna's mountain tomb.

This hidden spot in the middle of nowhere, a three-hour hike from Grondère, was rarely visited and totally unspoiled. He knew that Lucy and Poppy were planning to visit it in the summer to pay their respects to Genna. He shook his head smilingly at the thought of this odd couple of English women, hiking about the Swiss mountains looking at flowers.

A shout went out from the team in the crevice. He scrambled over just in time to see a hand reaching over the edge, passing out a small backpack.

He watched as a member of the forensic team carefully brushed off the mud and sand. The colours had faded and the fabric was shredding but the contents looked as if they could tell them something. It had clearly been quite a sturdy bag.

Of course, Genna would have had a backpack; how come they hadn't thought of looking for it before?

Throughout the day a pile of ropes followed, a harness and some carabiners.

It was becoming very clear to him that someone must have thrown them into the crevice. Genna's skeleton had still been in its harness which meant there had to have been a second climber present.

Lucy, you little terrier, he thought to himself. Your instincts were spot on.

Resolving, however, not to tell her anything just yet, he rang his colleague, Inspecteur chef adjoint Blonnay.

'This crevice is a regular treasure trove. You'd better take this case on: I don't want to have anyone saying I have a conflict of interests.'

After a detailed analysis of the new finds, it was agreed that someone must have deliberately covered up their presence: a body can roll into a crevice but the climbing equipment would have been scattered, not all neatly at the bottom of the same crevice. The second harness confirmed it: Genna Hobbs-Davison could not have been alone when she died. There was one further anomaly: her backpack contained a leather folder with a map detailing the date, times and distances of her planned walk and climb and a leaflet for a talk to be given in Savigny by a local mountaineer on the following day with the bus times. The dates did not tally with those the police had been working with for forty years. It was time to reopen the Genna Hobbs-Davison case.

Later in the month, on a morning when spring was still struggling to make its presence felt, Poppy had received a surprise visit. When the doorbell had rung, Poppy wrinkled her brow trying to think who it could be. People rarely just 'popped round' in Grondère and she knew most of her friends, including Lucy, were currently away. Once the ski season was over, everyone disappeared, either on holiday or back to their home countries to see their families and to satisfy whatever ex-pat yearning they suffered from: pork pies, pickled herring, biltong. Poppy no longer made the annual pilgrimage back to her home country, she had long ceased to think of it as home and, since the death of her parents, she no longer felt anyone needed her pitching up just because she couldn't go skiing. She was well aware that it was the busiest time in the academic year, with exams looming; she would rather go back when her friends and family were less stressed. The spring flowers didn't seem to mind that it was a damp and foggy time of year, and she would have been sorry to miss them. Besides, if the weather got too oppressive it was only a couple of hours' drive over the border to Italy where Poppy could always find warm lodgings with a warm friend.

No amount of speculating would have led her to expect to find Inspecteur chef adjoint Blonnay and Inspectrice Sylvie Jacquier standing on her doormat.

'Oh!' she exclaimed with dismay before she could stop herself.

The two police officers were not the slightest bit fazed by their chilly reception and stood there, smiling politely.

'May we talk to you for a moment?'

'Yes, of course,' she stammered. Flustered, she cleared a space amongst the clutter where she was busy cataloguing her latest photos.

'Tea? Coffee?'

'Coffee would be wonderful, thank you,' replied the senior officer who, despite his fascination for the English language and all things connected, had never been able to acquire a liking for tea.

She went through the coffee-making process in a blur.

What the hell can they want with me now? she wondered. Poppy's experiences with the Swiss police had, until recently, not always been agreeable and she felt the vestiges of unjustified guilt resurfacing.

'I know it's a long time ago Madame Smythe, but can you remember what you were doing on the day before Genna Hobbs-Davison went missing?'

'The day before?'

'Yes.' Inspecteur chef adjoint Blonnay gave her the exact date in the 1970s, one day prior to the day when her dear friend had gone missing.

'Thank you,' she replied, a little tartly. 'It is a date etched on my memory.'

'I am sorry,' he replied, jotting down the lovely word 'etched' in the little notebook he now always kept on hand when he was interviewing English speakers – the Grande Cour murder had been extremely fruitful in new vocabulary. 'But I have to be precise. It is important.'

She looked at him, puzzled. In forty years, no one had ever asked her what she had been doing the day before Genna disappeared.

'Actually, I remember very well. It was quite an eventful day and, because it happened the day before, I have always connected the two events.'

'Please go on.'

'I was woken at 7 o'clock in the morning by the Swiss Italian lady who lived in the flat above hammering on the door. She had gone into labour early, her husband had left for work, he was on a building site and no one in his works office was picking up the phone. I didn't have a car and so I hammered on the door of all the other flats but no one answered.'

Here she hesitated, she knew she was about to confess to an illegal act. Inspectrice Jacquier saw the hesitation and guessed the reason.

'Any prescription period for a minor offence must surely have expired by now, Madame Smythe.'

Poppy smiled.

'So, I "borrowed" a car from another neighbour and drove her to the hospital in Savigny.'

The officers looked at her with undisguised admiration and raised eyebrows.

'That old wire coat hanger trick,' she shrugged. 'My dad taught me, in case I ever lost my car keys, and a mechanic I knew showed me how to hotwire. Useful skills in those days but sadly obsolete now.'

'And then?' asked Inspecteur chef adjoint Blonnay managing only just to keep a straight face.

'Oh yes, I delivered Madame Castelli safely into the hands of the maternity nurse and waited until her husband appeared. He was dropped off by a work colleague in a work vehicle and had no car so I promised to wait for him in a nearby bookshop. I wandered around town and he turned up at about 2 o'clock, totally euphoric, shouting that they had had a little boy who they had decided to name Gianluca. I had been browsing through a beautiful book on Swiss flowers and as I went to place it back on the shelf he seized it from me, went to the till and bought it. I could never had afforded it otherwise at the time. Look, he wrote in it.'

She went to her shelf and took down the book. Forty years on, it was well-thumbed, a bit battered and faded but the bold flourish of handwriting on the flyleaf could still be read clearly.

Grazie mille! Alberto Castelli.

The young policeman held it in his hands for what seemed like an age: he could hardly believe it. He handed it to Inspectrice Jacquier and a big smile spread across her face: M. Castelli had also obligingly added the date.

'I'm afraid they were also a bit cooler towards me after Genna disappeared and some rumours implicated me.' Poppy could not keep a certain bitterness out of her voice. 'I lost touch with them when they moved. I think they're still around though.'

'I grew up in Grondère, Madame Smythe,' beamed Inspectrice Jacquier. 'Gianluca Castelli was my maths teacher at secondary school, his dad's retired now but he was on the local council.'

'And so your whereabouts,' Inspecteur chef adjoint Blonnay lingered on the word, a new one he'd been practising, 'on that day, can be easily verified by a respected member of the local community.'

'Can you please tell me what is going on? Why are you asking me about the day before?'

'Recently, as soon as the snow had melted, Capitaine Dupertuis sent a team of climbers, a drone camera and digging equipment to the Col des Fantômes to do a more thorough search. He felt that, in light of later events, we had maybe missed something when the body was first found.'

Poppy began to catch the sense of excitement.

'And you did discover something.'

'I cannot give you any detail, but, having seen this, I can see no reason not to tell you that we now believe that Genna Hobbs-Davison died a day before the day we previously believed and that we no longer believe she was alone.'

Poppy sat down, crushing some prints in the process but too shattered to notice.

'You think she was murdered.'

'We do not *know* anything but there are some unexplained elements that we are looking into.'

'So, you needed to check my "whereabouts".' Poppy suddenly realised how close she had come to being suspected again. She gave them a resentful glare. The look was not lost on him but Inspecteur chef adjoint Blonnay was far too pleased with himself to feel any sense of shame.

'I am very pleased, very pleased indeed,' he affirmed (he had heard BBC journalists using 'indeed' excessively in this way and thought he'd try it), 'that you can give such a good and verifiable account of your movements on that day.'

'Because …' grinned Inspectrice Jacquier, knowing she shouldn't but thinking it was about time the Swiss police cut Poppy some slack, 'Madame Sturridge cannot.'

After Poppy had showed the officers out she sat on a seat by the window. She rested her aching head in her hands.

So, Lucy's suspicions had been correct, Genna's death may not have been an accident.

All those years, she thought, all those years of suspicion and, if they're right, not only was I in the clear all along, but someone else should have been accused.

She did not linger on the injustice of it, she wondered instead what the police had found to make them so sure that Genna had died a day earlier. Desperate for someone to talk to, in Lucy's absence, she called Johnny. Half an hour later, Johnny sat nursing a coffee on her balcony.

'Jeez, Poppy. This thing just won't go away.'

Johnny had lived in Grondère for almost as long as Poppy and remembered the time when Genna had gone missing and Poppy been indirectly blamed.

'Genna's certainly making up for lost time,' she agreed. 'It feels like everything is slowly unravelling.'

While events were unravelling in Grondère Alain Dupertuis left his colleagues untangling the Genna Hobbs-Davison case and headed for the hills above the resort. He gave the heavy front door to his mountain cabin a good shove. He had to acknowledge to himself that he felt a certain excitement: it had been closed up over the winter and he was eager to move back in. Lucy was back in the UK and, much as he loved her, he was happy to have this moment to himself. He had lovingly restored his mountain home from its dilapidated state and the physical labour had brought him comfort after the death of his father. He wasn't originally from Grondère but his mother was from the region and had moved to Grondère when she was widowed. Out hiking one day he had come across the old mountain hut for sale and bought it on the spot. It had turned into a major rebuilding project, and the concentration on learning skills such as carpentry and tiling had absorbed his thoughts and helped him through his grief.

It was ridiculous, he told himself, to feel so emotional about a building. But, of course, it wasn't just a building, it was his creation, his sweat and tears: it had absorbed his sorrow and yielded him solace.

He opened the shutters, let the light flood in and looked around. It looked completely undisturbed since the last time he had been up to check up on it in late winter, when he had unexpectedly encountered Lucy and shown her around: his hard work to seal all possible mice entry routes had succeeded. He went from room to room, opening all the windows, enjoying each time the light burst into the darkened rooms. Specks of surprised dust floated in shafts of sunlight, looking guiltily for some quieter place to settle.

There remained some rooms which he had not yet fully completed: he hadn't worked out what he wanted to do with them and so he gave these rooms a cursory clean and then closed the doors on them for the time being.

The chalet sat high above Grondère and was accessible only by a mud track in summer and for most of the winter it was not accessible at all. Over the morning he unloaded supplies and clothing from the quad bike he had hired for the weekend, did a bit of cleaning and then brewed some fresh coffee and took it out onto the south-facing deck he had built in front of the lounge. He sat and relished the view over the sleepy ski resort and down into the valley, sitting in a sodden cloud of mist. The sense of satisfaction and peace was tangible but not complete: he realised that something, or rather someone, was missing – Alain Dupertuis was ready to share.

He picked up his phone and called Lucy. He took great pleasure in holding out his phone to scan the view and the inside of the chalet, all opened up and waiting for her.

'It looks happy to be woken up!' she exclaimed. 'Mind, the weather doesn't look much better than here.'

'It feels good to be back. No, spring's been particularly gloomy, so far.'

Small talk, heavy with unspoken words of love, two people, each just happy to hear the other's voice. Alain felt the pleasure of having someone with whom he could share the mundane, someone who understood his pleasure in letting in light and breathing life into his sleeping home. They didn't talk for long, he didn't tell her about the one clear day the month had granted him and the discoveries it had revealed in the Col des Fantômes: she would hear it from Poppy soon enough.

Three

"Is the spring coming?" he said. "What is it like?"...
"It is the sun shining on the rain and the rain falling on the sunshine..."
Frances Hodgson Burnett, The Secret Garden

On the first day of June, Alain picked Lucy up from the train station in Savigny. Back at the beginning of May, as soon as the ski season had ended, Lucy, like most of the seasonnaires, had gone straight back to her home country to catch up with family and friends. After almost a month away her eyes were glued to the window as they climbed up the winding roads towards Grondère. Entering the valley below the resort she looked up to see the clusters of chalet roofs and windows twinkling in the sunshine and the familiar peaks in the background. After the village of Pattier (otherwise known as Ex-Pattier due to its large international population) at the foot of the final climb, each familiar hairpin bend filled her with a growing sense of excitement and homecoming. They raced back to Alain's summer chalet, perched loftily above the resort, passing the little chalet she shared with Tommy and Eddie on the way.

'You can see them tomorrow,' he laughed as he saw her looking at it. 'I have a bottle of *Petite Arvine* on ice and it (and I) can't wait.'

'I have something special for you too,' she laughed. 'A haggis.'

'That I can wait for. Is it still living?'

'No, but if we don't get it into a fridge soon, it may spawn new life.'

'You're not selling it well.'

'I don't mind eating it all myself, if you're that squeamish.'

'Huh, some gift!'

Lucy just laughed and looked across at him fondly. She still couldn't quite believe that this tall, handsome young man loved her, but then Lucy had no understanding of her own many attractions. 'It's good to be back,' she said.

She smiled down with pleasure on the wide, sunny bowl of Grondère now below them. Their climb finished and levelled out as they took the dirt track that hugged the contour of the mountainside. Lucy looked hungrily up at the steep inclines surrounding the ski resort that had become her home. She could not wait to put on her walking boots and lose herself in the mountains.

'*The mountains are calling*,' she declared. Alain completed the well-known John Muir quote – that unofficial creed of mountain lovers:

'*And I must go …*'

'Why aren't you leading this enquiry?' Lucy asked Alain a few days later when she heard from Poppy about her visit in May from Inspecteur chef adjoint Blonnay and Inspectrice Jacquier. 'It was your idea to send the climbers back to the gorge. Is it because of me?'

'It is,' he smiled. 'I took myself off the team because of my relationship with you and, indirectly, Poppy. However, I can assure you that Inspecteur chef adjoint Blonnay is extremely competent and never hesitates to consult his senior officers when he needs guidance.'

She looked at him appraisingly.

'I see. So you can keep an eye on the case without any fear of being accused of having a conflict of interest. Very Putin-esque.'

'Thank you for that most flattering comparison.'

'But Poppy's in the clear?'

'I cannot comment,' he grinned, aware that Lucy was craftily digging for information.

She glared playfully at him.

'Okay. I can't comment on any other potential suspects but you have no need to worry about Poppy. Her alibi is one of the best I've ever come across.'

'And Swiss,' she teased.

'Most satisfyingly Swiss,' he agreed.

The poor weather in May had meant that the *inalpe* had been delayed and Lucy got back just in time to watch, from the balcony of the little chalet she shared with Tommy and Eddie, small herds of black Herens cows being escorted up to the mountain pastures. There they would form larger troops whose dominant females would lock horns to establish the hierarchy of the herd over the summer months. It was a gentle, natural process which local farmers had turned into an annual sporting event that Lucy and her friends had enjoyed in April but now the cows indulged freely in their unique democratic process on the hillsides before settling down to a summer truce. The jangling bells of jousting cows in the mountains accompanied by the squealing whistles of marmots, announced loudly that summer had finally arrived.

The Alpine flora, having been a little delayed by the cold May, seemed to all burst into bloom upon Lucy's return which coincided with the arrival of June and warm settled weather. The grazing meadows were rich in flowers: a multitude of yellows – buttercups, daisies and dandelions – danced in the new grass.

Gentians of all forms lit up the mountains. Large, tall yellows and reds punctuated the meadows and smaller varieties lit up the higher slopes with their vibrant blues and purples. Some were so tiny that an unobservant hiker would have passed them by, but Lucy's sharp eye saw them all and loved them for their quiet but confident beauty. She walked every day and rejoiced at the long summer days ahead. But first, she had a job to finish.

'I'm glad I've got you back.'
Sally, Lucy's best friend, hadn't been able to afford to return to her native Australia at the end of the ski season and had been desperate for Lucy's return.
'Mind you're looking a bit thin!'
'I have lost a few pounds,' Lucy confirmed, 'despite gorging myself on pies and fish and chips. It must be my northern metabolism.'
'You're not sick or … anything?' Sally looked at her tummy pointedly.
'Oh jeez, no, I just seem to burn off the carbs of British stodge better than Swiss stodge,' Lucy joked.
'It's all that rushing around you did, trying to see everyone,' Sally smiled.
'Yes, and pleasing no one,' grimaced Lucy.
'I'm sure you did, really. Anyway, now you're back, Tommy can fatten you up with his nice healthy salads.'
'Do you love him for him or for his cooking skills?'
'Hmm, good question. The cooking is definitely a factor.'
The two friends chuckled, happy to be together again, talking nonsense.
They were sitting in the lounge of the little chalet which, since Tommy and Sally had formed a couple, Sally now spent a lot of time in too. Sally, who was a bit of a wine buff, was helping Lucy make sure she understood the origins and uses of the different varieties of grapes. As Sally told her about the qualities of the unique grape

varieties found only in Valais, Lucy pored over the pages for Malcolm McDonaghue's book, sorting them into their final order: every available surface and piece of floor was taken up. Malcolm had been working on the book prior to his murder and Sebastian, Malcolm's son and Tonita, Malcolm's former fiancée, had asked Lucy to complete the book for them as a tribute to Malcolm.

Lucy had set aside the first two weeks of June for finalising the text before sending it to the printer for the first proof which would then go to Sebastian and Tonita in New York, for their comments. After that she was due to go hiking in the Bernese Alps with Poppy and then she wanted to really focus on learning for her first set of mid-mountain guide exams which she was due to take at the end of the year

'Eddie and Émilie seem to be getting on really well,' Lucy chattered casually as she turned the pages.

'Yes, she's been here quite a lot while you've been away. I think she's good for him, she's much more outgoing than he is.'

'I'm happy for them, at least something good came out of that tragedy.'

Eddie and Émilie, like Lucy and Alain, had only been together since the end of the ski season, brought together by the tragic death of Eddie's best friend and Émilie's brother Danny. Émilie was a downhill ski racer and her training with the Swiss national squad took her away a lot, even in the summer.

'I guess this is a crucial period for her.'

'Yup, make or break time, she says.'

'Imagine being that good. I'll never get to that level.'

'You wouldn't want to anyway.'

'No, not dedicated enough. I guess you have to really want it.'

'She has a good chance: she's managed to stay injury-free so far. But the competition's tough.'

'At that level, it's all down to mental toughness.'

'She seems almost too sweet.'

'Don't you kid yourself. Danny once told me she had got both her and his share of the family ambition. He said she wouldn't let anything or anyone get in her way.'

'I hope Eddie doesn't get crushed in her wake then.'

'I think she has a good heart. Besides, every sports star needs a support team and she couldn't have a more dedicated one. He's planning on following her as much as he can.'

'Looking after her for Danny's sake?'

'Nah, I think it's true love, like you and Tommy.'

'And you and Alain?'

Lucy just grinned and shrugged.

'Oh, come on, stop playing it down.'

'Okay, okay, I confess. I'm in love. I think I'm just struggling to believe it's happening.'

She hid her head in the pages to hide the fact she was blushing.

'I've had an idea,' Sally said. Lucy looked at her inquisitively.

'You should visit all the vineyards mentioned in the book, so you can really get a feel for what Malcolm is describing and make sure you are accurate with all the names of the wines and the winemakers.'

Lucy looked at her knowingly. Lucy had already carefully checked the spelling of every word in the book: what Sally really meant was that *she* wanted to visit all the vineyards. However, regardless of Sally's own vested interest, her suggestion was perfectly logical. Of course, all these people would need to approve what was written about them, and what better way of securing their good will than by visiting them personally.

'You're right,' she replied.

Sally looked very pleased with herself. They immediately drew up a list of the ten main vineyards featured in Malcolm's book, searched for their contact information and shared the phone calls.

Over the next two weeks, between drafting and proofing sessions, Lucy and Sally had a glorious time strolling through vineyards in the spring sunshine, tasting the winemakers' latest creations in cellars and verifying they had the most up-to-date information. Day after day, they drove down the hill from Grondère in whoever's vehicle they could borrow for the day, sometimes Eddie's, sometimes Poppy's, into the valley below, along the Rhône valley, adorned by endless terraces of vines on one side and fruit trees on the other. By the end of a fortnight Lucy had almost completed the final document for the printer; there remained just one vineyard to visit.

They had deliberately left what they both felt must be the best, for last. High in the foothills above the Rhône lay a large vineyard, described by Malcolm as 'a jewel', of which the photos were exquisite and of which his words had carried great affection.

They were welcomed in the car park by a young woman who introduced herself as Sandra Guérin, the trainee manager. The vineyard had recently changed hands and Sandra Guérin was being trained by the previous owner to step into his shoes.

It was clear, as she showed Sally and Lucy around, that she was highly qualified, extremely knowledgeable and passionate about her wine.

New fencing had recently been erected to hide the car park and office and a rambling mixture of golden hops, honeysuckle, clematis and native vines had been planted at its base to provide quick and lush camouflage. Lucy saw that in a few months it would look and smell glorious.

Walking through the vineyard closest to the office, Sandra explained her hopes and aspirations for the vineyard and the wines she wished to create. Every so often, as she chatted on, she unconsciously leant down to inspect the vines, then in early leaf, and squash the odd ant. She then showed them the office buildings, grabbed a couple of open bottles of white wine from the fridge in the tasting room and led them uphill. They wondered where on earth she was taking them but, as they reached the very highest row of vines, overlooking the vineyard and the flats of the river plain below, they entered the most enchanting spot imaginable. The slopes ended abruptly against a sheer cliff wall down which spurted a glistening waterfall. The water fell into a shallow, clear pool where a clever sluice system similar to the mountain *bisse* irrigation system controlled the flow of water into the sun-baked soil where the vines sat. The pool itself was in the shade and there, in a small nook, where no vines would flourish, someone had planted a small Japanese-style garden with Japanese maples, moss and tall grasses. Tables, armchairs and statues had been carved from old tree stumps and ornamented with ancient, gnarled vines.

Lucy gawped at it in admiration.

Sandra smiled, 'Beautiful, isn't it?'

'Truly.'

'M. Mayoraz the previous owner built this over many years. We come here at the end of the day to rest, talk things through and, of course, have an *apéro*.'

Sally was equally, if not more, enamoured.

'And the water … '

'Is, of course, the secret behind our fat, juicy grapes,' laughed Sandra.

A fast friendship formed between the three young women as they sat and sipped on their wine, watching the red sunlight fade to dusk.

At the end of the following day, Sally drove Lucy down to the printer in Savigny where she handed over her proofs and her USB key with the PDF for the preparation of the first proof. Her job done, Lucy headed up to spend the weekend with Alain at his place, taking her rucksack for her hike with Poppy with her and leaving the crowded little chalet to Eddie, Tommy and Sally for the rest of June.

Four

The awful power of those rocks as we crept under their beetling walls made one tremble as they irresistibly forced upon the mind thoughts of the end and the upheaval of all things.
Jemima Morrell, *Miss Jemima's Swiss Journal*

Nature in Switzerland in mid-June was in a hurry: the weather was glorious and settled In Valais the fruit blossom that had brightened the winter-dulled floors of the valleys had blown into the Rhône, leaving behind swelling apricot buds. Lucy and Poppy were in the Bernese Alps on the second day of their hike. Everything seemed to glisten with water gushing down from the melting mountain snowfields. Fields and trees were lush and green with spring water and constant sunshine.

Sitting outside the rustic refuge nestling in the prairie at the foot of the Eiger, dipping croissants into bowls of milky coffee, Lucy and Poppy watched as the sun burnt off the cloud cover, to reveal a glorious view of the mountain, without a single person in sight. They had a lighter day ahead of them, and were both excited at the prospect of new discoveries.

They set off in buoyant mood, following the sign marked 'Eiger Trail'.

Within what seemed like the shortest time they were traversing beneath the north face of the Eiger, some 1,700m below its peak. They had read that evening in an old book they had found in the refuge about the Eiger's *Mordwand* or 'death wall' which had defeated so many alpinists.

As she looked up at its sheer cliff, Lucy found it hard to believe that anyone had ever wanted to climb it, let alone succeeded.

'Fantastic!' uttered Poppy, stopping to look up at this legendary face and touch the darkened limestone. 'But,' she added, 'that doesn't quite capture it, does it?'

'No,' Lucy replied frankly. 'There are just some things you cannot describe. Tommy once asked me to describe the feeling of riding powder and I realised how poor my words were.'

'Yes, you're right, I feel verbally inadequate right now,' Poppy laughed. 'It seems to generate an almost emotional charge, and a simultaneous magnetic pull. Loads of writers have tried to describe the lure of the mountains, their beauty, their attraction and although some have got pretty close I think you really have to be here to feel it.'

When planning their hike, they had considered taking the little cog train which disappeared into a dark tunnel in the Jungfrau and resurfaced at the highest station in Europe, but the late thaw with the certainty of snow still covering the higher paths (and the cost of this popular tourist attraction) had caused them to decide against it and restrict themselves instead to the lower reaches of the Bernese Alps. Poppy had done the trip many years earlier in bad weather and seen nothing of the famous Aletsch Glacier.

'We'll save the high peaks for settled weather,' Poppy had said.

'And when I've been paid for editing the book,' Lucy had laughed.

Once they were able to drag themselves away from the Eiger Trail, they scrambled up the sunny high trail along the ridge of the Kleine Scheidegg where they finally had a complete view of all three great peaks of the Bernese Alps: the Eiger, the Jungfrau and the Mönch – a mighty wall of rock which held their gaze as they walked.

Descending through the woodlands down to Wengen, an unusual sound caused Poppy to stop still. She cocked her head.

'Listen!' she hissed.

Lucy listened. She heard a melodious warbling sound she hadn't heard before.

'It's beautiful, what is it?'

'Really, Lucy, your birdsong recognition skills are appalling, you'll need to work on that.'

Lucy grinned; she was working towards her mid-mountain guide qualification and, with Poppy, she was getting the best possible tuition, even on aspects that weren't in the exam.

'So? What is it?'

'A golden oriole, duffer.'

'Wow.'

'It's worth a detour to try and see it, it doesn't sound too far away.'

'We have loads of time, let's try.'

They headed into the woodlands and spent an hour chasing the melodious song of the elusive bird, heads craned towards the treetops, but to no avail. Once or twice they imagined they saw a flash of yellow in the forest canopy but Poppy, ever-pragmatic, knew when to give up.

'We'd better get back onto the trail now, we've given it our best shot.'

'It's so frustrating,' Lucy exclaimed. 'We can hear it but every time we get close, it seems to call from further away, as if it's teasing us. It's too high and well-hidden.'

'I think it's a ventriloquist,' agreed Poppy. 'Sorry, I shouldn't have got you so excited: in my forty years in Switzerland, I've only seen a golden oriole twice.'

'Really?'

'Really. This is not the first time I've been on a "wild golden oriole" chase.'

Lucy laughed at the term.

'Well, our wild oriole chase has taken us well off-track. I'm quite disorientated.'

35

Poppy got out her compass and made Lucy work out a bearing to steer them back to their original path, taking some recognisable peaks as her reference points.

As they rambled through the undergrowth, compass in hand, the two friends had to fight their way through in parts. Their fruitless pursuit of the oriole had led them into a dark thicket but as they approached the path, the trees thinned out and they came to a glade with a small pool at its centre. Specks of sunlight filtered through and danced on the water and the surrounding brown carpet of shed pine needles. Lucy inhaled the scent of sun-drying earth and foliage with appreciation.

'Oooh, what a beautiful hidden spot. Let's have a tea-break here.'

'You and your tea-breaks! We'll never get to Wengen before sundown at this rate.'

Lucy looked at her pleadingly.

'Oh, okay,' Poppy laughed. 'There is an extremely convenient log over there, just check for ants first.'

As they sat, sipping their tea, a flash of black and yellow flew past their noses and the black and yellow oriole landed on a nearby branch overhanging the pond. The two women kept perfectly still and the bird jerked its head in all directions before landing at the water's edge and dipping its beak to drink. Poppy's arm reached slowly for her camera, she raised it to her eye and pressed her finger on the trigger and kept it there. The whirring of the camera made the bird stop and look at them but Poppy didn't care, she wasn't going to miss this opportunity. The oriole seemed to hesitate, it hopped back onto a branch and warbled its melodic flute-like call. It took another look but, clearly thirsty, it flew back down to the ground, drank again, then took to the skies and vanished into the treetops.

Poppy stood and danced a gleeful jig around the clearing, before sitting back down to go through the photos. There were hundreds and some of them were sensational.

'Clearly a male,' Lucy assessed.

'Well done.' Poppy was impressed.

'I may not know calls but I have studied appearance.' Lucy laughed. 'And that's one call I'll never forget now.'

'Well, I promise you one thing. I'll never refuse you a tea-break again!'

They headed back to the beaten track which would lead them to the resort of Wengen, nestled at the foot of the Jungfrau, overlooking the Lauterbrunnen Valley.

'It's funny, isn't it?' Lucy commented. 'I'm used to thinking that it is small, insignificant birds that have the sweetest song, like nightingales, robins and blackbirds, but the oriole is pretty large and looks and sounds stunning.'

'True, although I have to confess, I've never heard a nightingale in Grondère.'

'Really? Never?'

'Never.'

'Too high?'

'I guess, I've never really thought about it. Although it's remotely feasible, I think that your chances of ever hearing one in Grondère are close to zero.'

The third day of Poppy and Lucy's hike in the Bernese Alps took them deep into the Lauterbrunnen Valley with its vertical walls and many cascading, silver waterfalls.

Above them, bare cliff walls capped with lush greenery rose either side of the emerald meadows and woodlands clothing the narrow valley floor. It was yet another place of immense beauty.

'What never fails to amaze me,' Poppy said, 'is how the scenery can vary so much from one valley to the next, from the heathlands of the Grosse Scheidegg to the rolling hills of Grindelwald to this "Middle Earth".'

'Lauterbrunnen really is a fairytale setting, it's not surprising it inspired Tolkien. We're so lucky to be here.'

'I tell myself that every day.'

'Me too, Switzerland never disappoints.'

'Do you think you're here forever?'

'I haven't really thought that far ahead. I couldn't get a decent job in marketing at home, that's why I decided to do a season. Now I'm hooked. I can't really see myself anywhere else, I think I'd miss the mountains too much.'

'And Alain?'

'I love Alain, but he's not my reason for being here. Anyway, it's early days yet. He might go off me.'

Poppy grinned; Lucy really had no idea what a catch she was.

The mixed forest of broadleaf and conifers they were walking through shone with spring green. Lucy kept stroking the beech leaves as she passed, they were so soft and silky at this stage in the season.

'I'd love a dress made of fresh green beech leaves,' she joked. 'Imagine fluttering and floating in the breeze and reflecting the sunlight like this.'

She shook a branch to illustrate her point.

'Like a little tree fairy.' Poppy smiled at the idea of Lucy dressed in beech leaves. Her Celtic colouring was, of course, perfectly suited to green. 'Maybe an idea for Mardi Gras next year. Didn't you and the others go as roses this year?'

'We did. Now there's an idea. Me as a beech tree, Sally would have to be a eucalyptus because she's Australian – we could shove a koala on it –, and what about Jodie? What tree would she be, I wonder?'

She cocked her head to the side as she thought about it.

'A willow, of course, a tall, graceful weeping willow. Now you, Poppy?'

'You know I'm far too old for fancy dress.'

'But you can still be a tree.'

'Oh no, I know exactly where you're going with this one.'

'You're right, there is only one possibility, a trusty old English oak.'

'You cheeky baggage, I'll give you trusty and old.'

Lucy laughed, 'Sorry, I've now got this image of you wearing dangly acorn earrings.'

They laughed and chattered as they descended through the meadows, brushing against the long grasses dotted with tall ox-eye daisies, yellow knapweed and purple field scabious. They also spotted occasional wild orchids and bright yellow gentians.

'I feel like I ought to burst into song, something like *The Hills are Alive with the Sound of Music.*'

Poppy looked at her askance: she had never heard anyone sing as tunelessly as Lucy.

'Don't worry, Popps, I won't, but I can still *feel* full of song can't I? I mean, if I'm happy inside?'

'Of course,' Poppy replied, 'the injustice of tone-deafness has never occurred to me before.'

'It isn't fair, is it? In fact, it should be treated as a disability, like being deaf.'

'Yes,' said Poppy, for whom the pleasure of singing the entire score of *Joseph and the Amazing Technicolour Dreamcoat* from start to finish under the shower was a pleasure she could not imagine living without.

'I wonder if anyone has ever thought of trying to find a cure for it. Ah well, maybe when they've found a cure for cancer and everything else, it might occur to someone. I wonder if birds suffer from it?'

Poppy gave her a stern look.

'Taken the theme too far? Okay.'

Lucy grinned, shut up and looked over at the rocky trio of the Eiger, Mönch and Jungfrau opposite. Climbing up to the sunny terrace of Mürren, bare grey peaks, some still harbouring deep couloirs of snow, seemed to look down on them contentedly: they looked happy to be free of their winter cladding and basking in the sun.

The trail led them on through lush Alpine pastures, before they climbed a jutting promontory called Bryndli. It was a slightly precarious path but when they reached the crest, they found a little bench where they sat, drank a cup of tea and took in the most stunning views over the Lauterbrunnen valley and the Bernese Alps. Retracing their steps back down to the main path, a little further on through grassy meadows they arrived at their overnight stop: the Rotstockhütte at 2,038m. That evening, after supper, someone got an accordion out and there was a sing-along around a bonfire. Poppy forbade Lucy to sing but she gave a rendition herself of the traditional folk song *The Oak and the Ash* that was well applauded and made Lucy a little nostalgic for her native Northern England.

Day four had them climbing beyond the green mountain meadows to the stony Sefinenfurgge Pass at 2,616m where, as they passed through this small saddle in the ridge into the Kiental they said farewell to the Eiger, Mönch and Jungfrau. It was stony and icy and the women fixed spikes to their boots to avoid slipping down the steep wooden steps that led down the other side of the pass. The landscape as they crossed the remnants of the Gamchi glacier was a grey and stony desert where their spikes were sadly redundant. Poppy was shocked to see first-hand the effect of the rapid retreat of the glaciers.

'I came here fifteen years ago and the river that flows from the melting ice from the glacier above had formed arches, bridges and caves in the ice. It was truly unique and now it's almost all disappeared.'

'It is depressing to think how fast we're losing the ice.'

They trudged on a little gloomily but, soon afterwards, were once more crossing cheerful green fields before tackling the rugged and steep trail up to the 2,778m-high Hohtürli Pass. It was a hard slog up a landscape that turned more and more lunar as they climbed; here they encountered snowfields and donned their spikes once more. The Blüemslialphütte was like nothing Lucy had ever seen: perched on a ridge at 2,840m, from below all they could see was a lone block of stone, perched on a sea of moraine.

'It looks like it's sitting on a giant slag heap,' she said.

Poppy laughed.

'It feels like we're climbing up one too.'

They were helped by countless steps and occasional fixed ropes set into the stony slope. The final steps were so steep it felt more like climbing a ladder, an exhausting final challenge, but worth it as the views when they arrived, just in time for supper, were spectacular.

The refuge had magnificent views of the little-known peak, the Lesteraarhorn. That night a mighty storm broke and they stood at their dormitory window looking out as lightning, thunder and fresh snow assailed its peak.

'I wouldn't want to be up there right now,' Lucy shuddered.

'No, scary stuff: it's as if the entire mountain is an almighty lightning rod.'

'I need the loo.'

'Good luck!'

Headlamp on, Lucy clung tightly to anything she could as she slid carefully over to reach the outside toilets. It wasn't easy in a storm. By the time she returned to the protection of the refuge, despite wearing waterproofs the damp had managed to creep underneath to her clothing. She stripped off and carefully hung her sodden clothing close to the radiators where they would dry overnight.

And yet the next morning the day was fresh and the sky bright blue and the Lesteraarhorn stood quietly composed as if to say, 'it'll take more than that little storm to ruffle my ancient armour.'

'It is a bleak place,' commented their hostess, seeing them looking at it. 'I was offered the post of guardian up there, but it's too lonely for me: it's not a popular peak, army mostly.'

It was easy to see why: the Lesteraarhorn looked like a dark, forbidding pyramid with its steep and featureless inclines clothed in dark green moss, rippled with treacherous veins of grey scree that shone silver in the early morning sun. Lucy shuddered.

'You okay?' asked Poppy.

'Yes, thanks, my clothes must still be a little damp from last night.'

But she lied: her clothes were perfectly dry. She had just had a sense of foreboding that she couldn't and didn't want to explain.

That morning, they zigzagged back down the sea of grey moraine to the narrow ridge of the Hohtürli Pass: the steep path consisted entirely of loose stones and was quite dicey in parts. Poppy was glad of her walking poles and Lucy, concentrating hard on not slipping, resolved to buy some as soon as she got the chance, for she now saw that Poppy was not decrepit – just savvy. The fringe of the Blüemisalp glacier seemed to reach out to them from the left as they clambered down the grey and white flank of the pass. Their surroundings gradually assumed a green tinge and the steep cliffs shouldered a covering of grass. They wound their way down the trail hugging the cliff sides where they smiled to discover each hairpin bend had its own name carved in calligraphy on wooden plaques. By the time they reached the gentler path, the trail's vista opened upon a lush green bowl, edged by cliffs with a glimpse of the beautiful Oeschinensee lake at its heart. They had left themselves a lot of time for this section of their walk because they had been told by Grondère's hiking expert, Hilly, that it was the most beautiful place he had ever been.

He was right: with every step that took them closer, the cerulean blue mountain lake presented a scene of beauty that took their breath away.

'I think this must be what paradise looks like,' sighed Lucy as they stood in awe before the mountain lake surrounded by steep cliffs, with plumed waterfalls cascading into it and pinewoods running along the opposite banks.

'It is truly, truly beautiful,' Poppy agreed.

Rocky walls, curved and folded layers in shades of slate and sand, enclosed the lake, and great slabs of whitened stone sloped inwards to be reflected back in the mirror of blue. At the water's edges, shaly beaches melted into dark green forests of pine that cloaked the gentler inclines. It was a perfect blend of greys, blues and greens that made you want to immerse yourself in it.

'Don't you just want to dive into that lake?'

'I wouldn't if I were you,' cautioned Poppy, 'it's a little early in the season yet, you'd freeze your tits off.'

They followed the path under the overhanging cliffs towards the far end of the lake where they sat on a rock looking back across the lake towards the mountains they had come from. From this angle the dreamy blue water now ended abruptly against a wall of rock – folded, twisted and bent by the earth's movements, eroded by time, the glaciers and the elements, but still the silent lord of the lake. Poppy carefully unwrapped the two crystal glasses that she kept for such moments and opened a small bottle of white wine.

They spent a long time wandering round the lake, and only after Poppy had taken photos from every angle, and Lucy started to have hunger pangs, did they reluctantly continue down into the village of Kandersteg, where they had splashed out on a hotel for the night. Kandersteg was another delight: as they descended, the village buildings seemed to be sprinkled like daisies on the valley floor with the River Kander meandering through the centre like a silver ribbon. The valley was surrounded entirely by glens and towering peaks. Poppy and Lucy were glad they had left themselves time to enjoy it. and they went for a wander before supper. Lucy bought herself some walking poles.

'It's a little late for those, isn't it?'

'I'm investing in my future security: I'm not going to get caught out like that on moraine and scree ever again.'

'Very wise.'

Poppy smiled inwardly to herself but said not a word.

As she lay in bed that night, Lucy closed her eyes and recalled the beautiful scenery she had seen during their first tour of the summer. She tried to impress the images upon her memory so she would never forget them. But, if she did, there would always be Poppy's photos …

———

Happy but a little footsore, the women left Kandersteg early the following morning for the final day of their trek: they had left themselves plenty of time to make it to the Gemmi Pass cable car before 5pm. They were retracing the path of a famous old trading route through the mountains linking the cantons of Bern and Valais. They walked upstream along the winding banks of the river Kander, enjoying the lush and pretty scenery before commencing a gentle ascent into woodland. The gradient increased steadily as they climbed towards Sunnbuël and they were pretty hot when they reached the summit. From there on it was an easy gradual climb and they were able to admire the scenery. It was like nothing Lucy had ever seen before. She was full of wonder.

'What rock is that? Look at those folds! How on earth did those cliffs get to look like that?'

Lucy was right – it was all about the rocks. Suddenly, geology, which had previously seemed to her a fairly dull subject, came to life. Here, deposits of ancient oceans and movements of the earth's crust were more apparent and easier to comprehend than in Grondère: they were staring you in the face.

As they walked through the centre of the high plateau, limestone cliffs loomed above them on either side, where the exposed faces, folded, raised and compressed by the collision of continents, then worn by the glaciers, carried lines, ridges and slopes of moraine reminiscent of the Grand Canyon. This was artistry of no human invention, but the majesty of nature in its purest form. Slabs of rock of every shape and size littered the plateau floor like scattered tombstones and toys. At staggered heights, matted grasses, lady's mantle and various evergreens turfed the cliff ledges.

'Extraordinary!' Lucy gasped.

The colour of the rocks grew darker and the climb grew harder as they wound around the path, hoping around each corner to reach the Berghotel Schwarenbach, one of Switzerland's oldest hotels. Suddenly, as the path levelled out, they turned a corner and there it was, a vast stone-built rectangle, with its back to a mound of crumbling schist, facing the Gemmi and the elements with insolent solidity. The women sat and lunched: it would have been a crime not to.

'This place just oozes history, *n'est-ce pas*?' Lucy commented.

'It's incredible to think of all the famous feet that have passed this way and stood here just like us: Mark Twain, Picasso, Wordsworth ...'

'Really?'

'Yes, there's quite a bit of literature written about the Gemmi.'

'I had no idea.'

'Oh, trust me, once you start digging, there's a wealth of material. Twain is my favourite on the subject, although I see great beauty in the bleakness of the Daubensee where Twain saw only "hideous desolation". And of course, they had to work harder for it than us: no easy trip in the cable car for them.'

Lucy looked at Poppy, fascinated.

'And then there's the less famous Jemima Morrell.'

Poppy told Lucy the extraordinary tale of a young woman called Jemima who had climbed the Gemmi Pass in 1863 on the first Thomas Cook 'conducted tour of Switzerland'. It was a remarkable tale: this young woman and three girlfriends had treated their ascent of the Gemmi – no small feat in the long skirts of the Victorian era – as a bit of a lark and had a snowball fight when they reached the top. *Miss Jemima's Swiss Journal*, only released one hundred years after the trip, recounted, in a jaunty style, how they had walked on glaciers and narrow mountain tracks. Lucy resolved to read it as soon as she could get hold of a copy.

As they continued their walk however, it was the ghosts and echoes of the traders of the past that sparked Lucy's imagination. How hard must it have been to drive your mules over these mountains to eke out an existence. The country folk of Switzerland had been much poorer in those pre-tourism times and Lucy, a sensitive soul, centuries later, felt for their hardship.

Poppy woke her from her reverie.

'By the way, I've noticed that there is one fact on which many of those pioneering writers of Swiss tourism agree, it's that their guides were all half-cut!'

Lucy laughed at this crushing of her idealism of the humble peasant as they rapidly covered the relatively easy ascent through the upper Alpine valley and over the Seestutz crest to their first view of the metallic grey Daubensee.

It was a bleak, barren place in contrast to the picturesque Kandersteg, but Lucy agreed with Poppy: it had its own stark beauty. Deprived of vegetation, the giant mountains of dark, shiny schist tilting inwards towards the lake dominated the lonely scene. Where the fissured layers of schist had broken off, their shining surfaces were smooth and bare: slopes of shattered shards formed skirts of scree all around them and a carpet of grey beneath their feet. It seemed as if no bird or animal resided there but the odd flutter told of hidden birdlife.

From the end of the lake a short ascent gave them a view opposite of the dwindling Lämmeren Glacier on which they turned their backs as they finally reached the top of the Gemmi Pass. Looking down the vertiginous drop, rocky protrusions, thickly clothed in grass, challenged the knowledge that the ancient pathway of the Gemmi lay below. The viewing platform gave them a glorious view of some of the highest mountain peaks in the canton of Valais from Mischabel over the Weisshorn, Zinalrothorn, Matterhorn, Dent Blanche and Mont Collon.

It was the end of a week of emotion and wonder and they both felt slightly sad as they posed for selfies before taking the last cable car down to Leukerbad. As they descended they got a clear view of the climb up the Gemmi Pass. It was an almost vertical zigzag up sheer cliffs: the hairpin bends were strewn with loose stones and looked extremely precarious. Where there was no path, just perpendicular cliff, a man-hewn galley snaked through the rock like a worm tunnel, with a sheer drop to its side – it looked terrifying.

'I feel we've cheated,' Lucy stated.

'I've nothing to prove: I've done it, and once was enough for me.'

I shall come back next summer and climb the Gemmi Pass, Lucy promised herself. If Jemima could do it then so can I.

'Did Mark Twain say anything about having tired legs after he'd done the Gemmi Pass?'

'Don't tell me your legs are tired?'

'Well, yes, they are a bit.'

Poppy exclaimed, 'You should be ashamed of yourself. At your age, I never had tired legs!'

'Really?'

'Really! And I don't have them now.'

'They just don't build them like they used to, do they?'

'So it would seem.'

'Well, I feel totally inadequate now.'

'Never mind, Lucy: what you lack in stamina you make up for in beauty and a trip to the hot springs tomorrow will sort out your tired legs.'

They both burst out laughing at the absurdity of their conversation, confirming the belief of the Swiss Germans sharing the cable car that English humour was completely unfathomable.

That night they slept like logs in the ancient Roman spa town of Leukerbad and the following day they treated themselves to a dip in the springs before catching a bus and then a train home to Grondère, feeling chilled and happy.

'It was a wonderful trip, Popps.'

'It was. I was just thinking about something Mark Twain wrote from his *A Tramp Abroad* that really rings true.'

'And that is?'

'*Even the finest scenery loses incalculably when there is no one to enjoy it with.*'

'Oh, I like that. It's much more special when you can share the glorious things we've seen over the past week.'

What Lucy and Poppy did not know was that their week in the Bernese Alps would cast a long shadow over their summer.

Five

Absurdly improbable things are quite as liable to happen
in real life as in weak literature.
                              Ada Leverson, The Twelfth Hour

Curled up on Alain's sofa the evening after she and Poppy
had returned from their hike through the Bernese Alps,
glass of wine in hand, Lucy was telling Alain all about
their adventures. When she recounted the Sherlock
Holmes re-enactment she had seen he suddenly went rigid.
'Which day was that?'
'Monday morning, why?'
Alain groaned.
'Oh Lucy, why does it always have to be you? A body was
found at the bottom of the Reichenbach Falls on Monday
afternoon. I remember thinking that you would have been
almost at Grindelwald by then. This means it was no
accident and I have an awful suspicion you could be the
only witness.'
Lucy was stunned.
'That's not very funny.'
'No, it's really not.'
'You're going all policeman on me.'
'I can't say anything else Lucy. I'm going to give you a
number, you must ring it right now and ask for Herr
Schmutz. Thank God it's not my case.'

The next morning, Lucy and Poppy were back on the first
train to Bern to give a statement to the Bern
Kriminalpolizei. From the train, they could see the distant
peaks of the Eiger, Mönch and Jungfrau but they could not
muster the same enthusiasm for them as they had felt

during their hike. Talk of murder had taken a little of the shine off their happy week in the Bernese Alps. They were a good two hours in the police station as the police were completely baffled as to how anyone could witness a murder and think they'd been watching a performance.

Lucy's inability to give them a description of either of the men she had seen grappling at the falls, other than one of them was wearing jeans and the other a deerstalker and a 30s-style tweed country outfit frustrated them even further. However, it was clear, as the victim had been in jeans, that the man pretending to be Sherlock Holmes must have been the murderer.

'I was on the other side and I didn't actually see anyone fall. There was a big camera, I just assumed it was one of the many film crews or tourist re-enactments you must get at that spot.'

It was true, thought Herr Schmutz, tourists grappling with each other at the site was a common occurrence and had caused the authorities to install a barrier. Sir Arthur Conan Doyle might have consulted the Swiss police before he killed Sherlock Holmes on their territory. They could have told him that nothing so outrageous could ever occur in their clean, safe country. However, it did bring in the tourists, the film crews and their precious revenue. But now, no thanks to the British author, a real murder had occurred on the very spot.

'And you saw nothing?' he insisted to Poppy.

'No, I was lagging behind: by the time I had located the spot with my binoculars the two men had been replaced by a group of Asian tourists so I assumed that filming was over.'

'So, you also thought this was acting?'

'Yes, why should I think anything else? It's a much more feasible explanation than murder.'

Herr Schmutz was at a loss as to how to respond: at least the Asian tourist sighting enabled him to assess that Lucy was telling the truth and allowed him to pinpoint the precise time of the murder, as the first Japanese tourists had walked up to the site and reached it at exactly the time Lucy had given. They, unfortunately, had met no one. The murder must have occurred half an hour before the first funicular arrival of the day. This meant that the murderer and his victim must also have arrived on foot.

Finally, he gave up and let the women go. He had been advised of their recent involvement with the Grondère murders and had to believe his French-speaking colleagues that they were reliable witnesses, although the Swiss French, especially in the Canton of Valais, were a little too laid-back for his liking.

'The Swiss German police are a bit scary, aren't they?'

'Yes,' Poppy agreed ruefully. 'Shame they don't have nice titles like the *Police judiciaire*. I don't think Herr Schmutz was very impressed with us.'

'No, if we're the only witnesses he's got, we haven't given him much to go on have we?'

'No, although he does now know the time and that it was staged as a Sherlock Homes reproduction to ward off suspicions.'

'But why go to such theatrical lengths? There must be quieter spots to push someone off a cliff.'

'Like the Col des Fantômes, for example?' Poppy raised her eyebrows.

'Ooops, sorry Poppy, I am a tactless cow.'

'It's okay,' smiled Poppy, 'I keep telling myself to get over it, but I think Genna's ghost will always be at my side even though she doesn't haunt me anymore. And anyway, you're right: why pick such a popular spot? There are many less-frequented waterfalls in Switzerland that would have served as well.'

'Ah well, we can only speculate. At least this time, it's nothing to do with us and we can go back to Grondère and forget about it.'

'Indeed. But Lucy, he's right about one thing.'

'What's that?'

'You are a useless witness; you couldn't even tell him if the men were bearded or not.'

'I think I might recognise them if I saw them again but I'm rather hoping I won't. Anyway, Herr Schmutz must know what one of them looks like. He found him floating at the base of the Falls.'

Poppy grimaced.

'So he must. Anyway, now we're in the capital, I have a plan for two country bumpkins who have a free afternoon and hate shopping.'

Lucy gazed ruefully at the Federal Palace: she was a self-confessed and unrepentant nerd when it came to tourism and politics. She had been to Bern the previous autumn with Sally and had already seen most of the main attractions but she had failed to get her visit inside the home of Swiss government; it was too late to visit it that day too. Never mind, she smiled to herself, another time. She asked Poppy what she had in mind.

'A run down to the bear pit, lunch at the old tram depot and then a visit to the rose garden, but before that we're on a mission.'

Lucy was intrigued.

'You remember I told you about that book, *Miss Jemima's Swiss Journal*?'

'Yes?'

'Well I've been trying to find you a copy for your birthday but it's out of print and there are no second-hand copies available on the internet. You can get it in French or German strangely, but not in English. But I've been digging around and discovered The Swiss National Library has a copy.'

An hour later, they were crossing the Kirchenfeld Bridge back into the centre of Bern with *Miss Jemima* on a USB key.

'Extraordinary,' Poppy smiled.

'Yes.' Lucy could only agree.

The 50-year-old book had been waiting for them at the information desk. They had been allowed to take the book and employ some very swanky technology to scan the 112 pages. Nobody had asked them for any identification nor, more importantly, any payment. Poppy had also located Mark Twain's *A Tramp Abroad* and copied the pages relating to Switzerland from that.

'An hour well spent.'

'Yes, definitely going back there. I can't wait to get reading.'

The joy of having obtained so much reading material for free made them bounce down the arcades of the old town towards the other side of the river which encircled the city. As the bells chimed midday, Poppy and Lucy crossed the bridge to the Old Tram Depot, admired the bears ambling around their large enclosure on the banks of the Aare River and treated themselves to a huge lunch which they then walked off in the nearby rose gardens. By the time they plonked themselves down in their seats on the train to Savigny, they had almost completely forgotten the sad reason for their trip to Bern.

———————————

Two days later, Inspecteur chef adjoint Blonnay arrived in the headquarters of the *Police judiciaire* and timidly placed two newspapers from the German-speaking part of the country in front of Capitaine Dupertuis.

'You're not going to like this.'

Capitaine Dupertuis didn't like it. His German wasn't great, but it was good enough to see that someone had been indiscreet.

MURDER AT REICHENBACH FALLS
WITNESSES COME FORWARD

The article revealed that the witnesses had taken so long to come forward because they had thought it was a Sherlock Holmes re-enactment. The Sherlock Holmes theme was explored with relish.

'*Merde!*'

'Precisely.'

'So now, whoever did this, knows that he was seen. I bet he saw Lucy and Poppy too. He was probably staking it out when they were there. They're a pretty distinctive pair. He must have been concerned their presence would wreck his plans.'

'He doesn't know *who* or where they are though. If he did see them, he'll have heard them speaking English and probably concluded they were tourists. I've read it carefully, there's nothing in it to link them to Grondère, or to Switzerland even.'

'Well, we can be thankful for small mercies then. Wait until I get hold of Schmutz!'

The officer from Bern was most apologetic, confirming that he knew exactly who had leaked the information and that the press would not be getting any more: Lucy and Poppy's names would be deleted from all files, both physical and digital, to protect their identities. By the time Alain Dupertuis put the phone down, he was still seething but a little calmer.

'But, I never asked you, why is Mlle Wilson so sure the murderer was deliberately trying to look like Sherlock

Holmes. If she couldn't see his face, how come she's so sure of that?'

'I think she did see his face, she just can't remember it: she didn't know she needed to. As to the Sherlock Holmes bit, she said he was wearing old-fashioned walking clothes and one of those funny hats, you know, like he has in the films – look here, the newspaper has him wearing one: what did she call it? We had to look up the French word. Ah yes, you are going to love this one…' he grinned at his anglophile colleague, whose obsession with the English language led him to keep a notebook by him at all times, ready to jot down new and fabulous vocabulary employed by the native English-speakers they encountered during their investigations, 'a deerstalker.'

Blonnay's face lit up with pure joy.

'Deerstalker,' he repeated the word with relish. 'What a beautiful word, full of poetry and historical significance.'

Alain allowed Blonnay a good ten minutes of internet investigation to uncover the full etymological and historical origins of the deerstalker hat. It was a fruitful one: by the time he decided to call him back to order, his colleague had a screen-full of the objects, manufactured by a firm in Scotland.

'Look at those!' he gestured to the display of curiosities. 'Only the British could have perfected such an object.'

'Only the British could contemplate wearing such a monstrosity!' Alain laughed.

'You are so conventional, Dupertuis, you shouldn't be so easily put off by a little eccentricity. The deerstalker is a most versatile garment: it can be worn with the flaps up or down to keep the ears warm and the peaks both front and back offer the ideal protection in a snowstorm. It is a wonder it has never caught on in Switzerland. Look at this array. Which tweed do you think would suit me best?'

'I can't believe anyone still makes the things, let alone buys them! Blonnay, you are already ugly enough! Don't even dare think about ordering one of those things! I will be demanding your immediate dismissal for loss of reason.'

Blonnay grinned; he had no intention of buying a deerstalker at that time, but he might consider it on his forthcoming trip to Scotland. He quite fancied himself traipsing across the Scottish moorlands pretending he was on the trail of the Hound of the Baskervilles or whatever the Scottish equivalent was. This thought he kept to himself, saving to his files the details of the manufacturer's shop in Edinburgh.

Alain was also keeping a thought to himself: Lucy, in her description, had mentioned the word 'knickerbockers' but he didn't want Blonnay going off on another tangent just yet. He would keep that word in reserve.

Six

The streets of New York I consider more dangerous than the Matterhorn to a thoroughly competent and careful climber.

Annie Smith Peck

Sebastian McDonaghue put the phone down, reeling from the news he had just been given. He stood at the window of his office which looked out over the wall of concrete and glass that was Wall Street. Row upon row of tower blocks crammed together competing to scrape the sky whilst their occupants competed to make money. The dark streets below were filled with darkly clad city workers making their way home, pouring into Manhattan's exit holes like streams of ants retreating into their nest. These were the smaller cogs in the Wall Street machinery heading home. Those making the big money went home in limousines when the streets were dark and empty: Sebastian was one of these.

At one time, it had all mattered to him, this intense, work-driven, competitive environment. He had worked hard to climb the echelons of the American investment bank that had given him that opportunity, but the truth was, it seemed to have lost its magic for him. He had made millions for his employer and himself, he was the head of one of the most successful equity desks on Wall Street, but, since his father's death, he was beginning to wonder why.

He looked at the endless rows of windows stretching out before him. It all seemed so dark and soulless. Those weeks in Switzerland, sorting out his father's affairs and arranging defence lawyers for his mother and sister had unsettled him.

It was the sky he missed; in Grondère the sky was a part of the landscape. In the streets of Manhattan the sky was divided into rows and grids above and between the tall buildings that rose towards it. You had to crick your neck to see it. The wind, likewise channelled, whistled through the brick and concrete canals. Yes, the city never slept, it had a buzz and dynamism like no other place on earth: it was a cultural hub and he was surrounded by some of the brightest and most creative people in the world, but how much time did they really get to apply those talents to any task other than making money.

This latest information was another hard blow. If true, his mother had not only killed his father, but forty years earlier had also disposed of her love rival. It was unthinkable that the woman who had given him life could have such little regard for the life of others: how could such a murderous streak be part of his own flesh and blood. As he stood there shaking his head he remembered his father talking affectionately about his first love, the mountain-climbing Genna, for whose loss the lovely Carla had consoled and, eventually, compensated, and in whose memory his sister had been named.

Hang on a minute, he thought, the extent of his mother's treachery fully sinking in. This means my mother actually named her daughter after the woman she killed; she must have a heart of concrete. This is too awful to digest.

Sebastian kept a bottle of whisky in his office, but he didn't trust himself not to down it in one. Instead, he dragged himself away from the window and tried to concentrate on the task in hand; he had a pricing meeting with his team and then a conference call with the syndicate of banks underwriting a new share issue. Sebastian was having a problem working up his enthusiasm. He knew that his younger team members could sense his disengagement and they were all eager to take his place, but he just found it mildly pathetic.

He knew that this signified it was time to step aside, before someone, sensing a weakness, seized their chance to stab him in the back, discredit him and take his place. He had seen it happen to many before him and it was always preferable to leave before you were pushed or made a mistake and had to leave in disgrace. The standard announcement 'leaving to dedicate himself to charitable causes and spend more time with his family' would soon be circulating with his name on it. The trouble was, Sebastian had no family and had never been particularly philanthropic. The other popular option for retiring bankers, high political office, held no attraction and he was still a British citizen so not technically eligible.

Sebastian was already as rich as he'd ever need to be: he had an apartment overlooking Central Park which he shared with his equally successful girlfriend Ellen, a beach house on Long Island, a chalet in Aspen that he'd only used once and, due to his father's demise, he now owned a small hospitality business empire in an exclusive ski resort in Europe. He had initially thought to liquidate these assets but now, it was to the mountains of Grondère that his thoughts turned more and more often.

He looked down at his desk and smiled. On it was a glossy brochure for Tonita Shalott's first own-name collection. He and Ellen would be at the launch that Friday evening after which Tonita, his father's former fiancée, would leave for Geneva. A pang of regret for his father brought him back to reality just in time as, at that moment, his team knocked on the door.

The young bankers filtered in, gathered around the table in Sebastian's office and the pricing discussion began. One of his protégés had collected the views of the other syndicate members and they went through them one by one to assess the overall view. As the discussion progressed Sebastian found his mind wandering.

What does it matter? he asked himself. Really, here we are discussing percentage points as if it was the most important issue in the universe and it's just not.

His team seemed to smell his apathy.

They're almost sniffing the air like blood hounds, he thought, they can smell blood. They can't wait to execute me and yet, every person in this room owes their career to me.

And the worst thing of all, he realised, was he just didn't care. They could have it.

He hastened the meeting to its close, managed to summon up an appearance at matey comradery, and sent them all off to their desks with various tasks which should hold the hounds at bay for a while. But he knew it could not be long.

Tonita was glowing as she greeted them at the glitzy gallery where her first collection in her own name was being launched.

'Ellen, Sebastian, I've been desperate for you to arrive, I can't spread myself around enough, everyone wants to talk to me and I just can't manage it.'

Her smile said it all: she was a hit. Thanks to Ellen's contacts, every fashion magazine editor in Manhattan was present, and, thanks to Tonita's talent, they were liking what they saw.

They divided up the room between them and worked it all night.

It was late before all the canapés had been eaten, the last champagne glass drained and the three of them were able to regroup and assess the evening.

'I think we should get some good reviews,' smiled Ellen. 'I got some great feedback.'

Tonita was grinning to herself and could no longer keep her news to herself.

'The buyer from Tiffany's wants to meet me to discuss an exclusive collection. I can't believe it, my own counter in Tiffany's. Oh, Ellen, thank you! I would never have made all these contacts without you.'

'You only have your own talent to thank, Tonita. You're on your way now.'

'That's great, Tonita. Dad would have been so proud.'

They all thought of Malcolm, Sebastian's father who had been murdered that March in Grondère by his ex-wife (and Sebastian's mother), Carla Sturridge.

'I wish he was here to see it.' Tonita agreed sadly. But the truth was, she realised, she was really enjoying herself and had been so busy getting ready for the launch, that she hadn't really thought much about her former fiancé over the past few weeks. A little pang of guilt came over her, which Ellen and Sebastian mistook for grief.

'Come on,' Sebastian said. 'I've booked a table at the Red Hare Running to celebrate.'

Arm in arm, the threesome headed outside to a waiting taxi and made for Manhattan's hottest restaurant.

The next morning Tonita sat in the Swiss business lounge at JFK with coffees and pastries and a pile of newspapers. Her name was all over the pages of the Saturday fashion supplements.

She leafed through them incredulously. I'm a brand!

Seven

Think of all the beauty around you and still be happy.
Anne Frank

Tonita felt her stomach churn as her taxi turned into the courtyard of La Grande Cour. How strange being a visitor in the place that had been her home and of which, had things turned out differently, she would, by now, have been the co-owner. Its elegant wooden façade, louvered shutters, graceful balconies and wide, elegant portico entrance seemed untouched by the tragedy which had taken place there just months earlier. What on earth had she expected, it was, after all, just architecture; shaking her head at her own stupidity, she took a deep breath and stepped out of the car as the porter opened the door for her. He smiled in recognition and took charge of her luggage.

Tonita had deliberately chosen La Grande Cour as the venue for her first rapprochement with her half-brother and sister: being in unfamiliar territory she wanted to be at least on familiar ground. Until recently, she had been estranged from her father. Losing Malcom had made her re-think her stance for the sake of these much younger siblings, as yet, still strangers to her. It wasn't any more convenient for her to fly back from New York than for the children's parents to fly over from Dubai for the children's half-term from boarding school in England, but Tonita had recently become their guardian and wanted to get to know them. They would arrive later that evening, but in the meantime, she wanted to see Lucy again and show her that her overtures of friendship were genuine.

'Come on, Lucy. It's time to face your demons,' she pleaded over the phone. 'I've just done it: you can't live here and keep avoiding La Grande Cour. The person

63

responsible for Malcolm's death is behind bars, you can't blame a building.'

Lucy hesitated; Tonita was right, of course. She agreed she would join Tonita for a drink that evening.

Tonita greeted her in the lobby with a big hug and led her into the bar where a bottle of champagne was waiting on ice. Lucy's friend, Anya, who had been hurriedly promoted from manager of the hotel spa to manager of the entire hotel after Malcolm's untimely death, came over, opened and served the champagne, accompanied with a long, large wink at Lucy.

Lucy smothered a grin: she had been a waitress the last time she had been in Grondère's only five-star hotel and accused of serving poisoned soup to its owner. Unmaterialistic as she was, she was not totally immune to the pleasure of sitting in the plushest bar in the resort, drinking a champagne that, having formerly worked as a barmaid, she knew was well beyond her means. It was exquisite and she allowed herself to savour its taste as Tonita fussed over her.

'So how's life in New York?' Lucy finally managed to say, after savouring every sip of her first glass of champagne.

'It's going really well,' Tonita replied, refilling Lucy's glass. 'I just launched my own brand: Ellen and Sebastian have been so supportive. Thanks to the launch party Ellen organised, I was approached by a buyer from Tiffany's and they want to discuss me creating an exclusive range for them.'

'That's awesome,' exclaimed Lucy, 'Tiffany's! Even I know what that means.'

Tonita nodded happily.

'And I've got my own apartment now, in Greenwich Village. I just love it.'

Lucy looked at her. Tonita really was a different person; she still had that hard edge to her, but she was more open, more natural and was displaying an affection towards Lucy of which, a year ago, Lucy would have believed her incapable.

'How are you? Tell me what is happening in your life. Any man on the scene?'

Lucy was stunned: Tonita had never shown any interest in her personal life before. Lucy decided to drop the bombshell that she was going out with Capitaine Dupertuis.

She enjoyed watching the effect of her revelation reflected in Tonita's shocked face.

'Capitaine Dupertuis?'

Lucy nodded.

'How astonishing,' Tonita commented, re-filling their glasses as she reflected on the idea of the detective in charge of the investigation into her fiancé's murder and Lucy falling in love. 'It is an interesting pairing,' she continued, 'you: lively, open and natural, and him: haughty, proud. Like a modern-day Mr Darcy to your Elizabeth Bennet.'

'My friend Bethan would be happy to hear you say that: she told me my Mr Darcy was out there somewhere.'

'Two hundred years on, we have the vote, equality, financial independence and we are still obsessed with Mr Darcy. Why do you think that is?'

'Possibly because it's just a great love story.'

'You must be right.'

'And your Mr Darcy?' Lucy asked gently. 'Was that Malcolm?'

'I could only say this to you Lucy, because you already know what an awful person I am, but no … I loved and respected Malcolm and I promise you, I would have made it work – though I am not sure the person I was then would have made him happy. Maybe now, I would, but it's too late. I have to confess that I do not miss him as I should, if I had loved him as I should.'

Lucy was shocked, not by the revelation, it wasn't really one to her, but by the avowal of it. Self-knowledge and honesty were not qualities she would previously have attributed to Tonita. Suddenly, rather from what Tonita had *not* said, she had an intuition that there was someone. 'So who is he? Your Mr Darcy?'

'Oh Lucy, sometimes I wish you weren't quite so astute. Someone who is so out of reach that I must just keep it to myself. Hopefully the feeling will fade with time.'

Lucy thought she knew the subject of Tonita's impossible love, but she didn't say. If it was who she thought, saying it would only cause pain. She changed the subject.

'I must admit, I wasn't sure you would ever return to Grondère.'

'It wasn't an easy decision, but it's the perfect place for me to entertain my siblings. I'm hoping you can give me some suggestions.'

They chatted for a while about suitable activities and arranged that Lucy would take them on some nature hikes. When the hotel driver called to say he was only ten minutes away with the children, Tonita immediately started to feel and display her nervousness and Lucy made to leave.

'Just one more thing.' Tonita asked, 'Does Sebastian know about you and Capitaine Dupertuis?'

'I don't think so. Why?'

Tonita gave her a wicked wink.

'Because I cannot wait to tell him.'

Eight

*Mrs. Rachel Lynde was one of those capable creatures
who can manage their own concerns and those of other
folks into the bargain.*
L.M. Montgomery, Anne of Green Gables

As the good weather firmly settled in, The Pub Mont
Grondère opened its doors, giving the returning residents
a place to congregate and socialise. Tommy and Eddie had
both just secured lucrative full-time jobs on the White
Snowflake project which would be starting soon and so
they had something to celebrate.

On opening night, Lucy and Eddie arrived to find a tall,
glamorous blonde woman holding court to their friends.
The stranger had her back to the door as Lucy entered, as
did Jodie and Sally and Tommy, so she couldn't see their
expressions, but Poppy and Johnny were facing her and
their faces were a sight to behold: Poppy's wore an
expression of polite resignation but Johnny looked really
riled.

'What this place needs,' the stranger was saying
confidently, 'is some proper structure.'

'Structure *is* provided by the local municipality,' Poppy
explained.

'I mean for the ex-pat community,' stated the newcomer.
'I mean. Where are the clubs, the societies? Where is the
action?'

'Most of us came here to get away from the *action*,' spat
Johnny whose tolerance was visibly close to cracking.

'But what do you all do out of season?' she asked. 'You
can't just hang around in The Pub all the time?'

Johnny, who did, just glared.

'There are some clubs and such down in Pattier,' tried Sally, in an attempt to be constructive. 'Some mothers' groups, book clubs …'

'How dull, I was looking for something more tailored to my artistic talents. I'm thinking of starting a choir.'

Johnny groaned. At this point, the others noticed Lucy and Eddie and turned round, glad of the distraction.

'You must be the famous Lucy Wilson,' the woman held out her hand. 'Laeticia Braythwaite, call me Letty.'

Lucy, bemused, shook the offered hand and confirmed that she was indeed the 'famous' Lucy Wilson. How long, she wondered, was it going to be before people stopped associating her with the Grande Cour murder.

Eddie introduced himself and beat a hasty retreat to the bar.

'I was just telling your friends how we needed something to liven things up around here when there's no snow on the ground. Don't you agree?'

'I can't say I'd thought about it,' Lucy skilfully sidestepped the question.

'You see, that's exactly what I mean. You need someone with organisational skills around here.'

Lucy could see Poppy suppressing a laugh; Eddie, clinging to his fresh beer, stayed in the shadows, looking on in horrified fascination. Letty, however, seemed impervious to any negative vibes.

'So, how about it? Who's up for joining my choir?' She turned on Eddie who had clearly failed in his attempt to become invisible.

'Eddie?'

'Tone deaf, I'm sorry to say,' shrugged Eddie, not sorry at all.

'Same here.' Lucy, grateful for the first time in her life for her lack of musicality, shook her head. 'Music teacher used to tell me to mouth the words.'

'Maybe that's why your birdsong recognition is so poor', offered Poppy who, despite her lovely singing voice, had no intention of joining Letty's choir. She also shook her head when Letty looked in her direction. Lucy gave her a wry look, she had heard Poppy singing beautifully in the Rotstockhütte, but she could see that it was unlikely a pushy personality such as Letty would ever win favour with Poppy – she knew Poppy so well she could actually feel her bristling under her forced smile.

'I might be interested,' said Jodie, who loved to sing and missed her school choir days.

'Yes, I'll give it a go,' Sally volunteered, 'I was in the choir at school but I can't read music.'

'That's not a problem for chorus members,' Letty reassured her pompously. 'But we'll need some male voices. What about you?' she looked hard at Tommy who, although amused, thought it might be a nice activity for him and Sally to share in the summer months.

'I can hold a tune,' he smiled and looked at Sally complicitly. 'It might be fun.'

'Good man,' Letty congratulated. She didn't look at Johnny, she'd already dismissed him as an unsuitable candidate. Johnny was also a really good singer, but he doubted Letty wanted a Mick Jagger soundalike: all *he* wanted was for her to leave.

Once she had secured the contact details of those who had indicated an interest, Johnny got his wish and Letty moved on to her next target group.

'Thank God for that,' he said. 'Look at poor Louie, she's raised his hackles.'

'And yours,' Poppy grinned.

'What on earth just happened there?' asked Eddie. 'Who is she? Where did she come from?'

'She and her husband just moved here from London,' Poppy, who was always the first to know anything, replied. 'They've bought one of those huge chalets above the sports centre. Apparently, they've both made a fortune in the City, no kids and they've moved here for a "gentler existence". They're going to continue some sort of trading business from here, but at a more "leisurely pace".'

'I don't get these people,' ranted Johnny, 'who leave their country for a new way of life and then just recreate the life they had at home in the new country.'

'Johnny, the British have been doing that since the 17th century,' laughed Poppy, highly amused by the irony of his comment. 'And what do you think we're doing right now? Exactly what we would be doing back in the UK, having a gossip over a pint in The Pub.'

Johnny saw that he's been outwitted and had the good grace to laugh.

'You got me there, Poppy. Guilty as charged. But, in my defence, I didn't come here to get away from my country, I came here because my country's *only* failing is its lack of mountains.'

'That woman is a shocker, though,' said Eddie. 'I hope she's not going to try and hang around us.'

'I doubt that,' Lucy said, looking across the room to where Letty was entering Sammy's details into her phone – another recruit. 'I'm sure as soon as Sammy's swanky bar reopens, she'll be more at home there.'

'You don't think we're traitors, do you?' asked Jodie.

'Of course not.' Poppy laughed. 'We know you love a good warble, and you never know, you might get some solos.'

'Well, I don't like her. Too bossy,' Johnny insisted.

Poppy smiled.

'You made me think of an old favourite, a Mary Wesley book I was just re-reading. There is a bossy woman in it and everyone refers to her as the Natural Leader.'

'How about NL, for short?' suggested Tommy.

'How about BL,' Johnny countered. 'Bloody L.'
Eddie snorted. 'I love it. It's even her initials backwards.'
And so, from that day forward, poor, enthusiastic, unpopular Letty Braythwaite was known, only behind her back, of course, as BL.

Proving the truth to her claim of those much-vaunted organisational skills, within a week BL had recruited her choir from the summer residents of Grondère. She had been proved right: the resort had many talented and aspiring singers who were glad of an outlet for their voices and something to do in the summer evenings. BL lost no time in finding a practice room and a musical director and the newly formed Grondère choir began rehearsals for a concert version of *West Side Story* every Thursday night. As Lucy had correctly predicted, thereafter BL was no longer found slumming it in The Pub. Both Sammy and Jamie, competent tenors, had been recruited for BL's choir and as soon as Sammy's bar re-opened for the summer season, the Braythwaite couple transferred their allegiance there, to the Bar des Deux Moines and anywhere else the 'smart set' hung out.

Letty and Henry Braythwaite were reportedly becoming fast friends with Charles Sidforth-Sykes who had been rather lonely since Malcolm had met his untimely end and his ex-wife had been sent to prison for precipitating it. Sammy and his friend Jamie, who was cheffing for him that summer, reported back on copious quaffing of champagne and lavish suppers.

The Braythwaites were also working hard to ingratiate themselves with Humphrey Watson, as this was where the real influence lay. Humphrey Watson was a local resident who had moved to Grondère in the early seventies, about the same time as Poppy and Johnny. Unlike Poppy and Johnny, Humphrey was extremely rich and shared his time between Switzerland and one of the Channel Islands, though nobody could ever remember which one. Humphrey was plugged into the higher echelons of Grondère 'society' but was unusual in that, unlike many of Grondère's more wealthy residents, he also liked to hang out with the ski bums, keep an eye on everyone and loved hearing the latest gossip. His eyes positively twinkled with mischief.

Humphrey only came into The Pub for the rugby. Otherwise he hung out in the Bar des Deux Moines with the posh set, but whenever he turned up, even when it was heaving, the locals always found space for him. He no longer skied but, as far as Lucy could tell, he seemed to spend a lot of time shepherding a flock of grandchildren to and from ski school. She thought he never looked happier than when surrounded by hordes of over-excited children. Sammy reported that despite BL practically throwing herself at him Humphrey was holding out: he would have a drink with her in the bar but every time she said 'we must have dinner' he had a ready excuse.

'What name did you say?'
'Braythwaite, Laeticia Braythwaite,' Lucy replied as Alain handed her a glass of decent white wine to stop her swigging the cooking wine she was generously stirring into her risotto, one of the few dishes she knew how to make. She had been recounting the story of the choir and BL's antics.
'Does she have a husband called Henry?'

'Now how would you know that?' Lucy's antennae were twitching.

'Oh, just some background checks we did when they arrived and started a trading business.'

'Oh.'

'You sound disappointed.'

'Well, yes. I was hoping you'd say Interpol had a global arrest warrant out on them for torturing innocent ski bums.'

'Sorry, just mundane police work.'

'Ah. Oh, that wine's much nicer.'

'I should hope so. If the five-franc bottle you've got tastes better, then that's all you'll be getting from now on.'

She laughed and kept stirring.

'I don't suppose you can just kick her out of Switzerland for being annoying.'

'I'm afraid not. I do not believe it is grounds for repatriation, although it has been used as grounds for refusing naturalisation.'

'You serious?'

'I am.'

'Don't you just love this country?'

Nine

If you should get there first
Save just a little space for me
                                    Emily Dickinson

Poppy called for Lucy early the next morning and the two donned their backpacks. They would just be away for three days this time as the purpose of their trip was to pay their final respects to Genna Hobbs-Davison at the Col des Fantômes where she had fallen, or, more likely, been pushed, to her death.

The hike could have been done in a day but they wanted to take their time and collect lots of plants for Alain's garden. They would overnight on the way there and back in the Cabane du Lagopède which must have been the only mountain refuge in the area Poppy didn't know. Since Genna's disappearance, Poppy had always resentfully avoided this part of the mountain, associating it with the day that had clouded her life. It was time to change that.

On the way, they collected plants that would grow happily in the south-facing wall that hid Alain's garden from the hikers on the old *bisse* path on its north side. He had created a beautifully secluded spot with a deck, a Jacuzzi and a natural cool pool fed by a spring, but he had left off at the hard landscaping. Lucy had promised to make it into a secret garden, including a 'flowerfall'.

Poppy and Lucy had discussed the ethics of taking wild flowers from the hills.

'We'd not really be taking them out of their habitat,' Lucy reasoned. 'We're just spreading them and multiplying stock.'

'It's a tough one, isn't it?' Poppy had agreed. 'I think as long as we take flowers that are common and where they're plentiful, we're not doing any harm.'

'In fact, you could argue that it would be worse to introduce alien plants from a garden centre into the mountain flora.'

'You could,' Poppy smiled. That settled the question.

Nevertheless, they always looked around to check no one was watching each time they stopped to extract plants from plentiful clumps as they walked. It wasn't that they felt *very* guilty, but they certainly didn't want to have to justify their behaviour to every passing hiker. There weren't many other hikers as it turned out and by the time they had reached the Cabane du Lagopède in the early afternoon they had filled two old plastic ice cream containers lined with damp cotton wool with plants.

The hike took them away from the familiar walks of Grondère, over the ridges that, in winter, led to the remote off-piste ski areas, and in summer were natural wildernesses unfrequented by the summer herds. Ibex and chamois seemed plentiful here and the marmots didn't even bother moving out of their way.

From a long way off they could see the refuge in front of them but the path seemed to take a long detour around the hillside. They realised why when they spotted a large field of cotton grass below them: a sure sign of a boggy area, so they stuck to the circuitous path climbing the flowered inclines leading to the refuge.

They arrived before any other walkers and, for the rest of the afternoon, Lucy found a quiet deckchair set in a field of buttercups and fell asleep in the sunshine. Poppy disappeared and returned with all the ingredients for Chalet Soup which she and her new friend, Lilli Marchand, the refuge guardian, proceeded to make. There were quite a few other walkers booked in that night and Lucy and Poppy enjoyed the lively chat and cultural exchanges that you only get in that unique environment of the mountain refuge, where fellow walkers become the best of friends for one night and then never meet again. The early night is another feature of mountain refuges: Lucy wasn't sleepy, having dozed in the afternoon, and so she lay in bed listening to the gentle snoring of the other hikers in her dormitory and thinking how strange it was to be able to be so familiar with strangers up in the mountain who you would never speak to if you met them in other circumstances and certainly not share a bedroom with.

Capitaine Dupertuis was disappointed to receive a phone call from the Bern *Kriminalpolizei*: he thought he'd carefully sidestepped Lucy's scant involvement with the Reichenbach murder. He listened with increasing concern as Herr Schmutz revealed to him that his murder victim had finally been identified and was a Grondère resident. A warrant for searching his address had been issued, would the *Police judiciaire* of Savigny be so kind as to effect the search on behalf of the Bern *Kriminalpolizei*?

'This home town of yours is a magnet for trouble,' he complained to Inspectrice Jacquier as they sped up the hill on their way to search the home of a certain Sergei Kowalski, recently found dead at the foot of the Reichenbach Falls.

'It's getting like Midsomer,' agreed Sylvie. 'They'll be calling you Inspecteur Barnaby soon.'

He glanced across at her; she was grinning wickedly. That remark had been no mistake: it had been a well-aimed barb at a stinging comment Lucy had made to him when she was suspect number one in the Grande Cour murder during an uncomfortable interview he would prefer to forget. He nodded at her wryly to let her know that her arrow had hit home.

She felt a little ashamed of herself, but not too much. Capitaine Dupertuis could get a bit haughty and needed grounding from time to time.

'So, what's the address?' She took the printout of the warrant from Bern, most of which she skimmed over, it being in German. 'I'll see if I know it.' She looked at the address, the only part in French, and gasped.

'What's up?' asked Inspecteur chef adjoint Blonnay.

'It's Maria's address!'

'Maria, the maid from La Grande Cour?'

'Yes. And look, this guy had the same surname.'

Maria had been instrumental in helping them clear up the Grande Cour murder: this was a worrying development. Sylvie Jacquier had grown fond of the timid Polish chambermaid who had found the courage to admit to the minor wrong of stealing a hairbrush in order to help them uncover a greater wrong. The hairbrush had been used by a Lord Shilton to do a DNA test which proved that Malcolm McDonague was the illegitimate son of his father. It transpired that there was no connection between this and Malcolm's death but Maria's subsequent discovery of a dry-cleaning ticket in Genna McDonaghue's purse had helped them establish the true murderer's identity and clear Lucy.

Capitaine Dupertuis winced, 'I don't like the feel of this.'

It was with a certain amount of trepidation that they pushed open the door. It was already ajar. Blonnay entered first, gun at the ready and Capitaine Dupertuis covered him. The scene that greeted them was worse than they could have imagined. Maria lay in a pool of dried blood in the centre of the floor of the bedsit: she had clearly been beaten up pretty badly prior to being shot. The furniture was overturned, ornaments broken and a framed print of the Madonna lay on the ground under her hand. A trail of bloody fingerprints smeared the wall, where Maria, sure she was dying, must have reached out for her beloved namesake saint.

Sylvie Jacquier, normally a very controlled police officer, broke out in gasping sobs and took herself outside.

'*Merde*!' said Inspecteur chef adjoint Blonnay.

'As you say,' agreed Capitaine Dupertuis. 'What a mess!' He cast his eye around the scene but there was nothing he could see that helped him understand what had caused someone to dispatch the gentle young Polish woman. The violence of the scene told him that the murderer had been trying to get information out of Maria before making sure she never shared that information or his identity with anyone else. He wondered if her torturer had been successful.

Sylvie Jacquier put her head round the door.

'Apologies for my reaction, I really liked that girl.'

'She was a sweetheart,' agreed Capitaine Dupertuis.

'I've called the lab,' she added.

'Thanks, good work.'

They were about to withdraw from the scene and stand guard outside to wait for the scientists to arrive when Alain Dupertuis detected a movement from behind the breakfast bar which separated the sitting room from the kitchen.

Signalling to his colleagues, gun in hand he slowly edged round the bar. Cowering behind the rubbish bin was a small dog. It whimpered when it saw him.

'You try, Sylvie, I don't think it likes men.'

Sylvie bent down and urged the little dog to come to her. Nervously it tiptoed towards her and nuzzled her hand.

'Looks very thin. Can't have eaten for days. Shall I take it down to the rescue centre?' she asked.

Alain hesitated. He had an awful sense of foreboding and suddenly an image flashed before his eyes of Lucy deep in the forest and in grave danger. Instinctively, he knew that the little dog was important, but he couldn't explain this to his colleagues.

'No,' he replied, reaching for a more rational explanation, 'it's our only witness for the time being and dogs can be very intuitive. We'll take it round to my mum's and I'll ask if she can take it to the vet and look after it for a while.'

'Mlle Wilson?' asked Inspecteur chef adjoint Blonnay. 'The little dog would certainly not lack for exercise roaming the mountains with her.'

Capitaine Dupertuis looked at him askance. Blonnay was right: Lucy was the perfect candidate to look after their chief witness and this had actually been his initial thought, but it was hard for him to acknowledge this new relationship to his work colleagues.

'You're right,' he nodded reluctantly. 'I'll ask her when she gets back from the Col des Fantômes.'

His two colleagues grinned at each other behind his back. Mlle Wilson was definitely a good influence on their formerly haughty colleague. He would never have admitted to them before that he had a girlfriend.

The next morning, Poppy and Lucy were up for sunrise and breakfasted outside with homemade croissants, bread, *sérac* cheese and apricot jam. With fresh water in their bottles, tea in Lucy's flask, and a small bottle of champagne that Poppy had stowed in the fridge overnight, they set off for the Col des Fantômes.

After an hour and a half, they entered the col. It was a straight narrow pass, lined either side with high sheer cliffs, giving it the feel of a gorge. At the far end, having been told where by Tommy and Eddie, they looked for the steep ledge underneath which lay the crevasse which had hidden Genna for so long.

Lucy looked up at the walls of rock towering above her and shuddered: it had been Tommy and Eddie's last climb. They had been with Danny, Eddie's best friend, climbing these very walls when they had looked down and spotted the skeleton the previous autumn. The following winter Danny had been killed in an avalanche.

'You're thinking of Danny?'

'Yes, and the boys: they haven't climbed since. Without Danny, they seem to have lost their appetite for it.'

'They'll come back to it, it's a bug that's hard to lose.'

'You stopped after Genna died.'

'Only because no one would come with me. I still keep my skills up on the climbing wall down at the Sports Centre.'

'I didn't know that.'

'No, the caretaker lets me in every so often before opening.'

'You are full of surprises.'

'Aren't I just? Still, the boys seem to have kept themselves busy in the bike park since it opened.'

'Yes, they love it. They spend the whole day going up in the gondolas and racing down those tiny tracks, then they come back home very muddy and sweaty, strip off outside and shower themselves and their bikes under the garden hose.'

Poppy laughed.

'I'm glad they've found another occupation to entertain themselves, but you wouldn't find me hurtling down the mountain on two wheels – terrifying.'

'Yes, isn't it? And yet we think nothing of hurtling down the mountain on two skis – why is that?'

'Not a clue.'

'Mind, if we were true athletes we would do what Émilie does and bike up and not down.'

Eddie's girlfriend, Émilie, as an elite athlete, had explained to Lucy that she only cycled uphill: she didn't want to risk an accident going downhill, slipping on a stone and missing out on a season and so, when others were unloading their bikes to race down the mountain trails, she was loading hers, having ridden up.

'I just couldn't do that. She must have legs of iron.'

'She must have.'

'Come on, let's find the spot.'

It wasn't hard to find: the overlying vegetation had been ripped away by a landslide which was how the boys had come to notice her and since then, the police had cleared the site completely. If there had been any doubt they were in the right place, it was quickly eliminated by the small cross someone had made of stones by the edge of the gaping crack in the col's rocky floor.

'That's nice, must have been the police.'

Poppy smiled and started to build a larger cairn of rocks into which she inserted a small Celtic cross she had brought with her to pay tribute to Genna's Scottish roots and threw some dried rose petals into the darkness of the crevasse. Lucy watched on from a little distance – she didn't feel that this was her ceremony – but she came and stood beside Poppy as she recited the Emily Dickinson poem, *Going to Heaven*.

Finally, after kneeling a long time beside her friend's hidden tomb, Poppy opened her little bottle of champagne, took out her two crystal glasses and they drank a toast 'to Genna'.

They didn't speak on the way back to the Cabane du Lagopède but Poppy sang *The Banks of Loch Lomond* as they left the gorge.

'You do have a lovely voice, Popps. You should join BL's choir.'

'No fear!' Poppy replied indignantly and the sombre mood was broken.

'I was thinking, back there,' Lucy paused. 'I love native plants but do you think it would be terrible if I planted some cultivated plants in Alain's garden.'

'Depends what they are,' came the reply.

'Roses,' Lucy said. 'It was seeing you scatter those dried rose petals that got me thinking. I've always loved that fairy story, you know, *Snow White and Rose Red* where the mother had one rose bush of each colour beneath her window to represent her two daughters.'

'You old romantic, I don't see why not, they're not exactly going to self-seed and invade the forest, are they?'

'No, that's what I thought.'

'Mind, they'd have to be pretty robust to survive up there. You should look at the Canadian Parkland cultivars, they're bred for hardiness and they grow on their own roots, not grafted, so if they do get hit by a hard winter, they grow back true.'

'Okay, I will,' Lucy said brightly. Poppy always had a solution.

On the way back to the refuge, they stopped off for a picnic at a small mountain lake. All around the lake was a springy carpet of Achemilla alpina, Alpine lady's mantle.

'It's lovely to walk on,' said Lucy. 'I wonder if I could create a "lawn" of it around the cool pool?'

She left Poppy to collect a good stock of plants for her while she went for a swim. Swimming in the mountain lakes was an activity she was getting addicted to: she loved the icy feel of the clear water but she never stayed in for long, as it took a while to warm up afterwards. If, on that occasion, she had known that one of the local photographers had been in the vicinity, she might have kept her T-shirt on.

'What a peculiar little dog. What is it?'

Lucy looked at the little dog standing looking timidly at her in the lounge at Alain's mother's flat.

'I believe it's an Italian greyhound,' replied Anne Dupertuis.

'It's not very grey.'

'No.'

Lucy looked at the small, caramel-coloured creature before her, trembling as if it knew its fate lay in her hands.

'What does Alain want us to do with it?'

'He wants us to look after it for a while: it is the witness to a murder.'

'Oh.'

'Yes, oh.'

Anne told Lucy the little she knew about Maria's murder. The two women looked at the poor animal whose owner had been brutally struck down in front of her.

'It's quite pretty,' suggested Anne.

'Yes,' admitted Lucy, whose idea of a dog was considerably bigger than this one-foot-high specimen. The greyhound had a white bib and big brown eyes which looked at her in a deliberate appeal for sympathy. It worked.

'I suppose I could take her walking with me during the day but I don't think I can take her back to the chalet at night, we're already cramped enough.'

'That's okay, I can take her in the evenings. It's just the days when I'm at work that are a problem.' Anne Dupertuis taught part-time at Lausanne University and Lucy could imagine the difficulty of taking a dog into the lecture theatre.

'Do you think it can do long walks?' Lucy was working towards her mid-mountain guide exam and spent most days learning the local walks, flora and fauna.

Anne laughed, 'It's called a *lévrier* in French. I think there's a clue in the name.'

Lucy grinned back: if the species had been used to hunt hares, then it must have a considerable amount of stamina. Lucy bent down and looked at the medallion on the dog's pink, sparkly collar.

'Słowik.' The dog didn't respond.

Anne pulled a face. 'I think there may be a pronunciation issue.'

Anne was a language professor but her talents were limited to English, German and Italian.

'I could call someone in Poland for you.'

'I'll get back to you on that, I think I can find someone closer to home. Do you think Alain would prefer to be on his own this evening?'

'He was on his own yesterday: I think he could probably use some company but you'd have to ask him.'

Alain texted that he was desperate to see her.

As they drove up the hill she asked him if he thought Maria's death was connected to the Grande Cour case.

'We don't think so: Maria's evidence is not essential to get a conviction in the Grande Cour case. But it's definitely connected to the Reichenbach Falls murder: it looks more like there's some Polish criminal connection. Her cousin seems to have been a small-time villain who stumbled into something too big for him.'

'That's almost scarier.'

'Yes, let's hope whoever it is has finished at two murders and returns to their own territory.'

'This is getting a bit close to home. Nobody knows about me seeing what happened at Reichenbach, do they?'

'No. The electronic files have been deleted, only the investigating officers know your name: Herr Schmutz knows I will kill him if that gets out, but be watchful.'

'I will.'

She was silent for a moment, processing it all and then she asked, 'I didn't know Maria, but did she suffer?'

'She must have been terrified and I'm afraid he beat her up to make sure she had no information, but I think, once whoever it was had found out what he wanted to know, he dispatched her pretty quickly.'

'What awful things you see.'

'Yes, and I can't tell you what a difference coming back to you at the end of the day has made to my life.'

'That's a lovely thing to say, thank you.'

They spoke no more on the subject that night. Lucy just held Alain tightly in her arms until he slept. As she listened to his steady breathing her mind went back to Poppy and Genna and the Col des Fantômes. How sad, one friend had died young and one had grown old and yet the friendship had never faded. Eddie, she knew would always remember and cherish his friendship with Danny, whom he had watched swept to his death in an avalanche. Who, she wondered, would treasure the memory of Maria?

The following day Lucy found out the phone number of the only Polish person she knew in the resort, a barmaid from The Pub Mont Grondère and took the little dog to meet her.

'That's Maria's dog!' exclaimed Maja as Lucy walked into the café.

'Yes,' Lucy replied hesitantly. She hadn't thought of that; she should have checked with Alain who knew what before making contact. Maja, however, had clearly heard all about it.

'What bastard would do such a thing?'

'I'm so sorry. Did you know her well?'

'We're a small community here, of course I knew her, but just to say hello. I didn't see her socially. I think she had a more conservative upbringing than me: she was very religious. I doubt she approved of me.'

'Do you want the little dog?'

'No thanks. That's the last thing I need. Is that why you called me?'

'No, I just offered out of politeness. What I actually need to know is how to pronounce its name and the commands in Polish. She's not responding to French or English.'

Maja laughed gaily.

'A quick lesson in Polish, no problem.'

She bent down and looked down and looked at the dog's medallion.

'Swovick.'

The dog's ears pricked up immediately. Lucy repeated it and the little dog ran towards her and licked her hand.

Lucy made Maja repeat the name and the basic commands into the recorder on her phone for Alain's mother: noga – heel; siad – sit; zostan – stay; waruj – down; do mnie – come here; aport – fetch. Słowik had been well-trained and responded obediently to each command.

'Good luck,' Maja wished Lucy as they said goodbye. 'I hope your boyfriend catches whoever did it. Poor little Słowik, what must she have seen?'

'I hate to think,' shuddered Lucy.

'What's it mean? Her name?' She called after Maja as she was leaving.

'Oh, I don't know what it is in English, that little brown bird with the beautiful song at night.'

'Nightingale,' smiled Lucy, 'how pretty.'

Thereafter Słowik followed Lucy wherever she went during the day, trotting beside her in the mountains, watching her as she studied or worked on the book which had now come back from the printer for proofing. She sniffed around as Lucy cleared the garden surrounding Alain's chalet and started plugging plants into the stone wall to create her 'flowerfall'. Lucy grew used to having her at her side: she did indeed prove to be capable of walking all day, and was nimble and quiet so she didn't disturb the wildlife.

Lucy began to appreciate having the company of a dog and became aware of a change in her status on the mountains. People who had previously nodded curtly at her in passing now stopped to say hello and stroke Słowik. Słowik loved the attention and played up to it beautifully, batting her eyelashes and presenting her haunches exactly where she wanted a scratch. Dog walkers looked at Lucy with renewed respect on seeing that she had joined their club: they also now stopped to exchange dog talk, usually about the best walking terrain or where the electric fences had been moved to enclose grazing cattle. In short, Lucy learned that a dog was not only a companion but was also an ice-breaker, socialiser and networker.

Occasionally she would meet Johnny and Louie on their early morning walk and they would amble along together for a while. Lucy enjoyed listening to Johnny's tales of Grondère when he was a young lad and Louie and Słowik seemed to get along quite well, probably because Słowik was totally submissive to Louie's dominant personality.

In the evenings, worn out, Słowik was happy to abandon Lucy and curl up at the foot of Anne's armchair.

Ten

What the detective story is about is not murder but the restoration of order.

P.D. James, The Face, 1986

The Polish murder investigation team sat around the table, on a conference call with their counterparts in Bern. The team in Bern had, in conjunction with the Polish police, been investigating Sergei Kowalski's past. They confirmed he was Maria's cousin, her father's brother's only son. He had had a brief, inglorious career in the army, before descending into small-time criminal activities such as blackmail, theft and doing the occasional bit of intimidation work for a protection racket.

'Nice guy,' commented Alain.

'We think he got into trouble with one of the gangs, not sure why but the word on the street is he needed to disappear for a while to avoid disappearing for good.'

'So he comes and plants himself on his sweet, God-fearing cousin who would have felt it her Christian duty to offer him refuge,' Inspectrice Jacquier said with bitterness.

Alain looked at her carefully. Was she taking Maria's murder too personally? He looked at her steely face and concluded she was angry but not over-invested emotionally.

'I think we can speculate that far,' agreed Herr Schmutz.

'So one theory is that he didn't cover his tracks well enough, someone came looking for him and Maria was collateral damage?'

'It's the only avenue we have so far. You?'

Alain gave a brief summary of Maria's part in their investigation into the murder of Malcolm McDonaghue.

'So do you think this Lord link could be another line of enquiry?' Herr Schmutz was full of scorn.

'No idea,' Alain said truthfully.

'Well, we can't dismiss it but it seems a bit far-fetched. Anything else?'

Blonnay took over.

'Shortly after *we successfully resolved* the Grande Cour case,' he spelled out, 'Maria resigned from the hotel and took a job as a maid in a private chalet. Looking at her pay slips it seems to have been a profitable switch and easier work. Her employers are a wealthy couple from England who haven't been here long but the wife does have Polish origins.'

'Another link to Poland. So, we need to look into their activities?'

'Yes, so far, it seems they have some private trading and investment company. We're looking into all that. Maybe Maria discovered something, her cousin started blackmailing her employer and needed shutting up?'

'That sounds like a more realistic scenario.'

'Maybe,' agreed Inspectrice Jacquier carefully. 'I can certainly see a Brit getting dressed up in this ridiculous Sherlock Holmes get-up, what did you call it?'

'Deerstalker,' Blonnay offered, allowing himself real pleasure in exaggerating the hard vowels of the word.

'And knickerbockers,' offered Alain, thinking it was time he gave the ridiculous word to Blonnay.

'Knickerbockers,' Blonnay repeated the word with a gleam in his eye.

Herr Schmutz could not believe the frivolity of his French-speaking colleagues. He thought it was time to restore some order to the proceedings.

'Whatever,' he said. 'Can I leave you to dig more into the employer connection?'

After the call, the trio called the procureur to report back. They agreed that it was possible someone from Grondère had dressed up as Sherlock Holmes and lured Sergei Kowalski to the Reichenbach Falls to blur the Grondère connection. But then why the bloody killing of Maria in her own home when it would have been so easy to lure her away too?

'Maybe that was the idea. To make it look like she got caught up in his criminal dealings?'

'Maybe. It sounds a bit twisted to me.'

'But then, that's what we deal with, isn't it?' she sighed, 'The twisted?'

'Correct. Check out Maria's employers' movements. Leave Lord Shilton out of it for now,' the procureur ended his participation in the discussion.

'Are you okay, Sylvie?' Alain asked her after the call.

'Yes, thanks for asking,' she replied. 'I'm just sad for Maria. Poor kid, she leaves her country, comes over here and works really hard just to get killed by some criminal from her own country. It's not fair.'

'It isn't fair,' he agreed. 'But we don't get to decide, just to try to get justice.'

'Well, that's a promise from me: *I'm* going to get justice for Maria.' She grimaced as she headed out.

Blonnay, never a sensitive type, turned on his colleague as soon as they were alone.

'You! You have been holding out on me, that glorious word, knickerbocker.'

'Herr Schmutz didn't seem to appreciate its virtues.'

'Strange. For I can see him wearing such a garment.'

Blonnay held up his phone bearing an image of the baggy knee-length tweed trousers for Alain's admiration.

'Yes,' he confessed wryly. 'So can I.'

'Come on, let's pay a call on Maria's employers. It is a hard one to pronounce – Braythhhwaite.'

'Braythwaite,' Capitaine Dupertuis helped him out.

Blonnay looked at him, puzzled: he was used to being the English expert in the office. His colleague grinned.

'I heard Lucy mention them. My antennae immediately homed in *and* I picked up what I assume is the correct pronunciation.'

'Did Mlle Wilson have anything interesting to impart?'

'Just that the woman is a bit of a bossy type. She's got the whole of Grondère singing in a choir.'

'Gracious! Including Mlle Wilson?'

'No. My girlfriend has many fine qualities but she sings like a jackdaw, that's why I have nicknamed her *Rossignol*.'

'How sweet.' Blonnay couldn't believe Capitaine Dupertuis was disclosing such personal information. Neither could Capitaine Dupertuis: he emitted an embarrassed cough.

'Yes. Mme Braythwaite's nickname is not so sweet.'

'It is?'

'Bloody L – BL, for short.'

'The linguistic creativity of our guest residents never ceases to impress me,' Blonnay grinned.

'Come in officers, we have, of course, been expecting your visit,' Laetitia Braythwaite purred as she waved the two young detectives into her lounge.

The chalet was one of the most luxurious either of them had ever seen: it could have come straight from the pages of a glossy interior design magazine. The lounge was large, spacious and had plunging views over the resort. From the side windows Alain got a glimpse of his own little chalet, perched even higher, where, right then, Lucy would be working away in their secret garden.

Henry joined them and the couple dutifully expressed their horror and regret at the loss of their maid. It was correct but not heart-felt.

'Did you know her well?'

'As well as one can know a servant,' BL replied. 'She was very polite and respectful, performed her duties well, a good timekeeper. Much more than that I cannot tell you. She'd only been with us three months.'

'You say she was a good timekeeper: did you not then find it strange that she stopped coming to work?'

'I did, I kept calling her but she didn't reply. It was extremely annoying.'

'You didn't think to go round and check up on her?'

'Absolutely not. If she was ill I wouldn't want to catch it and I certainly wouldn't have wanted to have anything to do with that awful cousin of hers.'

'You met her cousin?'

'Briefly,' Henry replied. 'Caught him snooping around in here one day, he said he was looking for Maria. I made it very clear I didn't believe him and escorted him outside. I told him to wait for Maria at the end of the drive.'

'Yes, very unsavoury looking character.'

'You have a Polish maiden name Mme Braythwaite, the same as Maria and Sergei. Do you have any family connection with the Kowalskis?'

Blonnay had hit a nerve, BL's social aspirations clearly didn't align with having her Polish origins exposed.

'Kowalski, in Poland, Inspector, is like Smith in England. We did establish that both our families came from the same area near Warsaw, but beyond that, I can assure you, there is no connection. My family belonged to the higher echelons of Polish society and, other than a few distant cousins, I have no close family left in the country. I did, however, hire Maria *because* she was Polish and I feel a certain loyalty to the country my parents came from.'

'Can you speak Polish, Madame?'

'I can. What's that got to do with anything?'

'I do not know: it is my job to collect information.'

The two detectives left the chalet feeling that they had made no progress.

'Nice pad though,' commented Capitaine Dupertuis.

'Yes, we're obviously in the wrong business.'

'Maybe.' Alain looked up towards his home. It was 4pm, a bit early to stop work but a bit late to go back down to Savigny. He had never invited Blonnay to his mountain hideaway, now was the time.

'There's no point in me going back to the office now. I suggest we discuss progress on my terrace. I'll call Lucy to let her know we're on our way.'

Blonnay needed no second invitation: he was delighted. Capitaine Dupertuis really was defrosting.

Eleven

Next to happiness, perhaps enmity is the most helpful stimulant of the human mind.
Margaret Oliphant, The Perpetual Curate, Chronicles of Carlingford

Reports of Maria's murder rippled round the resort like the tremors of a small earthquake. The Grande Cour murder had held Grondère's residents enthralled but they had never felt concerned for their own safety. Here was a gory, vicious and inexplicable murder of an ordinary resident. This could have happened to any of them. Keeping it out of the newspapers was impossible and so the police spokesman concentrated his efforts on damage limitation and emphasising the foreign connection.

BL did not even try to disguise her delight. The celebrity associated with being at the heart of Grondère's latest intrigue vastly compensated for the inconvenience of having to find a new maid.

'Guess what,' she exclaimed to Jodie and Sally at choir practice. 'I've been questioned by those handsome policemen, you know? Of course, I must be a suspect. She was my maid after all. Soon I'll be as famous as your Lucy Wilson.'

Her friends knew that Lucy would be delighted to relinquish her 'fame' but said nothing; BL wouldn't have heard them anyway: she was off to discuss the gory details of Maria's demise with her musical director.

Sally recounted this cavalier reaction to the poor young woman's murder to Lucy who, of course, made sure Alain knew. Lucy didn't know why, but she had taken a decided dislike to Bloody L. She asked Poppy if it was jealousy she was experiencing.

'After all,' she said, 'the woman has everything, good looks, intelligence, talent, wealth, success, energy and dynamism. You can't deny she's throwing everything she's got at this choir project.'

'I wouldn't have put you down as the jealous type, Lucy, such a pointless sentiment. I have learnt not to fall for the public front people project: you never know what sad or bad secrets they're hiding. Do you wish you were her?'

'No, but a bit of her money wouldn't hurt.'

'Would you want to spend your time trading and juggling financial instruments or whatever it is she does to get it?'

'Not at all.'

'Then that's just a harmless and understandable bit of envy, not full-blown jealousy.'

'So why does she get up my nose?'

Poppy laughed. 'You're not alone, I think her greatest talent of all is for rubbing people up the wrong way. Johnny comes out in a rash at the mere mention of her name and Eddie's terrified of her: have you seen the way he cowers in the shadows when she appears?'

'Well, we'll have to get used to her. It looks like she's here to stay.'

'Yes, I'm afraid it does. Hopefully, she'll calm down once she's had her moment of glory.'

'Fingers crossed.'

Lucy wasn't so sure anything could ever calm BL down.

Poppy didn't let on but she had also taken a great dislike to Letty Braythwaite: she didn't mention it to anyone else for she knew it would be interpreted as jealousy. But it wasn't jealousy, it was realistic apprehension: after years of living in Carla Sturridge's shadow, Poppy had been enjoying having Grondère back to herself without somebody trying to do her down all the time behind her back and now she had the feeling it was happening all over again. Her fears were not without grounds: Letty, it would appear, had also discerned Poppy as a threat to her influence, and never missed an opportunity to undermine her 'rival'.

'That poor woman,' she would say to her wealthy cronies, 'how long has she been here? Still living the life of a ski bum and hanging out with people half her age.'

Such remarks, made repeatedly in a small community, can gradually damage their subject and when Poppy began to receive disparaging looks from certain quarters she had little doubt as to their source. Poppy was not immune to negative vibes and it was only a matter of time before she and Letty entered into open hostilities, but Poppy had been around long enough to know to bide her time. As Poppy saw it, BL had already made one big mistake: places and the people who live in them share a history, secrets and allegiances that incomers can never guess at. BL had barged in and asserted a place that she had not earned without any sensitivity to existing ties and loyalties. More than that, Poppy couldn't abide people who looked down on others because they had less money or luck in life or just didn't share their views. She always thought it was dangerous to feel too superior, for you never knew when your luck was going to run out.

Heaven therefore, she thought, must have been smiling on her the day she finally headed down to Savigny to buy some new smart clothes. Poppy wasn't interested in fashion and didn't like shopping. This was probably also a question of budget but, on this occasion, she had left the task far too long and it had become an emergency.

As she wrestled with some new-fangled fasteners in a changing room she overheard a loud conversation arriving and, as it was in English, she tuned in more rapidly than she would have done ordinarily.

'Look at this,' the loudest voice was exclaiming, 'what a find this little boutique is.'

The changing booth beside Poppy was clearly being filled with various items by Letty Braythwaite and whoever she was with: as the other person wasn't getting the opportunity to say much, it wasn't really important. Poppy held her breath and settled comfortably on the little footstool in her cubicle.

She listened in as BL tried on various outfits whilst criticising many of their common acquaintances – including Poppy, and eventually settled on her choice.

'This might work nicely for the concert on 1 August.' She flounced up and down the corridor in a gorgeous frock that Poppy was able to glimpse through the curtain gap.

'And look at this price? A snip.'

'*Ça va, Madame?*' asked the shop assistant peeping through the curtain at Poppy, wondering why her other client was taking so long and if she had gone to sleep.

'*Oui, merci*,' Poppy whispered back grinning and putting her index finger to her lips.

The assistant frowned at her disapprovingly but, at least this woman spoke French, unlike the loud, flashy one. BL, determined to remain the centre of the assistant's attention, thrust the selected dress through the curtain at her.

'I'll take this! Wrap it carefully please.'

She laughed gleefully, telling her friend, 'I'll save that little number for the 1 August concert and official reception. It's time someone showed all those oiks in Grondère some style. I swear that Poppy Smythe woman only possesses comfortable outdoor clothing and terry towelling pyjamas.'

Poppy, concealed only inches away, blushed a little. BL wasn't far from the truth. Maybe she had been living in the mountains too long. But shame quickly turned to indignation.

I'll give her 'oik', she thought, and there's nothing wrong with being more attracted to sports clothes than fancy town stuff I'd never wear: that's what suits my lifestyle ... But that doesn't mean I can't flash a bit of style when I want to.

Once she was sure BL had left she coolly returned to the shop rails and located the dress BL had bought. There was one left and, being a little wider than BL, it was in Poppy's size. She balked a little when she looked at the price tag but her resolve held.

She went and tried it on. It wasn't something she would have looked at but, in fact, it looked great on her and she could afford it – just.

The shop assistant did not utter a single word throughout the transaction but it was clear whose side she was on: she carefully wrapped the item, added a free matching scarf, skilfully adorned the bag with an extra-large bow, finally handing it to Poppy with an undisguised look of admiration.

Not normally a wicked person, as she left the shop it was a grin of pure wickedness that Poppy wore.

'I've been reading up on Italian greyhounds,' proclaimed Poppy as she and Lucy set off for a day's hiking with Słowik at their heels.

'Oh?'

'Yes, going right back to mediaeval times, they were a favourite with noblewomen. You see them in tapestries, renaissance paintings.'

'Of course!' Images of old tapestries came to her and the assertion needed no proof.

'So all you need now is a wimple and a chastity belt.'

Lucy laughed out loud.

'Ohmigod, no thanks. Anyway, why all the research into Słowik?'

The little dog looked up at the sound of her name.

'I was interested to know if we could train her to hunt for truffles.'

'And can we?'

'No, hopeless: she's more likely to chase after a rabbit.'

'Well that's okay, you don't often see a rabbit in the Alps. And she won't be chasing a marmot again.'

'Really?'

Lucy laughed as she described Słowik getting a lesson for her insolence from an affronted marmot.

'That piercing alarm whistle alone will make her think twice against chasing anything else. She hardly leaves my side now.'

Poppy laughed.

'Still, an odd choice of dog for a ski resort. It's okay now but they hate the cold apparently.'

'Oh. That isn't good.' Lucy was concerned. How were they going to deal with that once winter arrived? Oh well, they had the whole summer ahead of them to think of something. Hopefully Alain would have solved his case by then and his crucial witness could be released to warmer climes.

As the weeks of rehearsals progressed, Tommy and Sally regaled their friends with tales of BL's mission to knock them all into shape.

But even without inside informants, it would have been hard for anyone in Grondère to avoid knowing every small development, thanks to the marketing campaign conducted by BL herself. She created dedicated social media pages and regularly posted accounts of their progress, sharing them on all the local community sites. Thrilled and encouraged by the number of 'likes' and hits on these posts, she multiplied them, little knowing that the whole resort was increasingly enthralled by the awfulness of it all.

Military metaphors were a favourite: 'I rallied my troops back into battle', 'once more unto the beat, dear friends', referring to the choir members as 'my worthy little chorists' and 'my brave singing soldiers'. At the same time, she spoke of herself in the most glowing terms: 'Thanks to my timely intervention, we won the day,' – it was all very cringe-worthy. Her patronising comments about the 'slow but steady improvement' and 'increasing musicality' of her 'wonderful warbling warriors' were particularly relished.

'Why do you keep going?' asked Eddie, who wondered what was holding his friends to an activity that was attracting such ridicule.

'It's actually good fun,' confessed Tommy. 'We've got a real professional director and, when he's allowed to be in charge, it's brilliant.'

'Isn't he allowed to be in charge all the time?' asked Lucy, who had always thought musical directors were the boss of the orchestra.

'Not with BL around,' laughed Sally. 'She's paying for the whole shooting match and she's not afraid to keep reminding him. I don't think he likes her very much.'

'I don't like her very much,' said Tommy.

This created a moment of silence. Tommy didn't know how 'not to like' people.

'Why Tommy? She's a bit ridiculous but she's not malicious, is she?'

'I'm not so sure.'

'He's thinking of something strange that happened at our last rehearsal,' Sally explained. 'BL had to leave the rehearsal to take an important business call. "Sorry, darlings," she said, "but someone has to make the money to pay for all this." And the musical director asked Jodie to step in for her and sing her part. You should have heard her, Luce, it was just beautiful. I was almost in tears and the conductor looked dumbfounded. When BL waltzed back in she looked livid. She sent Jodie back to the choir ranks pronto.'

' "Dear, dear! What on earth was that? I suppose you were trying your best. Don't worry, the real singer is back",' added Tommy, imitating BL's patronising tone.

'How did Jodie react?'

'Oh, she just took it. I don't think she realises how good she is.'

'Well, I had no idea, I knew she'd done a bit of singing but I didn't know she was that talented. Maybe they'll give her a little solo.'

'Not if BL has anything to do with it,' Tommy grimaced. 'Anyway, it's not like this is the big time or anything, it's just a concert given by a few ski bums in Grondère.'

'With a proper orchestra,' Sally reminded him. He echoed her proviso.

'With a proper orchestra.'

Lucy and Sally were lounging over a jigsaw puzzle on the lounge floor one rainy weekend afternoon, still in pyjamas and on their second hot chocolate. Tommy and Eddie, excited by the prospect of getting themselves caked in mud, had raced off to the bike park.

'Not that I mind, but I haven't seen Gluey Hughey for ages.'

'No, he always seems to lie low during the summer months.'

'That man is a total enigma.'

'Don't worry. He's sure to turn up if there's a party on.'

Gluey Hughey was an inoffensive young man who had an inbuilt radar for parties and free drinks.

'Talking of missing persons, where is Jodie?'

'I have no idea. I think she might be having an affair. She's been acting all secretive recently and disappearing off without saying where she's going.'

'Do you think she's okay? Should we be doing something?'

'I don't know. When I think about it, we've seen a lot less of her since Tommy and I got together. I'm always at your place and you're often up at Alain's, I've been feeling a bit guilty about it.'

'Now you put it like that, I feel bad too. Do you think she's upset with us?'

'No. She seems okay, just a bit distracted. Maybe it's love.'

'I can't see Jodie having a secret lover.'

'Maybe it's Gluey Hughey.'

'Don't ever let her hear you say that.'

When Alain came home from work in the evenings he popped in to see his mum and collect his parachute from his early-morning paraglide, then picked Lucy up from wherever she was and drove up to his chalet. Lucy didn't spend every night at his place: sometimes he had to work late and occasionally she felt he needed to be alone to dispel whatever unpleasantness he had witnessed during his working day.

Situated just below the woodland section of the old *bisse* path that Lucy loved, Alain's chalet was even more remote than the chalet shared by Lucy, Tommy and Eddie and it was a peaceful refuge for him at the end of the day. In winter, it was closed up but in summer, he spent every moment he could there.

When they spent the evening together they would open a bottle of wine, make dinner together and watch the sun set from the deck he had built. There was a Jacuzzi but Lucy preferred taking a dip in the cool pool in his secret garden. There was only room enough to immerse a couple of bodies and float a bit in the small, dark pool whose water was constantly refreshed by the crystal waters of a mountain spring. Making love outside was a sensation they both appreciated but they were careful to make sure there were no paraglider pilots around. As one himself, Alain knew how, even unintentionally, it was easy to surprise people in illicit activities, from the sky. People rarely thought to look skywards.

Storms were a feature of life in the mountains in summer. Being caught in a storm in the mountains during the day was something to be avoided but they often occurred at night and provided the most dramatic natural spectacle. Forks of lightning would light up the entire sky and the dramatic backdrop of the mountains. When the storm was unleashing its fury on the opposite mountain range it was a thing of majesty to enjoy. Poppy loved a good storm and she would open the windows onto her balcony and lie in bed watching the electric show.

On her first stormy night in Alain's little chalet by the old *bisse*, Lucy felt more vulnerable than during storms in her usual lodgings in the hamlet lower down. She was almost shaken out of bed by a thunderclap which also left her ears ringing: it was terrifying.

'How can you be so relaxed?' she asked Alain who barely stirred from his sleep.

'Because I know that I fixed the sturdiest lightning rods available to man to this place,' he grunted.

'Oh, that's very clever.'

'Thank you.'

'What about falling trees?'

'I measured them: there isn't a single tree near the chalet tall enough to reach it if it falls.'

'Really? You measured them?'

'Of course.'

Lucy lay in bed and got the giggles.

'What's so funny.'

'You measured the trees, that's so Swiss.'

'What's wrong with being Swiss?'

'Nothing, I'm very happy lying here with my Swiss policeman in the knowledge that I am safe from lightning and falling trees.'

'Seismic activity and landslides.'

'Wait a minute: landslides too?'

'Yes, I got a digger and made a break above the chalet and trenches either side.'

'Is that allowed?'

'Yes, all cleared with the authorities. And you can stop that right now: I can feel you grinning through the darkness.'

'I don't know what to say.'

At that moment, a great crash of thunder shook the chalet and she snuggled up closer, feeling suddenly much more relaxed about the natural forces raging above.

Down in Grondère, Poppy had fallen asleep and missed the whole storm. She would wake up the following morning feeling stiff from the draught and with a floor to mop.

Charles Sidforth-Sykes was completely entranced by the Braythwaites. These were his sort of people, loaded with cash and happy to spread it around. He and Henry became inseparable and he introduced Henry to the Golf Club and the local Lion's Club.

One Sunday, the Golf Club held a celebration for its anniversary and the players were encouraged to wear old-fashioned golfing outfits. Charles thought he looked particularly nifty in some chequered knee-length knickerbockers, a lozenge-patterned pullover and a flat cap, all in that unique clash of colours favoured only by the British. Henry, though, outdid everyone. Clad in matching brown tweed knickerbockers, jacket and deerstalker, he stole the show.

'Henry, old chap, you look splendid!' Charles congratulated him on his look, while thinking privately that Henry's regalia was more suited to the damp moors of Devon than the sunny golf course of Grondère.

'Thank you, Charles. Ordered it specially from a tailor in Edinburgh. Swiss customs slapped a mighty import charge on it but worth the expense, I think.'

Henry wore his outfit impeccably all day, even though Charles could detect signs of overheating, and Henry inevitably won the prize for the best outfit at the end of the day. This Charles didn't mind a bit, he was delighted that his new friend was making an impression in the right circles and never left his side to make sure everyone associated him with this rich, successful businessman.

'How about letting me invest some money for you?' Henry Braythwaite asked Charles as they were sitting in the clubhouse celebrating with a glass of brandy.

'That's frightfully good of you, old chap.' Charles was delighted: this was exactly the invitation he had been hoping for after all the attention he had given the newcomers. This couple were obviously high rollers in the finance world. This could be a chance to make some serious money. Henry must have been one of the few people in Grondère who hadn't yet worked out that Charles was not quite as wealthy as he liked to make out.

The golf event did not escape the attention of the *Police judiciaire* and Blonnay popped up to see Lucy and show her a photograph of Henry in his outfit.

'No, definitely not Henry. My Sherlock Holmes was bigger and his face was rounder and the outfit, although almost identical, was a darker shade of brown.'

'But how can you be so sure when you can't give a description of him?'

'I don't know, Laurent. When you show me, like that, I can tell it's not him but I cannot conjure up his face in my mind.'

Blonnay looked disappointed.

'Do you think I imagined it all, Laurent?'

'No, Lucy. I know you are a reliable witness. I just hoped this might spark your memory.'

'Sorry. It is a great picture though, Charles and Henry look like something straight out of P.G. Wodehouse, what a pair of dandies!'

Blonnay still didn't have his man but he had a new author to investigate and a new word so it wasn't a totally wasted trip.

Jamie was engaged a couple of times to chef at the Braythwaites' chalet.

'Great gig,' he told his mates in The Pub afterwards. 'It's not often you're given free rein to cook up a feast, no expense spared. No quibbling over waiter's fees and all paid up front in cash. I can take a lot of shit at choir rehearsals for that kind of work.'

Jamie normally spent the summer in the Southern Hemisphere ski resorts but had decided to stay in Grondère for once. He had been uncertain as to whether he would make enough money staying but the private cheffing and working for Sammy in his bistro and bar was proving much more lucrative than he expected.

Lucy grinned. She enjoyed Jamie's outrageously camp attitude but she had another reason to be fond of him. He had been a waiter the night of the charity ball at La Grande Cour when it had all gone horribly wrong and she had found herself suspected of murdering Malcolm McDonaghue. Jamie had been one of the people who had remained a friend when others had turned their backs on her.

'Charles Sidforth-Sykes has been persuaded to join the choir,' he announced.

'You are kidding!' Lucy could not think of a less likely chorister.

'Scout's honour,' Jamie pouted. 'Heard it myself. Although I shouldn't really be telling you – most unprofessional of me. Anyway, he was boasting of his rich baritone over supper and so BL made him audition there and then. He actually isn't bad.'

'Crikey,' Tommy gulped. 'That's going to make choir practice interesting.'

Poppy was chuckling so much she couldn't say anything.

Of all Grondère's residents, Humphrey Watson was the person deriving the greatest pleasure from the choir. He read all of BL's Facebook posts with voracity and took to attending rehearsals with whichever grandchildren were currently in his charge.

BL was elated to be finally the focus of Humphrey's attention and made sure there was always a bucket of cold beers and wine for his exclusive use and squash and crisps for the grandchildren. During the breaks, if she wasn't haranguing the musical director or the choir, she would head over to him and fawn over him obsequiously.

He and Charles had known each other for decades and so Charles would also join in, saving himself from having to mix with the lower orders.

'I don't know how he can stand all that bowing and scraping,' Sally remarked. 'He may be as rich as Croesus but it's not his style.'

Jamie smiled knowingly.

'Humphrey's got his own agenda. Look at that grin on his face.'

Humphrey would just seat himself in the front row, chuckling and smiling broadly while his small charges ran around the hall pretending to be Jets and Sharks. Curiously, this didn't bother anyone: the children seemed instinctively to know when to be quiet and they stood enraptured during the quieter numbers.

When asked, all Humphrey would say was that it was the best entertainment to be had in Grondère, and all for free.

Twelve

The vineyards literally seemed to be sunbathing, lying back at an angle with eyes closed, willing the rays to kiss them.
Jancis Robinson, on the vineyards of Valais, in an article on Swiss Wines, 2015

In early July, Sebastian and Tonita flew back to Switzerland together. As they sat in the business class lounge in JFK, Tonita browsed through the latest glossies to check various promised photos of her collection had been published and Sebastian juggled phone calls from his equity sales team who were calling for advice about the latest share issue.

He was relieved when they finally sat on the plane and he could switch off for a while. It was his first trip to Grondère since April. After witnessing his mother and sister's arrests, he had put his father's affairs in the hands of his old friend and lawyer, Maître Aulnay, and left Anya in charge of the hotel. He was returning now to check up on everything, resolve some business matters and had timed his visit to coincide with the start of the summer holidays, the first two weeks of which Tonita would be spending in Grondère with Ruby and Leo, her half-sister and brother. He had again put the hotel at her disposal as he felt it was only fair; it had, after all, been her home before Malcolm's death. They both had another reason for returning to Grondère at this point in time: Malcolm McDonaghue had been preparing a book on the wines and vineyards of Valais before he was murdered and, at their request, Lucy had been working with the printer and publisher to complete it. They had seen the various proof stages of the book and Lucy wanted their final sign-off to go to print. This was their tribute to Malcolm and they wanted to be there with Lucy when she gave the go-ahead to print.

Sebastian looked across at Tonita who, having downed a couple of glasses of wine, was dozing. She looked happy and peaceful and he envied her: he had never felt less so. That April, she had come to him for advice about her estranged father and her half-siblings.

Prior to that he had known little about Tonita's past and he was flattered that she should feel able to use him as a sounding board. Malcolm had just died and it had made her reconsider an offer from her father to become the guardian of his children by his third marriage. Being no dupe, Tonita knew it was a self-interested offer on his part: the children were starting boarding school in the UK and, as she lived in Switzerland at the time, her father, being based in the Middle East, knew she would be closer to deal with the shorter holidays and any emergencies that arose.

Losing Malcolm had shaken her to the core and brought Tonita to have a good long hard look at her own behaviour and motivations. Her father had hurt Tonita all those years ago by leaving her cancer-ridden mother when she needed him most: it had hardened Tonita.

Malcolm's death had taught Tonita that shutting love out of her life might have protected her from pain, but it had also deprived her of its comfort. She was revisiting the matter from a different angle and as a changed person.

As they talked it through, Sebastian had seen that Tonita had a deeply rooted hate for her father that time was unlikely to erase: forgiveness for him was out of the question. They both felt however, that the children shouldn't be punished for that: in fact, knowing what selfish cruelty her father was capable of, she almost had a duty to put herself in a position to be able to protect them, should one day he also let them down, as he had her.

Sebastian and Tonita had arrived at the conclusion that she should let her father back into her life whilst keeping him at a distance, but allow herself to love the children. She obviously had grown fond of them, she talked about them all the time and was undisguisedly excited about having two weeks with them before they headed off to Italy to join their parents. The searing temperatures in Dubai drove her father and his third wife to Europe for the summer but they had not received an invitation to Grondère.

The meeting with the printer and publisher was over quickly. Lucy had done a great job and, thanking her, they gave the order to print. Promising to meet her the following evening for a celebratory drink at the hotel, Sebastian and Tonita dropped Lucy off at the station and made their way to the offices of Maître Aulnay, Malcolm's (and now Sebastian's) lawyer.

Sebastian and Tonita sat quietly in front of the lawyer and skimmed through the complete list of Malcolm's assets. Tonita was only concerned with the shares in the White Snowflake project which would soon be hers. Sebastian had already seen a draft of the transfer of ownership and, indeed had been partly responsible for drawing it up, so he expected this final review to be a formality only. Once the trial was over, his mother and sister, if found guilty, would be unable to profit from their crime, and all the assets could all be legally transferred to Sebastian, as Malcolm's sole heir. Sebastian, already wealthy in his own right, had decided to atone for Tonita's having been cheated out of a wealthy husband by the untimely death of her fiancé by respecting his father's original intention and giving the interest in the lucrative property development directly to her.

Sebastian, however, was puzzled.

'Maître Aulnay, there seems be an error here. It lists a large property in Valais which I've never seen before.' He pointed to the line item.

Maître Aulnay looked at him in even greater puzzlement. Firstly, the idea that Maître Aulnay might have made a mistake was inconceivable, but secondly, and even more perplexing, was it possible that Malcolm had not told his son of his greatest project of all?

'I can assure you, M. McDonaghue, there is no mistake. You were aware that your father, just before his death, had purchased a vineyard?'

Sebastian was speechless. He looked at Tonita who, equally baffled, shook her head.

The room was silent as they all absorbed this bombshell, then Sebastian burst out laughing.

'Brilliant! Brilliant! Oh, Dad! You really are still pulling the strings, after all.'

Tonita grinned at him.

'How typical of Malcolm, I should have known he'd never be satisfied until he was making his own wine.'

The three of them smiled as they absorbed this startling piece of information.

'So, tell me Maître Aulnay, as you seem to be the only person in the know, what was my father's grand plan and what on earth am I, living in New York, supposed to do with a vineyard?'

'For the time being, I do not think you need to do anything. The agreement was that the previous owner, having no successors, would train a young person he and your father had selected to run the vineyard. Your father had paid for the young woman to train at the Changins School of

Viticulture and Oenology and, when she completes her diploma this summer, she will gradually take over. It is a profitable outfit and Mlle Guérin has a good business brain.'

Tonita had a thought. She removed the final proof of Malcolm's book they had just cleared for print from her briefcase and turned to the final pages.

'It's this place, isn't it?'

Maître Aulnay looked at the open pages and nodded.

Sebastian took the proof from her.

'How did you work that out?'

'I always thought that sentence at the end was a bit cryptic. Read this: *This jewel of Valais will hopefully continue to shine as the next generation takes over. It is to be hoped that the new owner merits the confidence placed in him and takes good care of it.* Don't you see? He was talking about himself.'

'It's strange that Lucy didn't pick up on it. Didn't she visit all the vineyards?'

'But that's just it, she did. This morning at the hotel, she smiled at the logo I had prepared for the hotel and said what a great wine label it would make. She just assumed we knew about it.'

'Ask her.'

The two men sat as Tonita stepped outside and called Lucy, who expressed her surprise at their surprise.

'Well?' asked Sebastian, as Tonita finished her call, 'Were we really the only ones who didn't know?'

Tonita grinned widely.

'We were. Lucy said, of all the vineyards, she could see exactly why Malcolm had fallen in love with it. I asked her to arrange for us to visit, tomorrow if possible.'

It was all a bit much to take in for Sebastian. Not only was he the involuntary owner of a hotel in Europe that he didn't know what to do with but now his dilemma extended to a vineyard.

'Is that everything, Maître Aulnay? Are there any more surprises?'

'Everything I know about is contained in the papers you have in front of you. As to any further surprises … in light of what has just happened, I am reluctant to opine.'

Sebastian shook his head. He was used to making big decisions, striking deals and taking risks but this unexpected turn of events had him totally floored.

'I suggest we regroup when you have had time to consider this new matter,' proffered Maître Aulnay.

Sebastian thanked the lawyer and he and Tonita left, feeling slightly shell-shocked. As they drove back up the mountain to Grondère, Sebastian began to chuckle and didn't stop until they arrived.

───────────────

The next morning, Sebastian, Tonita, her two siblings, Lucy and Słowik drove down into the valley again, this time past Savigny, towards the hillsides of the Rhône Valley where Malcolm's grapes were swelling and basking in the generous Swiss sunshine. Lucy was looking forward to seeing the vines in full leaf and meeting Sandra again. She was also enjoying watching Sebastian the banker inside his father's comfort zone, but so clearly outside his own.

She couldn't work out if he was proud or horrified at finding himself in the middle of his father's rural undertaking but she was sure that the vineyard would work its magic on him, as it had on his father and, more recently, on her and Sally.

Lucy was right. As they stepped out of the car and looked around, Sebastian could see why Malcolm had used the word 'jewel'. The vegetation hiding the car park was lush and green and above them, up and up, curved terraces, with dry stone retaining walls, surrounded them. The slopes came to a dramatic halt at the edge of a cliff down which trickled a glistening waterfall. It felt secluded and private and yet, it was large.

Standing in front of the office, an elderly man and a young woman stood side by side, nervously waiting to hear what was to become of them and the vineyard they loved.

The children scampered through the rows of vines with the nimble little dog as Tonita kept a discreet but careful eye on them. Lucy nodded at Sandra, but, once she had introduced Sebastian, held back and walked behind them. Throughout the visit Sebastian said little: he listened seriously as he was shown first the vines, then the wines, the cellar and the plans Malcolm had drawn up for a new tasting room and hospitality suite and, finally, the accounts. He looked pensive as they then all sat down to take an *apéro* in the small Japanese garden at the foot of the waterfall.

'I am so sorry I have not contacted you before M. Mayoraz, but I had no idea …'

'So I understand. I am also guilty of failing to contact you but I attributed your silence to grief,' nodded the old man. 'I was, of course, at your father's memorial service but you were so distressed and it was not a time to be talking business.'

'Thank you for looking after things.'

'I owed this to your father.'

They were all silent for a moment, during which Sebastian heard the remembered sound of his father's relaxed laughter, which made him smile.

'However, I think Mlle Guérin would like now to know your plans for her and the vineyard.'

'Well, to be honest, M. Mayoraz, I'm still a bit shocked to find myself the owner of a vineyard. I wouldn't necessarily have expected my father to tell me all his projects but I am a little surprised he didn't take his fiancée, Mlle Shalott here, into his confidence.'

'It was to be kept secret from everyone until the new buildings were completed and he had produced his first vintage, a sparkling white, which was, and still is, to be named *La Dame de Shalott*. It was to be served for the first time at his wedding.'

Tonita smiled at Sebastian; she was grateful for this explanation. If Malcolm had deceived her it was only so he could give her pleasure at a later date.

'And so,' asked Sandra Guérin, 'what are we to do?'

Sebastian grinned.

'We are going to follow my father's master plan. We are going to make wine. There is just one condition …'

They all looked at him questioningly.

'The Lady of Shalott over there is an artist: I would like her to design all the labels and artwork from now on.'

Tonita nodded her agreement with evident pleasure and they raised their glasses to Malcolm and his crazy project.

On the way back to Grondère, Sebastian was pensive: it was his business instincts that had taken over. He eventually shared what was troubling him.

'We'll have to get someone in to do the books, we cannot expect Mlle Guérin to run the vineyard entirely on her own. There's no doubt she can handle the vineyard and the winemaking process but she needs to be able to focus entirely on that. If she has to handle sales, marketing and accounting too she will not be able to concentrate on making good wines: that cannot have been my father's plan.'

'No,' agreed Tonita thoughtfully. She was driving as Sebastian had done a little too much tasting of his own wine.

'What sort of person are you thinking of?' asked Lucy, whose mind was racing. Sally was, for her, the obvious candidate but Sebastian would probably not consider her qualified enough.

He looked round at her, craftily, thinking she was thinking of herself.

'Well, it would have to be someone of similar age, so that they could grow the business together and compatibility with Mlle Guérin would obviously be paramount. Someone with sales experience and able to keep the books. Preferably, also with some wine know-how.' As he thought out loud he realised that Lucy did not fit his description.

'You weren't thinking of yourself, were you?'

'No way,' Lucy laughed. 'My knowledge of wine extends only to the contents of the book.'

She proceeded to tell him about Sally, how she had explained all about different grapes to her and how it had been her idea to visit the vineyards. Sally had bookkeeping and sales experience and Lucy knew she was desperate for a change from working in a skiwear shop.

'She and Sandra also got on like a house on fire,' she said, closing her sales pitch.

Sebastian grinned. He was beginning to wonder how much of his destiny he was actually in control of.

———————————

The next day, Sebastian and Tonita met with Alessandra Rosset, who, since Malcolm's death, had taken charge of the White Snowflake project. Alessandra was a hard-nosed entrepreneur and the project was advancing well. She showed them the plan of works for the development, full costings plus projected revenues. They were left in no doubt that the consortium was in good hands. She also talked to them about other potential sites for development in and around Grondère. It was becoming patently clear that all Tonita had to do was leave her money where it was and this young woman would make it grow.

'There's just one more thing,' she asked as they were wrapping up the meeting. 'The hotel: will you be selling?'

'I don't know yet. I can't do anything until after the trial.'

'You can discuss price.' She pointed out.

'I can discuss price,' he concurred.

'20 million.'

'It's worth 40, as a going concern.'

She looked at him appreciatively; she liked a decent negotiation.

'You want rid of it quickly, 30.'

'I'll think about it.'

'Don't think too long.'

'Message understood.'

Mme Rosset shook hands, turned on her heels and left.

'Goodness.' Tonita sat back in her chair. 'She's intense.'

'She's come from nowhere in ten years to be one of the most influential property magnates in Switzerland.'

'I can see how. 30 million, you could retire easily on that.'

Anya watched Alessandra Rosset leave with dread in her heart. She had already been approached by Alessandra's headhunters trying to poach her away from the hotel. Alessandra wasn't stupid: she knew that it was down to Anya that the place had survived the blow of Malcolm's death. Feeling that it would be nice if someone would tell her what was going on, she called Lucy.

That night, once Tonita had settled her young charges to bed, she and Seb set out for a moonlight walk. It was a beautiful, clear evening and they both had much to digest. 'Do you remember the last time we did this?' Tonita asked him as they paused to look down on the twinkling lights of Grondère below.

'I do,' he grinned. 'We sneaked out to escape Mother and Genna during the murder investigation. I felt guilty at the time for being such a bad son. If I'd known what I know now …'

'I'm dreading the trial.'

'Me too. I'll just be glad when it's all over and I can work out what I'm going do with Dad's assets.'

'That's going to take a while.'

'You know? I feel more and more inclined to leave things as they are.'

'Really?'

'Dad's businesses were so sound, Tonita. Look at Anya: she's running that hotel just as well as he did – better without Mother's interference. When I went through the accounts, Mother was a taking a big chunk of the profits and Genna's allowance was much bigger than Dad had ever admitted to me. All the private suites on the top floor were occupied by family: I can see why you and Dad had one, but Mum and Genna both had those valuable rooms tied up. They're now permanently booked and earning a bomb. Anya has lowered the prices in the spa to bring in more outside custom and so that's now turning a tidy profit. His other business interests are all bringing in revenue and now the vineyard also looks like it could be a goldmine.'

'But I thought you wanted to cut your ties with Europe?'

'I did. Now I'm not sure. When I'm here, all that scrapping over shares, deals and percentage points seems a little pointless. Each time I come here I find it harder and harder to leave.'

Tonita was shocked. Sebastian was sounding more and more like his father.

At that point they both stopped still. Ahead of them on the path, bathed in a shaft of moonlight, stood a large stag. It looked directly at them and they could hardly breath at the beauty of the animal and the fear it was about to charge.

It must only have been about thirty seconds before the animal moved but it seemed like minutes. It put forward its right leg, lowered its antlers in a majestic bow and then bounded into the darkness.

It was a while before Sebastian spoke.

'Do you believe in signs?'

'I do. I'm not religious but you cannot deny that life is full of the strangest echoes and coincidences.'

'Last time we were here, at this very spot, I thought I felt Dad's presence. Now, it's almost as if I saw him. Do you think I'm crazy?'

'No Sebastian, I don't.'

He looked at her and knew she was being completely honest. They walked on in silence until they came to a clearing and a bench beckoned them.

'I wish I'd thought to bring a flask,' he sighed.

Tonita had thought of it. She grinned as she brought out a small bottle of port.

'I've been hiking with Lucy. She always brings little treats: she says it's something she's copied from Poppy. Apparently Poppy even travels with crystal wine glasses; I'm afraid I opted for plastic beakers.'

'No complaints,' he laughed.

They sat looking down on the lights of Grondère and Sebastian realised he hadn't felt this happy for a long time.

Before flying to New York, the next day Sebastian called Anya into his office, told her he had declined Alessandra Rosset's offer and offered her a pay rise.

'You're doing a great job Anya and, if you're willing to make a long-term commitment, we can continue to run this place profitably without Mme Rosset's help.'

'I have heard about her management practices and I could not work for such a woman, however much she offered. She has everyone on timesheets and aggressive targets. I understand it's very efficient but it makes for a horrible working environment.'

Sebastian looked at Anya knowingly.

'How much did she offer?'

'The person who called offered 30% more than whatever I was on here, but I told them I was not interested in talking to them.'

'That was brave. If I'd sold, you'd have been the first out the door.'

'It would also have been disloyal. You and your father do not deserve that. He gave me my first management opportunity and you my second.'

'I don't deserve any credit for that. I'm afraid I just took the easiest option in the circumstances.'

'I don't believe that. You could have called in someone with experience but you saw I wanted it and you let me try.'

'You're right. I also thought you had a head start because you already knew the establishment.'

'You see, it was a business decision. And it was a good one because I was the right choice.'

He smiled at her honest appraisal of her own competence. 'Profits are up, the staff are happy, the customers tell me it's a tight-run outfit. The internet site reviews are even better than before, so yes Anya, I chose well, or Dad did.'

'I was very fond of your father: when you're here it's a bit like having him around again.'

'That's nice to hear, thank you.'

'Although, you don't know your wines like he did.'

'That is something I plan to work on,' he grinned, thinking of the pleasure he would derive in the future when he presented her with *La Dame de Shalott* to put on the wine list.

'Anya, I have neglected you and I apologise. From now on, I would like us to speak more often. I do not want to interfere, I want us to be a team.'

'I would like that.'

As they shook hands warmly, she added, 'I spoke to Lucy yesterday, she told me you'd not sell.'

'I'd love to know how she knew when I didn't know myself.'

'She said the mountains were calling you.'

Sebastian shook his head in mock exasperation.

'Well, right now, Wall Street is calling and so the mountains must wait.'

Charles Sidforth-Sykes looked down upon the bulldozers tearing down the old wooden shacks of the former school holiday camp as diggers began opening up a huge hole in the ground. Work on the White Snowflake project had begun.

The aspect was a depressing one for Charles who had been a founding shareholder in the consortium. Believing the project to be a dead duck, and in keeping with his record of bad business decisions, he had sold his shares to Malcolm McDonaghue just weeks before building authorisation had been received. Those shares, he understood were now in the lucky hands of Tonita Shalott. He had also heard that the consortium, now headed by Swiss hotshot entrepreneur, Alessandra Rosset, was expanding and setting its sights on developing other sites in Grondère. If she could hold her nerve, Tonita stood to make a large fortune.

Tonita – now there was an idea: he'd always suspected her of harbouring a secret attraction for him and she'd had a few months to get over Malcolm's death. It was time for him to make his move before someone else did.

The prospect of simultaneously securing love and financial security cheered him up and he walked jauntily uphill to visit Letty and Henry.

He congratulated himself for having established this strong friendship with such lovely, rich and generous people: he knew he could look forward to a good supper and fine wines with the Braythwaites. He might also get a bit of advice from Letty on wooing Tonita: it had been a while since he'd seriously considered dating anyone.

'Charles, dahling, do come in, go and help Henry, he's just down in the cellar trying to find the right red: Jamie's here, we're having *chateaubriand*.'

Yes, thought Charles, my star is definitely on the rise.

Tonita stayed on for another week with Ruby and Leo. Every day she had Molly at The Larder prepare them a picnic and worked through the list of activities Lucy had put together for them. They hiked along the old *bisse*, explored gorges and grottos, took the cable car up to the top of Mont Grondère early one morning for a sunrise breakfast, hired downhill scooters and mountain bikes and raced down the mountain trails. She felt she was finally getting to know them as brother and sisters should know one another.

On the final day, they hiked up to the Lac des Bouquetins where Lucy and Poppy had said they would meet them for a picnic and a swim.

They were hot and sweaty when they arrived.

Lucy was already there and had laid out picnic rugs near a large flat rock that was clearly meant to serve as a table.

'It is a stunning spot.' Tonita looked around. Grassy meadows gently led down to the heart-shaped lake with grey mountains rising on either side. The far side of the lake sloped towards a descending mountain pass, giving the impression of a natural infinity pool. The still, dark waters mirrored the surrounding landscape and the cloudless blue sky but the lake still looked cold. 'The trick is,' Lucy told them, 'to go in slowly. Come out before you've had enough, and dry and change immediately, even if you want to go back in later. Once you get cold up here, it's hard to defrost, even on a warm day.'

Her advice was good. After a first swim, they all changed and tucked into the picnic. Molly, knowing it was their last day and that Lucy and Poppy would be joining them, had gone overboard. She had even put in a bottle of cider for Poppy who turned up with a bottle of *Petite Arvine* for Lucy and Tonita, which she served, as usual, in her crystal wine glasses: she had brought an extra one for Tonita.

'I'm impressed, Poppy.'

'Crystal belongs in the mountain, Tonita.'

'Indeed it does,' Tonita smiled, holding up her glass so that the engraved facets twinkled in the sunlight and the scenery made patterns like a kaleidoscope.

Other hikers soon appeared, swam and picnicked in their turn and the lake took on the aspect of a lowland lake at holiday time with squeals as swimmers entered the water and laughter as they exited. When Tonita, Leo and Ruby surfaced from their second swim, Lucy and Poppy were huddled over Poppy's camera.

'I think it's some sort of sedum,' Lucy was saying.

'I thought maybe a euphorbia of some sort.'

'Possibly.'

'May I see?'

Poppy showed Tonita the images that were causing such debate.

'What do you think?'

'I have absolutely no clue. I was just curious to see the cause of consternation. It's beautiful though, look at all those tightly clustered pink flowers, each one a tiny jewel. Will you send me a copy?'

Poppy and Lucy grinned at each other behind Tonita's back: who would have thought the Prada-clad, Chanel-shoed, Hermès-scarved, Tonita Shalott would have ended up hiking, picnicking and swimming in the mountains with a pair of ski bums. Not them, that's for sure.

'You're laughing at me, ladies, I can tell.'

'No, we're not, Tonita,' Poppy insisted. 'We're enjoying your company and we're laughing because we never thought we would. It's very different.'

Tonita blushed. It occurred to her that she had never imagined she would enjoy theirs either, but this thought, she felt, did not reflect well on her and so she kept it to herself.

Heading back down the hill, the happy party went past BL's chalet: she was, inevitably, in her garden and so an introduction to Tonita could not be avoided.

Letty was overjoyed to meet Tonita although she wondered what on earth she was doing with company so beneath her: she assumed she had hired them as guides. She could immediately see why this beautiful young woman of the world was completely suitable for her dear friend Charles and considered it her duty to befriend Tonita, not only for Charles' sake, but because Tonita's rightful place was in her circle, not the unambitious underachievers currently monopolising her.

'Such a pleasure to meet you,' she gushed.

Tonita was puzzled to know why.

'We have a dear friend in common, I have heard all about you from Charles.'

'Oh yes, of course,' Tonita, who hadn't given Charles a thought since she'd left Grondère for New York in April, smiled politely.

'Just the other night, he was saying over dinner how we must all get together.'

'That would be nice,' Tonita lied.

'Let's exchange numbers. Do you have a free night this week?'

'Oh, I'm so sorry: this is our last day.'

Tonita, highly accomplished in off-loading unwanted hangers-on, explained that she had been fully engaged all week, looking after her sister and brother. The children were duly called over to be presented and fawned upon. Poppy and Lucy made throwing-up faces at each other.

Tonita felt a growing dislike for this invasive, gushing woman who, she noticed, had barely acknowledged Lucy and Poppy once she had obtained her introduction to Tonita. Słowik sensed the negative vibe and trotted over to stand protectively by Tonita's side.

126

'What a sweet little dog, is it a whippet?' asked BL, bending down to stroke Słowik and promptly receiving a sharp nip on the hand for her troubles.

'Oh no, I am so sorry,' Tonita stammered.

'Oh, it's okay, it's just a little scratch.'

This was true: Słowik had judged her attack to perfection and had not drawn blood. Lucy rushed forward to drag the unrepentant creature away.

'I'm so sorry Letty. I've never known her do that before. She's usually so good. Słowik, you bad, bad dog!'

'Oh, so it's not your dog,' Letty looked at Tonita, as if to say she knew Tonita could never have such a badly behaved dog.

Tonita saw her chance to escape and seized it.

'You'd better get some disinfectant on that all the same. We'll leave you to it.'

'You don't want to stay for a little drink?'

'No, we'd better be off. We'll get the dog out of your way. Another time.'

Tonita, Słowik and the children at her heels, was five metres away, having adroitly dodged giving her phone number to BL. BL glared at Lucy and Poppy, clearly holding them responsible for the loss of her prey: they shrugged apologetically before following on.

Once they were out of sight and hearing, they all broke out into giggles and lavished Słowik with cuddles – entirely inappropriate dog-disciplining measures.

'Good work, Słowik,' laughed Tonita. 'You got me out of a tight spot there. What a dreadful woman. I felt like Mowgli being hypnotised by Kaa.'

Poppy couldn't resist a little tease.

'In the old days, Tonita, BL would have automatically been part of your social set.'

Tonita looked at her consideringly.

'True. And I don't think I have escaped the burning coals yet, Poppy. BL does not seem like a woman to be thwarted at the first hurdle.'

'You are right, Tonita. She is determined to have you, but having seen how neatly you wriggled out of your first encounter, I have no fear for your virtue.'

Lucy chuckled.

'At least we're safe from her attentions. Oh, the joys of being a ski bum.'

'Thank goodness I'm off tomorrow. What a lucky escape.'

Poppy had a thought and burst out laughing.

'Well, at least, Lucy, you know she won't get anywhere if she reports your vicious dog to the police. She's their bloody witness.'

Thirteen

Sweet poet of the woods…
Charlotte Smith, On the Departure of the Nightingale

The wild lupins around Lucy, Tommy and Eddie's chalet had finished flowering and the grass had grown very tall. Fearful that it might be inhabited by the odd snake, Lucy had cut it with a rusty old scythe she had found in the storeroom under the chalet. She had spent a delightful evening in the garden with a wire brush and a sharpening stone and the next day had scythed a space for her guests to spread out blankets and the few rickety deckchairs in their possession. She left a big pile of hay in front of the balcony and had enjoyed watching the deer tucking in early the next morning as she sat on the balcony drinking her first cup of tea of the day. The deer were used to her now and, as long as she kept still, they would bring their young and all graze quite happily in her company.

It was her birthday and, as it fell on a Sunday, she had decided to hold a barbecue party. The previous evening, she and her housemates had prepared everything except the food and, as she was not a talented cook, Tommy and Sally would be prepping everything that morning. Grondère was inhabited by many talented cooks, Molly, Sammy and Jamie included, and they had all promised to bring something delicious with them.

For now, all she had to do was sit enjoying the deer and contemplating the day ahead.

Tommy brought out a second mug of tea and sat beside her on the sofa.

'Just how I like it, as always,' she sighed, noticing that the deer had vanished.

'This feels like old times,' he smiled.

'You're right,' she agreed. 'How much has changed since I first moved in, and yet, it's only just over a year ago.'

'The family has grown.'

'It has.'

'But you, Eddie and I, we will always be there for each other.'

'We will. Are you going anywhere? Is there something you want to tell me?'

'Not specifically, but things are changing, I can feel it.'

'Yes, me too.'

She knew he was thinking about the time they lost Danny and he was right, it had created a special bond between the three of them that would always be there. Something good and lasting had come out of that terrible time shared.

'Happy Birthday!' Eddie and Sally joined them and handed Lucy her present from all of them.

'An old-fashioned Alpenstock! How wonderful!

'Just like the ones you told us Mark Twain, Jemima Morrell and all the early tourists felt compelled to buy!' Sally teased. 'You are properly equipped for the Gemmi Pass now!'

Poppy was first to arrive that afternoon, chuckling as she, in turn, handed Lucy her present. It was a CD of bird song. Lucy was ecstatic.

'Brilliant!' Lucy kissed her gleefully. 'I can't wait to listen to this!'

'Really?' said Jodie. She loved nature but she did think Lucy and Poppy were mildly odd in wanting to know every detail about it.

Molly arrived with a huge carrot cake and Sammy and Jamie each brought a lavish salad. Sammy had called his Grondère Goo and Jamie's was called Mountain Mush: they were both delicious.

Gluey Hughey, absent all summer, suddenly appeared out of nowhere. He hadn't been invited but then Gluey Hughey never was: it never seemed to deter him. The wonder was how he always knew there was an event to invite himself along to. He didn't bring a bottle but then he never did. He sat happily on a log, drinking beer and listening to everyone else's conversations.

As Alain and Lucy were at the water trough opening some fresh bottles of white, Gluey Hughey appeared at Lucy's side.

'Happy Birthday, Lucy,' he said shyly and handed her a grubby paper bag.

Lucy nearly fainted: Hughey had never been known to give anyone a present. She gave her stunned thanks and lifted a wooden object out of the bag.

'Did you make this, Hughey?'

He nodded, embarrassed.

'It's beautiful.'

She held it up to show Alain. It was a beautifully carved songbird.

'It's recycled wood,' he explained, eager to specify that he hadn't vandalised the forest. 'I only ever take fallen wood.'

'You're very talented. That's a good bit of workmanship,' Alain complimented him. Having renovated his own chalet, he appreciated the skill of a true craftsman.

Hughey blushed.

'It's not any bird in particular, I just follow the grain of the wood, the shape of the branch and the line where it broke from the tree.'

It was the hand of an experienced woodcarver. Lucy was touched and even felt a little sad. She had an image of Hughey spending many long, lonely hours wandering the forest and carving wood. She turned it over in her hands.

'It could be a cuckoo.'

'Tail's too short,' Poppy commented, coming over to find out what had happened to her wine. 'More like a nightingale. There you go, Lucy, you have your nightingale in Grondère.'

'You mustn't keep it inside,' Hughey instructed her earnestly. 'Some people think that's unlucky. It's well-varnished, you can keep it by your front door.'

Lucy looked at her little bird fondly.

'It's truly lovely. I promise you, Hughey, I will keep this by the front door of every home I live in from now on.'

Hughey blushed and retreated back to his log, with a fresh bottle of beer, of course.

'Do I have a rival?' Alain teased.

'I'm in a state of shock,' Poppy said. 'That man has hidden depths.'

Fourteen

In this world you've a soul for a compass
And a heart for a pair of wings
There's a star on the far horizon, rising bright in an
azure sky
For the rest of the time that you're given, why walk when
you can fly?

Mary Chapin-Carpenter

Ellen looked tenderly at her partner of the past ten years.
'Your heart isn't in it anymore, is it Seb?'
He looked stunned.
'In what?'
'In any of it, the job, this New York life … me.'
He looked at her, unhappy to cause her pain but unable to
lie.
'No. Is it that obvious?'
'Probably only to me. The fire has gone out of you Seb,
you've lost your edge. Ever since your Dad died, you seem
distracted … absent.'
'I know you're right. Will it blow over d'you think?'
'I doubt it. Tell me, when you look out at that Manhattan
skyline, where are you? You're not here with me, that's
for sure.'
He was all admiration for Ellen, she was so brave to tackle
the problem head-on whilst he had been unable to even
identify it. He thought long and hard about what he
dreamed of when he looked out of the window.
'I see mountains,' he confessed. 'I see snow, I see sun,
grapes and … I see children laughing and running through
the vineyards.'
She shook her head sadly.
'And Tonita?'
'Are you crazy? My Dad's fiancée! I'm not that big a shit.'

'No one's accusing you of being a shit. You can't help who you fall in love with.'

'I'm in love with you.'

'You were, and I with you, but you've changed Seb, and I have not. You're slipping away from me, you've gone all mellow and "Mother Earth", it's as if you're turning into your father.'

'I'm so sorry,' he said. 'There seriously is nothing between me and Tonita, I promise you.'

'Well then you "seriously" ought to think about it. She's still "child-bearing" age but the clock's ticking.'

He was staggered. It was the end of his relationship and all he could feel was gratitude that she'd made it so easy for him.

The next day, Seb instructed his lawyers to sell his share of the property to Ellen and arranged to move into a serviced apartment near his office. A week later he heard that Ellen was already seeing someone else, a recently-divorced partner of a major Wall Street law firm that they had both been friendly with for many years. It dawned on Sebastian that Ellen had already lined up his successor before their break-up and all remnants of guilt vanished.

Some of the things she had said began to irk him, particularly the remark about the fire having gone out of him. Sebastian felt she couldn't have been further from the truth: not only was his fire still burning but it was more akin to a volcano on the verge of eruption.

He called Tonita to update her on the change in his domestic situation. Apparently Ellen had even saved him that task and had told her over lunch earlier in the week. Tonita dutifully expressed her sympathy and uttered the appropriate lines: 'love you both', 'glad you're still friends', but when Tonita was absorbed in designing a new collection she really didn't have much emotional room for anything else. She was fond of both of them, and did at least realise that she ought to have felt a little sad. Maybe she was still the old, heartless Tonita because she didn't really feel any sadness at all. In fact, if she was honest with herself, she was rather pleased.

Fifteen

Police work is two parts routine, one part common sense and one part luck.
Margaret Erskine, *The Limping Man*

Alain Dupertuis and his team sat in the procureur's office. It was weeks since Maria and her cousin had been murdered and they had not made much progress. They went over and over the little they knew but they could not make a connection between Maria and anyone else in Grondère.

'Mme Braythwaite has Polish origins,' Sylvie Jacquier told him. 'She says that's why she hired Maria but it could be a bluff. It does seem to favour Herr Schmutz's Polish connection theory but so far, we can't find anything to connect them.'

'What I find strange,' Alain added, 'is the difference between the two murders. The almost comical staging of the Reichenbach Falls murder smacks of melodrama and chancy amateurism. But there was no attempt to dress Maria's murder up as anything other than what it was – a cold and brutal annihilation.'

'You're thinking, two different murderers?' asked the procureur.

'Perhaps even a hitman, there was something almost professional about it. To have beaten her up like that and not leave a hair, a print, no DNA.'

'I agree, it's odd,' Blonnay added. 'Sergei Kowalski didn't leave much to show for himself either. The only personal possession we found at Maria's that clearly belonged to him, other than his shaving kit, was a well-thumbed Polish copy of the complete Sherlock Holmes.'

'Really? That is weird.'

'Perhaps the Reichenbach Falls encounter was his idea.'

'Well, if it was, it didn't go according to plan.'

'No.'

'Have the Polish police come back with anything else?'

'No, apparently the Polish criminal underworld has clammed up. His family are denying even knowing he was with Maria.'

'They're probably telling the truth. He wouldn't have wanted anyone beating that information out of them. So where do we go from here?'

'I suggest we release the bodies and get the Polish police to follow funeral proceedings and see if anything comes out of that, but I don't hold out much hope.'

'I'll talk to Herr Schmutz. And the British connection? Maybe it's time we checked that out.'

'Blonnay is due to go on holiday to Scotland, M. le Procureur. I suggest we ask our British counterparts if he could accompany them to interview Lord Shilton in person, if he would agree. We would only need to pay the difference for some small changes to Blonnay's itinerary.'

'Okay, agreed.'

'Otherwise, we've reached a dead end.'

'For now.'

Alain and his team shuffled out of the room. This matter was dragging on interminably.

Then, Alain grinned and looked at Blonnay.

'Don't forget to pack your knickerbockers.'

Blonnay was straight on the phone to Scotland Yard.

Sixteen

Let your soul touch the earth… go walking.
Sarah Marquis

Rehearsals with Charles were providing great entertainment for the rest of the choir. He was the only one who dared to answer BL back, calling her 'old girl,' and saying 'don't be so silly'. He had a powerful baritone and the other men were glad of him, even if he did have a tendency to sing everything with the same enthusiasm and volume as if he were singing the national anthem at Twickenham.

Jamie had Poppy and Lucy crying with laughter, mimicking Charles asking the musical director if he was sure they weren't singing *Gee Officer Krupke* 'a touch too fast'.

'The MD looked like he was about to blow a fuse but he just replied, "No, Monsieur Sidforth-Sykes, have you listened to the original?" To which Charles replied, "I have, and I think it's far too fast".'

Sally piped in, nearly choking with laughter.

'We were all trying to hold it in and the MD said really venomously, "Monsieur Sykes, I would have been interested to hear Leonard Bernstein's reaction to your remark. Fortunately for him, he is no longer here to hear it but it is unfortunate for me, for that is a moment I would have relished".'

Jamie concluded, 'The MD then had to march out of the room before he exploded but Humphrey didn't bother to hide his glee. He just laughed out loud and long.'

Lucy looked at them all, enjoying the joke. It seemed that BL had, inadvertently, achieved what she'd wanted; she had livened things up for the residents of Grondère, albeit not *exactly* as she had intended.

Now that the book was with the printer, and not being part of the choir action, Lucy settled down to her two big projects of the summer: studying for her mid-mountain guide exam and creating a secret garden around Alain's chalet.

She also found she suddenly had more time for reading. She galloped through Mark Twain and Jemima Morrell's writings on Switzerland and then stumbled across a fat poetry anthology in the unwanted books box outside the Grondère library. She'd never particularly liked poetry but, having found a free supply, decided to give it a second chance. It was a revelation: this was no longer the dull, boring stuff of her schooldays. As she read, she realised to what extent poets drew on nature, not just as a source of inspiration but also for metaphors, similes and other tools of their trade. What had previously seemed tedious, now she could relate to; the things she saw and felt every day were here, described and expressed with beauty and understanding that she could never hope to match. She was also astounded to discover how many of these poets had visited Switzerland: Wordsworth, Byron, Goldsmith, they'd all been there centuries before her and had discovered and been inspired by the beauty of her adopted country. It was incredible to think that greats like Wordsworth had walked the same remote mountain route to the Gemmi Pass that she had walked with Poppy just a month earlier.

It can come as a surprise to a member of the current generation to discover that they are not trailblazing but merely following in the footsteps of their ancestors. Lucy withstood the shock well and revelled instead in learning from the writings that spoke to her from the past. In a way, the literary connections with the natural world she loved enriched her love of it – the two became intertwined. She picked up her anthology whenever she could no longer absorb any more Latin names of Alpine plants.

Wandering ever further on her walks, Lucy stumbled across a sheltered little vale, a few valleys away with its own unique appearance and microclimate. It had a wide, shallow stream running through it with little rock pools and stony beaches. Dotted around were large boulders covered with low growing evergreens, punctuated by stunted conifers which spent their winters under a deep layer of snow. Lucy wondered how many times she herself had skied right over them, with no idea they were there. After some research, she discovered that the spot was called the Japanese Garden and she could see why. It all looked as if it had been carefully arranged to some great artistic design but then, it was not the first place in Switzerland that had stirred that thought: the Oechinsee also had such ethereal beauty that defied description and belief. While Słowik paddled, Lucy sat on the boulders, dangling her feet in the babbling brook and felt inspired. She wondered if, by adding some smaller boulders and dwarf conifers to Alain's garden, she could create a similar look. She hugged her knees with glee at the thought of it and snapped lots of photos to keep the image fresh: a trip to a garden centre beckoned.

During a break in all their various activities, when the summer weather was at its most glorious, Poppy, Lucy, Sally and Jodie set off for a three-day camping trip a few valleys away. Champex-Lac was a small, pretty resort sitting on a high plateau surrounded by forest with a lake at its centre but it was its beautiful Alpine garden that was the major attraction for the amateur botanists. They left Sally and Jodie rowing a boat around the lake with instructions to set up camp and spent a couple of happy hours getting up close and personal with some miniature jewels.

Set on a gentle slope on the hillside, the garden was planted in a natural style, recreating the different habitats of the various plant groups. Little winding paths wove around the different areas, from tall Alpine thistles to small crystal pools surrounded with delicate pinks and rockeries housing the smaller varieties.

'Small but perfectly formed,' Lucy pronounced. 'It's like a little shop crammed with beautiful jewels.'

'It is, or a living library.'

'Exactly! The *Flora Helvetica* come to life.'

Once they'd had a good rummage around, they joined the others for a swim in the lake and cooked their supper over a fire pit in the forest. It was too hot to do anything too strenuous, and the surroundings were so beautiful that there was no need to go anywhere. During the day, the four friends went for gentle rambles, swam in the lake and had barbecues in the forest campsite in the evening with Lucy listening as Jodie played her guitar and sang songs with Poppy and Sally.

'Aren't you sad you can't join in?' Sally asked gently, feeling guilty that they were enjoying sharing their love of music without her.

'Not at all,' Lucy replied honestly. 'I don't feel I'm missing out at all, I can't miss what I've never had. I'm perfectly happy listening to you lot. After all, musicians need an appreciative audience and you couldn't have a more appreciative one than me.'

The other campers didn't seem to mind either: a few campers came and joined Lucy by the fire to listen in. One older camper brought a guitar over and strummed along.

He picked at the chords, searching for songs they all knew and, having exhausted the more obvious repertoire, went further back in time to some oldies that only Jodie recognised.

Lying on her back, looking up at the stars, listening to Jodie singing the 50s classic *You Belong to Me*, even her tone-deaf ear could tell that Jodie's voice was in a different league to the others.

It had been a while since Blonnay and Charles Sidforth-Sykes had met. This was a cause of regret for Blonnay as Charles was a great source of hitherto unknown vocabulary. His recent discovery of P.G. Wodehouse had somewhat compensated for this, but he was extremely happy to bump into Charles in Savigny market.

'What brings you down to Savigny, M. Sidforth-Sykes?' Blonnay congratulated himself on finally having mastered the pronunciation of this most difficult name.

'Is this a formal interview, officer?' Charles replied testily: he didn't much rate Swiss policemen and especially not this one who, he had discovered, pretended to be an idiot but had a hard edge to him.

Blonnay, however, was not the sensitive type and was impervious to the cool response.

'Of course not, unless you have something on your mind.' Charles was wary: was this a trap?

'I am waiting for a friend, officer. There is a stall here that sells British specialities and I thought I would wander along and see if anything took my fancy.'

'Oh?' Blonnay replied, already mentally noting 'took my fancy'. 'I would like to see this stall: will you show me?' Charles shrugged: he didn't seem to have much choice.

Blonnay wasn't as big a fan of English food as the language and the array of goods did nothing to tempt him but the saleswoman was extremely eloquent and eventually, having failed to convince him to buy a Battenburg cake, did persuade him to try a malt loaf.

'Lovely choice for tiffin. Remember to butter it,' Charles told him.

'Are you sure? She did say I could eat it without butter.'

'It's not quite as scrummy without a good lathering of butter.' Charles, who had been tempted by a discounted fruit cake, wondered why on earth he was bothering talking to this irritating man.

'Ah, there's Henry, back from the bank,' he uttered, waving at his friend with relief at his imminent rescue.

Henry wandered up, carrying a huge and heavy briefcase. He didn't look delighted to see Blonnay either but he shook his hand amiably enough.

'Ready Charles, old chum? Let's be off.'

And the two withdrew as politely and rapidly as they could.

Blonnay watched them as they walked away, astounded that people still employed the word 'tiffin'. Having seen it in his Jeeves and Wooster book he had checked his dictionary which had informed him the terminology was 'old'. He looked thoughtfully at Henry's briefcase, shrugged and returned to his office.

Alain's garden started to take shape: Tommy and Eddie brought Lucy some boulders that had been dug out of the White Snowflake construction site and placed them according to her design. Once she had finished the main planting, Lucy stood back to admire her work.

'Not bad at all,' came Poppy's voice behind her. 'I was just coming down from Old Folk's Rock and thought I'd stop by to check up on progress.'

'Yes, I'm pleased with it. Now it's just a case of making sure the plants don't go dry until they're established.'

A real secret garden, Swiss style.

'Yes, needs some edelweiss, but I daren't remove it from the wild and I can't plant the cultivated one.'

'I'll keep an eye out for some seed. You coming to The Pub later? Ally's playing.'

'I could pop down for a bit, Alain's working late on this horrible murder case.'

'It seems to have gone quiet.'

'Yes, I don't know. He hasn't mentioned it but he's distracted, it must be that.'

Later in The Pub, listening to Ally and Suzie playing on the terrace Lucy was approached by a local photographer whom she knew by name but had never met.

'I've been looking for you.'

'For me?'

He nodded and took out a fancy camera. He flicked through some images, found what he was looking for and then showed her.

There was Lucy, in all her glory, surfacing from the crystal-clear waters of a mountain lake.

'Ohmigod!' she gasped, her eyes wide. And then she looked at it again. It was stunning. This was no act of voyeurism, it was a beautifully crafted image with the mountains reflected in the lake and her in the centre, surfacing from the water like Botticelli's *Birth of Venus*, her long auburn hair capturing the glint of the sun. There were more.

'I promise I took my finger off the trigger and my eye from the lens when your tummy button appeared.'

She looked at him and saw he was telling the truth.

'Interesting, like a modern take on a Pre-Raphaelite or even Early Renaissance,' commented Poppy, when she was shown them.

Soon a crowd had gathered and there was a great deal of oohing and aahing. Ricky was lapping it up.

'Don't you mind?' Sally asked her. 'Everyone in The Pub is ogling at you naked?'

'It's only my boobs for goodness' sake and my hair covers them mostly anyway. But actually, it's really weird: I don't feel like it's me in the photos. When I look at them, I feel totally remote from them.'

'Well I think he's a bit creepy, going round the mountains spying on women like that,' Sally pulled a disapproving face.

'He didn't ask me to pose nude. He just seized his moment.'

'Speaking as a wannabe photographer, I have to say that in his situation, I would have done exactly the same thing and I'm not a perve,' Poppy argued.

'I guess I'm being a bit prudish,' Sally shrugged. 'It's true that I wouldn't go skinny dipping anywhere.'

'So much for you modern women – in my day we did that all the time,' Poppy reproved.

Ricky, revelling in the sensation his photos were causing, found his way back over.

'I could have already sold them several times over,' he told Lucy, 'but I've now had an offer from the Swiss Tourist Board that's hard to refuse and I need your consent. There would be a modelling fee, of course.'

Lucy couldn't retain her mirth and laughed. 'A model? Me?'

When he told her how much, she stopped laughing.

'Can you give me a couple of days to think about it?'

That night she discussed it with Alain, who was more inclined to purchase the photos for himself than share them with the rest of Switzerland and beyond.

'I don't know, Lucy, it's obviously your choice, but you are the witness to a murder. If the person recognises you, it could put you in danger.'

'Is that your only objection?'

'Yes, the photos are a work of art, it's you but it isn't you, if you see what I mean.'

'Yes, that's how I feel too, I'm just a small part of the whole, the real star is the scenery. And I could really use the money.'

'I think then that you have to say yes, but that you have a timing constraint and you'll let him know when he can release them. You cannot tell him the reason, but we both know that it's only once the Reichenbach Falls murder has been resolved.'

'Which may be never.'

'I hope you have a little more faith in the Swiss police than that,' he teased.

'Well, get a move on then.'

Seventeen

I don't like those chiffon nighties… they show your vest.
Joyce Grenfell

Blonnay was in paradise, or to be precise, Jermyn Street, London. He had heard before of this iconic place where the men of the British royal family (and anyone who wanted to be like them) came to purchase their clothes and now, here he was, peering through the windows, his nose pressed up against the small panes that made a discreet viewing impossible. He marvelled at the wonders and curiosities set before him and felt he had stepped back in time; the clothes looked a little that way too. He did not venture beyond the shop front: the very smart gentlemen inside looked like they would have had him measured up, suited up, bankrupt and escorted to the exit before he had found any will to resist. The discreet price tags in the windows ensured that the contemplation of such pleasures remained contemplation only. Blonnay sighed, he would need all his money for his Scottish trip.

He had spotted one very smart hatter but, squint as he might through the window, he could not identify any deerstalkers. It did not matter: once he had interviewed Lord Shilton he would be heading north on holiday and he had identified a shop in Edinburgh where he was pretty sure he could find an affordable deerstalker.

After his meeting at Scotland Yard he was to travel to meet the Leicestershire police who would accompany him to interview Lord Shilton. He was looking forward to seeing Lord Shilton again, but he was not sure Lord Shilton felt the same. His liaison officer at Scotland Yard had told him the meeting had not been easy to arrange.

Blonnay looked at his watch, the only timepiece a Swiss policeman could rely on when overseas, and saw he had

147

used up the time he had allocated himself for sightseeing; it was time to head to the new riverside offices of the Metropolitan Police in Westminster.

As he recounted the two murders under investigation, the Scotland Yard detectives wondered what on earth such a bizarre sequence of events had to do with them. They certainly weren't used to Sherlock Holmes being cast as the baddie. They, of course, promised to help the Swiss police, as they had with their previous case, but they explained that the bloodlines of the British aristocracy should not be a serious line of enquiry. Detective Inspector Ferguson, who had studied history at university, explained that once 'an heir and a spare' had been produced, the upper classes no longer considered marital fidelity necessary, or even appropriate. She reckoned that the legitimacy of many heirs and spares could be questioned.
'There are not many big families in this country that would survive a thorough DNA investigation,' she laughed. 'I'd love to see it happen though.'
Blonnay smiled.
'In Switzerland, the people are the sovereign: we have people with money of course, but we don't have aristocrats.'
'That must make things simpler for you.'
'Not really,' he grinned. 'We just seem to get everyone else's.'

The following morning DI Ferguson drove him to Leicester.
All the way up she quizzed him about the political structure of Switzerland (which foreigners always seemed to have a problem understanding), the laws, history and lifestyle and how this all impacted on policing.

'I've never been there for skiing,' she added, 'Would love to but I always go to France – cheaper.'

They discussed the discovery of the burial site of King Richard III during the excavations of a Leicestershire car park and Blonnay regretted that he wouldn't have time to visit the hunchbacked monarch in his final resting place in Leicester Cathedral.

The time flew and it was almost a disappointment when they pulled into the Leicestershire Police headquarters on the outskirts of Leicester where East Midlands Special Operations officer, DI Jackson was waiting for them. Introductions were made and then, together, they drove into the countryside.

DI Jackson gave them some background about the Shilton family. Unlike many of the landed gentry, the Shiltons had astutely avoided the erosion of land and fortune by diversifying into business at the end of the nineteenth century. Lord Shilton owned property all over the country and vineyards in France and, particularly, in the New World; it was an extremely profitable enterprise. The Shiltons had never needed to open their country house to the public and, as they approached Lunstag Hall, Blonnay began to suspect that this was DI Ferguson's true motive for having insisted on accompanying him. She seemed to know a great deal about the architecture and history of the house.

When he got his first sight of it, Inspecteur chef adjoint Blonnay understood why she had been so eager to see it and, more importantly, why Lord Shilton was so desperate to hang on to it. Entering through the arched stone entrance with bell tower leading to stable blocks and carriage houses stood a beautiful sand-coloured Carolean house. In the classic H-shape with Palladian-style pediment over its central bay, it was large but not overwhelming. It looked splendid, yes, but it also looked like a home. In front of the driveway, to the left a formal parterre, to the right a rose garden and behind the house stretched a large park.

DI Ferguson was entranced and began explaining the architectural features but the front door opened and they did their best to walk nonchalantly up the steps.

The entrance hall was marble and a large wooden staircase swept up either side. The walls were hung with large tapestries.

'They are beautiful. Arts and Crafts, maybe William Morris, not sure.' DI Ferguson spoke almost to herself. 'The unicorn hunt was a popular theme. That one is more unusual. You recognise the theme?'

'Ah yes, *She hath no loyal knight and true, the Lady of Shalott*,' Blonnay replied.

He had been entranced by the story of the Lady of Shalott ever since Tonita had explained to him where she had got her pseudonym from. He could now recite the poem in its entirety: he didn't need to – DI Ferguson was impressed with one line. She couldn't think of a single one of her British colleagues that could have quoted Tennyson, and this one was Swiss.

DI Jackson was less moved. 'Bloody hell,' he muttered under his breath. He was beginning to wonder if he'd actually picked up a couple of art thieves masquerading as police officers.

The butler returned and showed them into the library.

Standing in front of the fireplace, the current Viscount Lunstag, Lord Shilton, above it a life-size portrait of his predecessor. Blonnay couldn't take his eyes off it, it resembled Malcolm McDonaghue and his son, Sebastian, to a remarkable degree. It did not resemble the man standing before him, bearing witness to what they both knew, that he was not his father's son, but that Malcolm McDonaghue was. He was, thought Blonnay, sending out a deliberate message. Here, he was asserting his rightful place and demonstrating that he was in charge of the situation.

Lord Shilton invited them to sit.

'Three detectives, goodness, it must be important. Inspector Blonnay, you have come a long way: to what do I owe the honour?'

'I am here, Lord Shilton, with the kind cooperation of my British colleagues, to determine whether you are aware of recent unfortunate events in Switzerland and whether you have any connection with them.'

'This interview is off the record, sir,' clarified DI Jackson.

'Thank you.' Lord Shilton looked appreciatively at the local man. 'I can confirm that I am aware of your current investigation and I am truly sorry to hear about Maria. But apart from my brief and misguided acquaintance with her, I'm not sure how you can think I may be connected to what sounds like some Polish mafia payback.'

'We have to explore all possibilities, sir,' Blonnay said apologetically, carefully copying DI Jackson by adding the 'sir' which he knew was not the correct way to address a viscount but the way his British counterparts addressed every male they spoke to, in order to show respect and avoid appearing confrontational – a device that seemed to be pretty effective. 'Can you confirm that you had no contact with Maria since you left Grondère in April?'

'I can.'

'And no one has approached you, either offering you information or threatening to reveal information?'

'No one. You are concerned I may be being blackmailed with information provided by Maria?'

'That is one avenue of enquiry, yes.'

'And that I then dispatched the blackmailer and Maria?'

'Yes.'

'Then I can promise you that I have had no such contact. Since last April I have sought legal advice on the matter you are obliquely referring to and I have been assured that it is improbable that the claim of an illegitimate son would take precedence over that of the legally recognised heir born within wedlock, regardless of biological data. To accept otherwise would question the status of adopted children, for example. I was stupid to have ever worried about it and even more stupid to have taken the steps I did, particularly as I have since discovered that my father fathered at least one other illegitimate child. So you see, officers, if anyone ever did decide to challenge my legal position, I would be quite prepared to take my chances in court. I do not need to go about silencing people, through payment or any other method.'

'But, of course, sir,' added DI Ferguson, 'that deterrent only works if anyone wanting to misuse that information is also aware of that legal advice.'

'True,' smiled Lord Shilton. 'However, as no one has asked me, I cannot tell them.'

'Then I can only ask you to be on your guard and to inform DI Jackson if any such approach is made,' Blonnay answered, truly grateful that he could now dismiss this avenue and go on holiday.

There was nothing to do but thank his lordship and take leave. DI Ferguson took a longing look around the hall as they left, hoping Lord Shilton would take the hint and show them around but it was quite clear he had no intention of prolonging their visit. The butler showed them out with stiff formality.

Before they got in the car DI Ferguson drew his attention to the land surrounding the house and explained how it had been redesigned by a landscape gardener called Capability Brown. She explained how the land surrounding many stately homes in the country had been completely re-sculptured to create the 'natural' look. Blonnay was astounded.

'So this man redesigned your countryside to make it look more natural?'

'That's right,' she laughed. 'Didn't Switzerland have an equivalent?'

He was totally perplexed.

'I do not see how Switzerland could ever have had need of such a person. It is inconceivable that the countryside of Switzerland could be improved upon,' he replied.

They laughed as they got into the car from where Blonnay called Capitaine Dupertuis.

'It was a long way to come for that. We could have handled it for you,' DI Jackson said a little gruffly when Blonnay had finished his call.

'Agreed,' Blonnay nodded. 'But I was on my way to Scotland anyway and my superiors were glad to know that we did all we could. I don't think international exchanges are ever a waste of time and, personally speaking, it has been a delight to meet you both and…' he smiled at DI Ferguson, 'most educational.'

Blonnay had pre-arranged with his London counterpart that she would give him a lift to Peterborough: he had studied the vagaries of the British rail network and established that he needed to be on the fast east coast line to get anywhere within a sensible time frame. On the way to Peterborough, having deposited DI Jackson back at his offices, DI Ferguson advised Blonnay which side of the train to sit on and what to look out for on his way up to Edinburgh. Their drive was all over far too fast for him. Blonnay felt quite flat as she drove off but he had managed to extract her personal phone number and a promise that she would give Switzerland a chance and book her next ski trip to Grondère.

Blonnay cheered up as he sat on the train, chuckling to himself thinking about Capability Brown and how no one would ever have had the audacity to 'redesign' Switzerland. Carefully following Jilly Ferguson's advice, he settled down for the journey north on the right-hand side of the train in the direction of travel. As instructed, he looked out for the wonderful Victorian arches of York station, a tiny glimpse of York Minster, the long platform at Darlington, the castle and cathedral of Durham, the Angel of the North, the bridges over the Tyne and the dramatic Northumbrian coastline – he missed nothing. The daylight seemed to last forever and from Berwick onwards he could hardly sit still for excitement. Two days in Edinburgh, from there, the Highlands, the west coast and the distilleries of Islay. If ever there was a happy man, it was Blonnay at that moment.

On his second day in Edinburgh, Laurent Blonnay crossed the threshold of an authentic hatter and headed straight for a display of deerstalkers. The choice was extensive but he couldn't help but be attracted to a nifty little number which carried a reduced price tag of £15.

He turned it over and over to find a defect but he couldn't see anything wrong with it at all. He was absorbed in his examination of the object for so long that, eventually, an elderly salesman came over to see if he could help.

'Why is it so cheap?' asked Blonnay, mystified.

'It's just an end-of-line.'

'But the quality of the craftsmanship, the tweed, the stitching, this is handmade.'

The salesman realised he was dealing with a real enthusiast and it would be easy to sell him a more expensive one, but this unpopular model had been hanging around for a while and he wanted rid of it.

'It's the last one, sir. It's been a popular model but I have new stock and I need it gone.'

'Oh.' Blonnay looked at the newer models and couldn't see much difference. 'But this is a style that doesn't change, it is eternal.'

'But my suppliers and I need turnover, sir. That is also eternal.'

'I'll take it.'

'I'm glad to sell the last one, sir,' the salesman said at the till. 'It's a few months since I sold the other one. Also to a foreign gentleman funnily enough.'

'Really?' Blonnay's policeman antennae pricked up. 'Are they popular with foreigners?'

'No, not really. In fact, they're not *that* popular with anyone. They tend to sell mostly to trade: theatre and television, you know, costume dramas and the like.'

'Where was the other foreigner from? Switzerland like me?'

'No sir, Eastern Europe I'd guess. He was a bit dour.'

'Dour?' Blonnay hadn't heard this word before but he didn't want to get his notebook out in front of the salesman.

'Yes, you know, unfriendly like, didn't say much.'

'Oh.' Blonnay wondered how to get the salesman to say more without revealing he was a policeman. The salesman, though, needed no encouragement.

'Yes, weird, big fella, Scottish colouring but his face was more round, like a Russian or a Pole. Polish, I reckon, but they're normally quite friendly. This one, I remember him because when he came to the till with the hat, he avoided looking at me direct. Then just as he was leaving he looked at me and I wished he hadn't, it was as if he was looking right through me, like he was threatening me. I'll never forget him – he had the coldest eyes I've ever seen.'

Blonnay stowed his new headgear carefully in his backpack and walked right into the nearest whisky bar, wrote down the word 'dour' in his notebook, then called Capitaine Dupertuis.

'It's too convenient,' replied his colleague.

'And yet, I have a feeling this is our man.'

'We don't go on feelings Blonnay, remember, we go on evidence.'

'Well, I'm going to ask Scotland Yard to call Scotland and ask them to send someone to get a photofit of that purchaser, then we'll have a potential piece of evidence, won't we?'

'Yes, Blonnay, we will. If you're right, it does back up Schmutz's Polish theory.' Alain paused.

'Blonnay?'

Blonnay was already contemplating speaking to DI Ferguson again. 'Yes?'

'Did you really buy one of those things?'

Eighteen

There are no persons capable of stooping so low as those
who desire to rise in the world.
Countess of Blessington, Desultory Thoughts and Reflections

July was music festival month, one of the major events of
the summer season: a true example of diversification in
tourist attractions. An activity and culture further removed
from the outdoor, sporty world of Grondère, Lucy could
not imagine, and she wondered how it could possibly
work. Once though, she had stumbled across an outdoor
concert in the mountain: the music was perfectly in
keeping with the majestic peaks and vistas into whose
empty spaces it fell, rose and hung suspended. Suddenly,
Lucy had realised, it all made perfect sense. If you
managed to be sitting on a hot, thyme-encrusted rock and
have a glass of cool, white wine in your hand at the same
moment, as Lucy did, well, it was complete fulfilment of
all the senses. Just glorious!
The young musicians wandered around town to rehearsals,
looking as if they were about to disappear beneath the
large instrument bags they carried. It was strange to see all
these etiolated youngsters wearing the black and white of
the orchestra pit intermingling with muscular, bronzed
cyclists and hikers wearing the mud of the mountain trails.
The young musicians, no different to any other youngsters,
liked to party and, for a month, mingled with the locals
until the differences between them became less noticeable.
Much to the annoyance of Johnny, the musicians flooded
into The Pub before and after performances and quite took
over. He repeatedly told anyone who would listen how he
still hadn't forgiven the beautiful Canadian viola player
who had enchanted his favourite barman and taken him
home with her.

The locals didn't go to many of the concerts, the tickets were a bit pricey, but there were ways of getting into one or two of the concerts without paying the official rate. Quite a few got jobs driving VIPs or acting as hostesses or service staff which entitled them to cheaper or complimentary tickets. There were also some local sponsors who always had a few spare tickets to hand out. This created a small black market in Grondère but it was not a reliable source: it depended on knowing the right person at the right moment and a lot of begging. Eddie, who, having a Grondèrian girlfriend, was better plugged into the local community than any of them, got tickets to one orchestral concert and one piano recital and, having no interest whatsoever in classical music, promptly handed them over to Lucy who considered herself very lucky. Poppy attended a lot of concerts: she never revealed where she got her tickets from but Lucy suspected her of actually buying them and being too embarrassed to own up.

BL and Henry, of course, attended all of the big-draw events and made sure that everyone knew about it. They had joined the Festival Friends just in time to get their names in the programme and provided accommodation to famous opera singer, Michael Winnaker. They had bought a grand piano specially and placed it in front of their large lounge window which overlooked the whole resort. It was, Molly from The Larder told her friends, spectacular. Molly was delighted: BL had booked her to deliver three cordon-bleu meals a day for her VIP guest and his entourage to ensure she didn't have to waste any time catering for them herself. On the other hand, she refused to let him have a chauffeur and drove him everywhere herself with great display.
Jamie too was called in to cater a large celebratory dinner party for the star the night before he left.

'The funniest thing was …' he laughed, before adding as usual, 'I shouldn't be telling you this of course – most unprofessional.'

'Oh, come on,' they protested. 'You've started now.'

'Michael Winnaker kept getting her name wrong, he kept calling her Betty. I'm not convinced he wasn't doing it on purpose.'

'Oh nooo! After all her efforts to ingratiate herself!'

'It was hilarious because she just had to take it! And of course, she had to make sure he knew all about the choir and made a big deal that the piano was a present from her husband so that she could work at home. She actually made out she was a professional singer!'

'Crumbs!' replied Tommy. 'He would surely see straight through that: he must know everyone who's anyone in that business.'

'I got the impression he's heard it all before,' Jamie grinned. 'He looked like he was just tolerating one more sycophant! Quite right too: he lived it up at their place, five-star service.'

'Well, as long as she's happy, I guess it's money well spent,' Jodie added.

'I guess,' Jamie smiled. 'You wouldn't like what she said about you though.'

'Sorry?'

'She said some of the chorus members had ideas above their abilities, it was always the problem when working with amateurs.'

Poppy burst out laughing but Jodie was disconcerted.

'Why do you think she was talking about me?'

'Because, Jodie, you're the only one of us with any true talent. She can't feel threatened by any of us.'

'Silly cow!' murmured Johnny, almost to himself.

'That's unfair to cows,' laughed Tommy.

'Well, I can't say "bitch" in front of Louie: it is a word that gets him over-excited.'

'Really,' Jamie's eyebrows were raised, especially when, as he looked sceptically down at Louie, so were his.

The climate of the north-facing inclines of Valais was as suited to the growing of apricots as that of the south-facing slopes to the vine. In winter, dark-trunked trees with splayed branches stood out starkly against the snow. They lined the lower hillsides and occupied every available space in the valleys up to the forest line and stretched in neat lines along the valley floor. In spring the white and pink blossom lit up the gloomy earth and the nation held its breath for fear of late frosts attacking the newly formed buds.

At apricot time, stalls appeared along every roadside, with the amber fruits arrayed neatly to tempt the passer-by. Pickers perched their ladders against the trees by the roadside to verify the claim that purchasers were buying directly from the local producer. Despite this, apricot-laden cardboard boxes arrived daily from other producers to try and meet demand. And demand was strong: people crossed Switzerland in an annual pilgrimage to load their vehicles with the authentic article, whilst across the country, stalls, authentic and fake, conveniently appeared for those unable to make the journey to get their share of *abricots de Valais*.

During that period, Lucy and her friends gorged on the apricot in every form; raw, in salads, tarts, cakes and, most importantly, Tommy got out the big jam pan and filled jar upon jar with amber nectar. Tommy was famous for his apricot jam and everyone bought the ingredients in return for him doing all the work.

There were many different cultivars that the growers used to extend the season and, over his years in Valais, Tommy had got to know them all and still preferred the old familiar, Luizet, over all the newcomers.

'It just has that extra something special that makes the perfect jam,' he waxed lyrical as Sally was helping him ladle the latest batch into jars.

'Mmm, I agree,' she said, dipping her spoon into the pan. 'Isn't this nice and domestic, Tommy?'

'It is. The kitchen seems much smaller with you in it though.'

'Great compliment, thanks.'

'You know what I mean?' He gave her a squeeze.

'I know. This kitchen is a bit small for a man of your talents. One day, we'll have our own place.'

'Grondère or somewhere else?'

'I love it here but I reckon I can be happy anywhere.'

'Not like Lucy then: I think she will be here forever, like Poppy.'

'Yes, it's funny, Lucy seems the most unfettered of all of us and yet the most attached to place.'

'Like a little mountain wind. Destined to roam these hills forever.'

'You can be very poetic sometimes, you know?'

'I wonder where the wind will take us, then.'

Tommy had a plan for the future but he thought he'd wait until he was ready to put it into action before he asked Sally if she'd follow him on his next adventure.

'Wherever it is,' she grinned, 'the first thing we must do is plant our own Luizet apricot tree.'

Shortly after Lucy's birthday, Alain asked her if she would like to move into his chalet with him for the rest of the summer. This was not a difficult decision for Lucy: to say nothing of the attraction of living in his beautiful home, there was the added appeal of no longer having to shuttle her clothes and dirty washing to and fro between there and the crowded little chalet: without hesitation, she agreed. Dearly as she loved the little chalet and its occupants, their number was ever-increasing: Sally and Émilie's frequent overnight stays had changed the dynamics in the chalet and Lucy needed peace and quiet to study. She offered to continue paying her share of the rent and to move back in the winter when Alain's chalet would be impracticable for both her and him to get to work every day.

As they left the chalet with Lucy's belongings, Alain picked up the little wooden nightingale from the window ledge.

'Shall we take this too?'

When they got to Alain's, Lucy discovered he had made a special ledge by the front door for her wooden nightingale and he screwed the bird in place.

'Always the policeman,' she teased.

'I think you would be devastated if some passing hiker took a fancy to it and took it home with them.'

'I would,' she said, abashed. 'Thank you for being so thoughtful.'

Happily installed in the chalet, Lucy made the most of its closer proximity to the forest to get to know her way around it better. She began leaving the main trails and learning the network of smaller paths that led to lesser-known glades and pools where the sun flickered through the canopy, creating magical little spaces. She started planning her own routes where she could take future clients and show them something a bit different when she started guiding the following summer. She imagined she would call it 'secluded glades and hidden treasures: a forest trail'. The dark, cool woodlands offered a peaceful retreat from the punishing summer sun; its quiet and discreet flora concealed little gems which required a sharp and detailed eye to both uncover and appreciate. Small anemonies, ranunculi, sandworts, pearlworts, single-flowered wintergreen, tiny violas, the tall, airy plumes of goatsbeard and meadowsweet and the dainty stars of astrantia, swathed by a glorious array of shade-loving ferns: aspleniums, polystichums, gymnocarpiums. Lucy lost track of time amongst the wealth of beauty around her. Occasionally another walker would wake her from her reverie but otherwise, she pretty much had these secret parts of the mountain to herself.

When he came home in the evenings, Alain could not talk to Lucy about his work but he loved hearing about her rambles in the mountains, her discoveries and botanical studies with Słowik who now also spent most of her evenings in the chalet.

'You're not off again tomorrow, are you?' he asked one evening. 'The weather forecast isn't good.'

Lucy looked at him in surprise.

'I just looked at it a short while ago, it looked fine to me.'

'Really? I didn't think so.'

Lucy looked amused.

'What is it now?'

'I think this is cultural,' she replied. 'We have a totally different perception of the weather forecast.'

'We do?'

'I think so. A "good" day for you is sunny and clear?'

'That's right. Isn't it for you?'

'No. As long as it's not raining or blowing a gale, it's a "good" day for me.'

'And you think this "different perception" is because we grew up in different climates?'

'Exactly. Where I grew up, in the north of England, if you waited for a "good" day by your standards, you'd never do anything or go anywhere.'

'But in Switzerland we have severe weather.'

'Yes, but in winter, you're equipped for it: in summer, you expect it to be warm.'

'I do.'

'How sad, you have never known the joy of sitting on a beach, crouched behind a windbreak, picking the grains of sand off your hard-boiled egg, or had your mum rub you down after a swim in the North Sea, not to dry you off, but to get your circulation going again.'

'No,' he agreed. 'You poor thing, your "good" days sound like army endurance training.'

'Funnily enough,' she added nostalgically, 'they were magic.'

Alain laughed and shook his head.

'You and your theories. It does explain one thing, though.'

'What's that?'

'Your penchant for skinny dipping in freezing cold mountain lakes.'

Nineteen

The tapestry of high summer.

Beth Chatto

It was mid-July and rhododendron time. High in the hills, just above the treeline, small, scraggy bushes erupted into explosions of shameless pink. A smaller, more restrained shrub than its blousy Chinese cousins, the native *Alpenrose* was always a welcome sight, making up for what it lacked in perfume by packing a punch in colour; gladdening the hearts of hikers and filling the nectar pouches of the mountain bees.

The earth was bone dry after weeks of hot weather and Lucy grabbed the opportunity to wander high, exploring the tangle of sandy tracks that crisscrossed the mountainsides. In amongst the great rust-coloured iron-girdered avalanche breaks, only the odd dwarf pine tree punctuated the low-growing tapestry of blueberry, juniper and heather: a slippery, prickly mix that defied shortcuts and provided tough armoured protection for the miniature wildlife world hidden beneath its canopy.

The main flowering period was already over but that summer constant, the harebell, shook her radiant blue cups in the breeze from amongst the undergrowth and from craggy rock faces. The odd lemon-yellow pasque flower stood out against the heather before transforming into exotic seedheads floating airily above it. Lucy held her face into the wind and inhaled the heady Alpine perfume as the baking sun heated the oils of pine, juniper and wild thyme.

There was another advantage to taking the higher tracks at that time in the season – it took her away from the high-season traffic. On a summer's day in Grondère, the main trails could be as busy as the ski slopes at half-term. It was etiquette for hikers to greet one another as their paths crossed on the mountains but this could get mildly ridiculous when you were passing someone every five metres. Still, what could you do? Rudeness was not an option. Lucy found that having a pretty little dog with her made matters worse as people always stopped to admire Słowik and she felt mean dragging Słowik away as she revelled in the attention that Lucy wasn't very good at giving her. The higher, less-frequented paths provided an escape from the noisy activity of downhill scooters, mountain bikes and other hikers. High amongst the rocks Lucy had the mountains back the way she preferred them – to herself.

Nimble as she was, the little tracks could carry danger: loose stones, slippery sand and narrow rock crannies. Lucy was aware that a twisted ankle or fall could happen to the best of walkers and, particularly when she was on her own, she was cautious, glad of those nifty hiking poles she had purchased in Kandersteg, but even so, bending at times to hold onto a firm surface and be sure of her foothold. She rarely crossed wild animals on these higher paths; however light her tread, she realised that she must sound like an oncoming troop of elephants to shy creatures.

In the afternoons, she worked on the garden which was now in really good shape and in the evenings, until Alain came home, she studied for her exam and tried to plot the route for her and Poppy's final hike of the summer: a shortened version of the Tour du Mont Blanc. It was a more ambitious hike than the one they had taken in the Bernese Alps, it would take them much higher and was more physically challenging. It also required careful planning and, here, Lucy was running into difficulties. Most of the mountain refuges were fully booked for the rest of the summer and camping at that altitude was not something either of them wanted to do

'I'm really sorry, Poppy,' she confessed one afternoon as they sat sunbathing on the terrace of The Pub with a pitcher of Pimms in front of them. 'I think we're going to have to shelve it. I should have booked months ago. I had no idea it was so busy, the Bernese refuges were much more accommodating. I feel like a total amateur.'

'Don't worry about it,' Poppy reassured her. 'It's a busy route, I should have thought of it too. Just concentrate on your studies and book up now for next year.'

'Already done,' Lucy laughed. 'I realised I was on a losing streak and so the whole trip's booked for next August.'

'It's not like we're lost for walks here. We can go for shorter hikes in the surrounding valleys.'

'Yes, I'm happy to stay in Grondère.'

'And, of course, you have Wales to look forward to.'

'Ah yes, I have Wales.'

Lucy was happy to stay at home. Her relationship with Alain was making her truly happy and she cherished every moment he could get away from his investigations and spend time with her in their own mountain refuge. Alain did not even try to hide his delight when he heard the Mont Blanc trip was off.

'I'll take you to Chamonix for lunch one day,' he said, 'we can go up the Aiguille du Midi and you can step into the void, my little *rossignol*.'

She laughed. She knew he meant the glass cube suspended over a precipice overlooking the highest peak in Europe.

'*Rossignol*, why do you call me that, is it because I sing so sweetly?'

Alain laughed. He had never heard her sing but he knew from her friends that this was to be avoided: her defect had at least enabled her to adroitly avoid joining BL's choir.

'No, it's a bit of irony mixed with a wordplay on your red hair, my beautiful redhead. *Ma belle rousse*.'

'Oh, charming.'

'I thought so.'

'Isn't *rousse* also a slang word for police?'

'I can't get anything past you, can I?'

July was drawing to a close and the festival was also winding up to its grand finale. The closing concert was due to take place on 1 August, which was also Swiss National Day. The traditional village fête took place on the same day and so the resort, full of young musicians, festival goers, summer tourists and locals, was at its busiest of all the summer. The main street was closed to traffic and along its full length on both sides food and drink stalls were set up. The shops put out trestle tables with all their sales items and the ubiquitous yapping toy dogs and dream-catchers were also in evidence. The local council offered free pony rides to the children and face painters, clowns and magicians milled around, offering their services to a willing public. During the day it was all very calm and family orientated but in the evening the music volumes went up, the DJs appeared and the serious drinking began.

Lucy and Alain wandered up and down, eating *raclette* and drinking various local wines and cocktails. Lucy knew lots of the people on the stands and chatted happily away while Alain retreated to his mother's apartment every time he needed a break.

As concert time arrived, Lucy and her friends admired the finery of those rushing down to the last big orchestral performance. Poppy was amongst them.

'She scrubs up well, doesn't she?' Jodie commented.

'Hey Poppy,' Sally called, as Poppy pretended not to see them. 'You look fantastic!'

None of them could ever remember seeing Poppy wearing a long dress and shawl before. She looked really sophisticated, except for the long dangly earrings which clearly dated back to the 80s, ensuring her reputation for eccentricity remained untarnished.

Poppy just flapped her arms dismissively at them.

'I'm in a hurry, see you at the fireworks!'

All the young musicians would be performing together as an orchestra for the last time before disappearing back to the four corners of the world they had come from. Before that however, they would be having one last shindig at The Pub Mont Grondère which was closed off, even to Johnny, for the night.

'Bloody musicians!' he complained. 'I'll be glad when I get The Pub back to myself.'

Someone put a beer in his hand.

'Look at this though.' Lucy waved her arms at the outside bars. 'You just couldn't do something like this in the UK.'

'True,' Tommy agreed. 'There'd be fights, drunken people passed out all over the place, police, ambulances – chaos!'

'Sounds great,' Eddie offered.

'Yeah.'

The young women shook their heads despairingly.

Poppy didn't normally bother with the VIP tent but getting past the doormen was a breeze as they were both fellow ski instructors. The glass of champagne also turned out to be complimentary, courtesy of one of the seasonnaires she knew working on the bar. Fully armed and having ascertained that BL hadn't decided upon a different outfit, she moved in on her target.

'Oh, Letty,' she laughed loudly, 'SNAP! How hilarious!'

Poppy's timing was perfect. Letty was surrounded by local dignitaries and Grondère's 'high society', many of whom had frequently heard Letty deride the woman who was now standing before her wearing the same dress.

Poppy's skilful employment of the element of surprise prevented BL from concealing her horror. Surrounded by amused looks she stammered something lame about 'excellent taste' and turned away from the ghastly apparition in order to collect herself.

Poppy shrugged nonchalantly and walked away, swigging the dregs of champagne from her glass. If BL had thought Poppy was going to be a pushover, she was now under no such delusion.

'That, Poppy, was very, very naughty!'

Humphrey, sidling up to her, handed her a fresh *coupe* and winked. She took it with a triumphant flourish.

'Deliberate?'

'Perhaps!' she winked.

'Then I salute you,' he said, retiring with a bow.

As daylight faded at the street party, the local grandees gathered for an *apéro officiel* and they were joined in dribs and drabs by those returning from the concert. Lucy spotted BL and Henry flouncing past looking important and heading straight for some local celebrities who greeted them with the tolerant smiles of those used to smiling tolerantly.

'Isn't that the same dress as Poppy's?' asked Sally.

'OMG, you're right,' Jodie confirmed.

Lucy, whose finely tuned fashion ignorance had not spotted the duplication, giggled.

'I bet that went down well.'

The trio chuckled merrily and sipped noisily on their cocktails through the speeches that nobody could hear anyway and the singing of the national anthem, to which only those who had had to take an exam to receive their nationality seemed to know the words. Only when the firework show commenced did Lucy and her friends start to pay attention.

Poppy, looking very pleased with herself, and accepting lots of compliments for her new look, squeezed in between Tommy, Eddie, Émilie, Sally, Jodie and Lucy – Alain had taken one look at the crowd and informed Lucy that he would be keeping his mother and her partner, Maître Aulnay, company on her balcony.

Grondère had been starved of fireworks the previous 1 August because of drought and the risk of fire and was looking forward to a big show. They did not get it.

Whether the local council was bending to environmental or financial pressure, nobody knew, but the firework display had moved into the computer age. Clever 3D images were projected into the night sky in patterns and colours that mingled and merged in a technicolour sound and light show. Funnels and shafts of light had the crowd impressed and extolling the merits of the council's decision.

'Much better,' someone remarked.

'Much cheaper,' added another.

The 'safer and more animal-friendly' comment met with murmured approval as did the 'environmentally-friendly' one.

A fairly subdued crowd began heading back to the street bars when … *boom*!

One comet, then another, followed by a couple of brocades fired into the air. For the next ten minutes, the public were treated to a more traditional display, courtesy of no one knew who. As the final drop of golden rain fell to earth, the politically correct display had been categorically put in its place.

'Well, I don't know what to think,' Sally said. 'I was quite happy with the sound and light until that happened.'

'Yes, I'm a bit confused too,' Lucy admitted. 'I know I shouldn't say it, but the real fireworks were much more exciting.'

'I prefer the real thing!' Tommy was categorical.

'Me too,' Eddie agreed.

Johnny was strangely quiet.

'What's up Johnny?'

'Did you see that guy?'

'What guy?' They all turned around and looked but whoever Johnny had seen had vanished into the crowd.

'Never saw him before. Coldest bloody eyes I ever saw,' he shuddered. 'He was listening to everything we were saying.'

'Probably the guy who designed the digital display,' Eddie joked.

'Oh Gawd, that's probably it. If looks could kill …' Johnny laughed.

Alain appeared to drive Lucy home.

'Did you see the display?' she asked. 'What did you think?'

'From where we were, we saw nothing at all, it was too low.'

'Oh, that's a shame.'

'We enjoyed the unofficial display though.'

'You see,' said Tommy, 'even the police prefer proper fireworks! Can we have a lift home too, Alain?'

And so it was that Alain ended his evening wondering what had happened to change his life to such an extent that, on *his* national holiday, he was driving three drunken Brits and one Australian up to the hills above Grondère.

Twenty

People may say I couldn't sing, but no one can ever say I didn't sing.
Florence Foster Jenkins

August took Grondère into high summer. As the weeks passed, it became clear that, whatever anyone else thought, BL was not treating the choir concert as an amateur gig in an aestivating ski resort. Money, it would appear, was no object. Social media posts and posters around the resort and beyond bore witness to a major marketing campaign.

'Have you seen it?' laughed Poppy. 'You'd think it was happening at the Royal Albert Hall, not the church in Grondère.'

'Don't we know it,' groaned Tommy. 'It's totally escalated out of proportion. BL's hired professionals for all the other major parts except Maria, she's the only amateur soloist. She's got the press coming, it's being live-streamed on YouTube. The pressure at rehearsals is huge. She's gone mad.'

'I don't think so,' Lucy assessed. 'I think this was the plan all along. This is an attempt to turn herself into a star overnight. It makes me think of that film with Meryl Streep, what was it called?'

'*Florence Foster Jenkins*.' Sally smiled wryly, 'Only unfortunately, BL can actually sing. I don't think she has a particularly remarkable voice, but she is technically excellent.'

'Oh,' pouted Lucy. 'Shame.'

'Quite,' Tommy sulked. 'I can't wait for it all to be over. I thought this would be a bit of fun but it's clear we're just being used to help BL springboard herself to fame.'

Lucy and Poppy grinned at one another smugly, glad to have ducked out of the enterprise.

Johnny just took a sip of Guinness, looked down at Louie and grimaced.

'We warned you that woman was a fucking nightmare, didn't we Louie?'

Was it a remarkable coincidence or had Louie really understood? At that moment, Lucy could have sworn he actually nodded his head and barked in agreement.

Alain and his team had news of some unusual phone traffic between Letty Braythwaite and a Polish number. Then, before it could be traced, it stopped and all record of the number vanished. The Swiss police by now had a good understanding of all the Braythwaite's activities and this was highly suspicious: it was out of pattern with Letty's other calls.

The officer assigned to keep the Braythwaites under partial surveillance told them of a visitor who, unusually, the Braythwaites seemed not to want anyone to see. The guest himself was also discreet and a clear sighting of him could not be had. One Sunday Alain flew over their chalet to have a look himself but, other than a fleeting shadow, there was no indication that the Braythwaites had company. Usually when he flew, he passed unnoticed but on this occasion he had a feeling that, though he may have seen nothing, someone had taken a good look at him.

Anne Dupertuis and Jacques Aulnay were dining quietly at La Grande Cour one Friday evening when a terrible din broke out.

'What on earth can that be?' Anne asked her companion. He raised his eyebrows as he looked towards the lobby but all he could discern was a great deal of gesticulation and discussion. He gradually understood from various pointing gestures, that he and Anne were the problem.

Anya, looking mildly irritated, whisked in with the maître d' and had a large table swiftly moved to a secluded corner and deftly set for a party of six.

A tall blond woman then flounced in as if she owned the place, loudly placed her guests, and took possession of the room.

'I'm so sorry,' she told her companions and the entire room, looking pointedly towards where Anne and Jacques were seated, 'I always have the oval table in the window, I can't think what went wrong with my reservation. That spot's far too large for a table for two.'

Until then, Anne and Jacques had been enjoying a quiet tête-à-tête in the beautiful restaurant which, owing to its formal environment and high prices, could usually be counted on for a civilised and tranquil evening meal.

Jacques was bothered by the distraction, but Anne watched on, amused.

'As free entertainment has been provided,' she chided him, 'it would be rude not to enjoy it.'

He grinned wryly and nodded. Their main course was served and they tucked in, with half an eye and ears open to the antics of the new arrivals.

BL scanned the room for anyone of importance to impress. She spotted a few local VIPs and waved to them conspicuously before dismissing the other diners as being unworthy of her attention.

Fortunately for them, she did not know that Anne was a professor at Lausanne University (and Alain Dupertuis' mother) or that Jacques Aulnay was one of the most eminent lawyers in the canton of Valais. Jacques, however, did know one of BL's guests, the highly acclaimed conductor, François-Xavier Bleuer. The men acknowledged one another with a brief and discreet nod: it was clear that neither wished to bring attention to the other.

Anne looked at him curiously.

'What's that all about? Do you know those people?'

'I know one of them,' he whispered. 'I do not know the others, although I think I may know who they are.'

'You're being cryptic,' she teased.

'In my line of work, it is called, client confidentiality,' he winked.

'Ah! Between you and my son, I am not blessed in gossip, that's for sure. So who is the loud English woman?'

'I believe her name is Laeticia Braythwaite.'

'Ah, the choir lady. At least Lucy tells me a little of what goes on around here.'

'My apologies for my deficiency. Perhaps Mlle Wilson is a better source of scandal?'

'Lucy is often the subject of gossip but I never hear her spreading it. She is, however, most entertaining on the subject of this choir. Apparently, Mme Braythwaite thinks big and everyone else thinks she has got the whole thing totally out of proportion.'

'Excellent! We must attend. Lucy is not participating?'

'No, apparently she has no musical talent but she seems to be quite relieved about that. She has lots of friends who are in the choir and wishing they weren't.'

'So, why are they?'

'It seems they have a professional orchestra and conductor and most of them have never sung at such a high level before.'

'I must admit, I enjoyed chatting to Lucy last Sunday. She was very funny about Mark Twain's account of the Swiss guides taking him through the Gemmi Pass.'

'Lucy always has something interesting to say. I like her a lot, Jacques. She is good for Alain. His father's death hit him hard. I was worried about him being so serious; she has really livened him up.'

'He seems very happy. And you too.'

'Yes, me too. I look forward to her bringing Słowik round and telling me where they've been exploring. My neighbour is less impressed though.'

'Really?'

'Yes, she asked me if he couldn't have found a nice local girl – I think she had her eye on Alain for her daughter.'

'How did you reply?'

'I told her that Lucy was local. I mean, what a cheek, her daughter lives in Geneva so she's not exactly handy. She then made some snide remark about her being mixed up in that nasty murder that took place here.'

'That's a bit below the belt.'

'I thought so.'

'You're smiling. Go on: tell me what punch you landed.'

'I didn't need to: at that moment Lucy raced up the stairs with Słowik, gave me a huge hug and a bunch of dried herbs. She gave Thérèse a charming smile and a polite hello and then dragged me inside to ask me a grammar question. I am so lucky, Jacques, I see my son and Lucy so often but Thérèse's daughter visits infrequently – too busy being a high-flyer her mother tells me. As she closed her door with her nose in the air, all I could feel was pity.'

The volume increased again as the table across the way gave its order. Anya and the sommelier were in attendance as the best of everything on the menu and wine list were ordered.

Jacques looked across at Anne fondly and thought how lucky he was. They had known each other when they were young but their paths had separated and it had been the death of his great friend, Malcolm McDonaghue, that had brought them back in touch. Both widowed, they had been lucky, he thought, to find love again.

Anne looked across at BL's table.

'Your friend looks like he's there under sufferance,' she surmised.

'Yes,' Jacques smiled widely. 'Doesn't he?'

'Ahhh. Now I recognise your musician friend, what's his name?' Anne asked.

'Nemesis.'

'That BL woman is outrageous,' Anya told Lucy when she popped in to have a coffee with her one afternoon. 'She marches into the lobby one night without a reservation and demands the best table in the house. It was a quiet night and we'd already put a table for two there.'

Lucy had already heard Anne's version of the encounter.

'Yes, Anne told me she'd seen her. She said she made quite a stir.'

'Can you imagine? She was loudly insisting that we go and ask your boyfriend's mum and her friend to change tables! They must have heard her.'

'They did. It was a bit cheeky.'

'Arrogant, you mean'

'But you managed to talk her into taking another table.'

'Yes, but we had to re-arrange the furniture to do it! Honestly! I'd been on my way home when she arrived: I had to stay and give her my personal attention so that the maître d' could deal with the restaurant's other clients.'

'I guess she's good for business though.'

'Not if she frightens away all the other customers. Whenever she turns up, my main objective is to make sure she causes as little disturbance as possible.'

'I think BL likes to cause a disturbance.'

'I think so too. She's going to be unbearable after this concert is over.'

'We're all hoping that some impresario will whisk her off to stardom and leave us in peace. Are you going?'

'Of course. We have tickets for the Saturday night performance.'

The hype surrounding the performance had created such a demand that a second concert had been scheduled.

'BL gets on my nerves, but it sounds like it's going to be pretty special.'

They had no idea, just how special.

_____

With the concert approaching, the non-singers, Lucy, Eddie, Poppy and Johnny dutifully reserved their tickets. Lucy asked Alain if she should get him a ticket.

'I'm afraid I have to work on Friday night. A long-term project is coming to a close. But can you get me ten tickets for Saturday night?'

'Ten?'

'Yes, team outing to celebrate the end of the project. I have included you, of course, if you would like to come.'

'I'm not sure I can bear watching BL's consecration twice.'

'But Tommy and Jodie have small solo parts don't they? Otherwise it is of no interest to me either.'

'Yes, they do. Okay, ten tickets. You'll have to give me the cash. They're 40 francs each.'

'Really?' he joked. 'I thought BL was financing the whole thing.'

'I don't think that extends to the audience.'

'Oh, Florence Foster Jenkins paid for hers.'

'If *I* was singing that would be necessary. Apparently BL can sing in tune.'

'Okay, I'll go to the cashpoint before I go to work and leave the money at Mum's for you.'

'Great. Supper?'

'Anya, how's it going at La Grande Cour?'

'It's going fine, thanks, Mme Rosset.'

Anya crossed Alessandra Rosset in the street as she was walking to work. She got the distinct impression it was no accidental meeting.

'Alessandra, please. I was very disappointed, Anya, that you decided to stay there instead of joining my team: I think we could offer you a much more exciting career path.'

'I'm very happy with my current position.'

'Well, they're lucky to have you. I hope they are paying you what you're worth.'

'I hope you understand that I can't possibly discuss my salary.'

'Take my card. One day you might tire of doing all the work just so someone else can live off the proceeds.'

Anya took the proffered card and Alessandra continued on her way.

What on earth was all that about, Anya wondered. Was she just trying to sow the seed of discontent or did she have another objective. She clearly hadn't given up on the idea of getting hold of La Grande Cour. Anya shuddered at the thought.

She decided to tell Sebastian when they had their weekly call.

'So, she's still sniffing around?'

'Well we're seeing more and more of her in resort. The White Snowflake construction is well underway and so I guess she has to be here to keep an eye on that. I don't know why but I'm nervous, Sebastian. I think she's up to something. That was no chance encounter.'

'Well, my guess would be that if she can't get you to leave of your own accord, she may resort to more underhand tactics to drive the price down and get me to sell.'

'More underhand?'

'Dad would have known what she was up to, but then, she would never have tried it on Dad: she thinks I'm a novice. Anya, you must be vigilant: watch out for any signs that your integrity or that of the hotel is being threatened.'

'I see. Bad reviews, rumours, staff leaving, sudden kitchen inspections by the authorities.'

'Yes, exactly.'

'I'll try and cut it off before it begins: I'll have a briefing with the staff.'

'Good idea. And Anya?'

'Yes?'

'Thanks for being honest with me.'

'I like these discussions.'

'Me too, we're learning together.'

Anya was shocked to discover a few red faces amongst her key staff members when she asked if any of them had been approached by another hotel group. In particular, her marketing and spa managers looked very uncomfortable. Anya decided to play it generously.

'If you are tempted by what seems to be a better offer, then I cannot prevent you from leaving. But ask yourself one question: when so many people from the same hotel have been approached, is it really about you, or is someone targeting the hotel? Please remember, if it doesn't work out, I will consider re-employing former staff members but that will depend on your position still being available and your not having behaved in a detrimental way towards La Grande Cour.'

She looked hard at them, the message had gone in. She knew she couldn't prevent some departures but she had at least issued a warning which should deter anyone from using their knowledge of the hotel against it.

The following day, her spa manager and chef told her they had decided to stay but Sandy Jennings, her marketing manager, handed in her resignation. Anya did not feel this was a great loss: Sandy was one of Carla's old cronies and had resented Anya being promoted over her head. The chef would have been hard to replace and the spa manager was Anya's own protégé so she was glad she had managed to make her think again. No one else indicated an interest in leaving and the whole team worked out a strategy for monitoring every review and comment published about the hotel.

Strangely, the idea that they might be under attack united them and they appreciated Anya involving them.

Sebastian also kept a close eye on things. The idea of someone trying to take the hotel away from him had made him realise just how much he wanted to keep it.

When the negative reviews and comments started appearing Anya recognised the unmistakable style of her former marketing manager. She was disappointed but not surprised that her warning had gone unheeded.

She and her team didn't let a single comment pass: they slammed back into every negative review, questioning their source, validity and motivation. It was a textbook exercise in dealing with negative press and eventually the attacks dwindled out.

Alessandra appeared in the restaurant one evening with a man Anya hadn't seen before.

'Let me introduce you to my new marketing director,' she said shamelessly as Anya seated them.

'I thought Sandy Jennings was hired for that position?'

'She has been moved to a less demanding role. She wasn't able to convince me of her abilities during her trial period. Truce?'

'I should be glad not to have to waste so much time putting out fires I didn't start,' Anya replied.

'You are a worthy adversary,' Alessandra replied. 'There's a job for you on my team anytime you want.'

Anya just smiled. 'I will send your waiter over, enjoy your evening.'

She sent the waiter over with two complimentary flutes of champagne and nodded at Alessandra when she held the glass up and looked in her direction.

Rightly she concluded, trouble had been averted for now.

How ruthless is she? she thought, glad that she hadn't placed her future in Alessandra's power like poor, misguided Sandy.

She sent Sebastian a text message to update him, warned her maître d' to keep an eye on Alessandra and went home to have supper with her husband for a change.

When, a few days later, Sandy Jennings called to ask for her job back, Anya gently told her that she couldn't take her back because she had broken her trust. She also made sure that everyone knew that she had stuck to her word.

It was Anya and Sebastian's first bout in the hard-nosed world of the hospitality business. They admitted to one another that they had both rather enjoyed it although they knew it was only the end of the first round.

The friends took their seats in the church. It was packed and they had to squeeze to all get into the same pew. The hall was noisy with that unique electricity created by the excited chatter of concert goers and instruments being tuned.

A large camera was in place for the live-streaming and strange-looking people who Johnny said could only be classical music critics, sat, pens poised, in the front row.

Lucy recognised several members of the local council and various dignitaries and celebrities. BL had clearly worked hard to make sure everyone who mattered was present to see her shine.

The orchestra went silent, the chorus filtered in and filled the back of the stage, then the first violin arrived followed by the musical director. Suddenly all eyes were on Tommy who left the chorus ranks and approached one of the soloists' microphones.

'Ladies and Gentleman, if I could have your attention for a moment. I regret to announce,' he said, grinning from ear-to-ear, 'a last-minute programme change. The part of Maria will now be sung by Jodie Scott.'

A loud gasp echoed through the building but there was no time for discussion. The professional soloists, with Jodie in the middle, walked onto the stage to polite but muted applause, took their seats, the MD rapped his baton on the music stand for silence and the music began.

As Jodie stood to sing her first notes, Lucy saw the professional mezzo-soprano singing the part of Anita give her hand a firm squeeze for courage and that set her off: Lucy cried from that point on. Jodie's opening bars were nervous but accurate and, with each assured note she grew in confidence. Her voice had a beautiful, clear tone and, not only to Lucy's untrained ear, but to many trained ears in the room, it was not out of place amongst the professionals at her side.

Lucy managed to gulp down some wine between sobs in the interval but she couldn't join in the discussion as rumours filled the hall.

'I'm hearing,' said Poppy, 'that BL and Henry have been arrested.'

'Arrested?'

'Well, all I can say is the Swiss police have impeccable timing.'

'Yes, one might almost say *uncanny,*' they said, looking pointedly at Lucy, but she was too happy crying to defend her lover. By the time the concert resumed, the reasons for BL's no-show had been ascribed to every crime under the sun from white slavery to smuggling and Maria's murder. Humphrey was standing by the bar, beaming.

'A most entertaining evening,' he could be heard saying to all around him. 'Who could have imagined such a satisfactory turn of events? What a delightful voice that young woman has.'

Standing side by side with the professional soloists, Jodie held her own for the second half of the performance. Her final notes were so touchingly and beautifully delivered that even Johnny was dabbing his eyes. As the music faded, the audience roared and jumped to their feet. The glory, intended for BL for herself, was all Jodie's: she was applauded by her fellow soloists and pushed forward to take a bow. Blushing but composed, she didn't quite seem to understand how well she had done.

As the crowds drifted out and the friends waited for Jodie and the others to arrive so they could have a communal hug, Alain drifted in.

'How long have you been there?' asked Lucy.

'Didn't miss a note,' he grinned.

'You knew, you knew what was going to happen.'

'Of course. You don't think I could allow illegal trading, money laundering and tax evasion to continue unheeded on my patch?'

'Ohmigod! That bad? So, is this the "long-term" project that you were talking about?'

'It is.'

'But why tonight? Couldn't you have arrested them earlier, or later?'

'Ah, I cannot go into that, but, if anyone was influential in the timing it was that gentleman over there.' He nodded in the direction of the musical director.

Lucy was puzzled.

'All I can say, Lucy, is – never get on the wrong side of a musical director, especially a Swiss one.'

Back at the chalet, they sat out on the terrace looking up at the stars twinkling above and the lights of Grondère twinkling below. Over a glass of port, Lucy playfully quizzed Alain.

'So, they didn't have anything to do with Maria's death then?'

'We cannot find anything,' he replied cautiously. The search of the Braythwaites' chalet following their arrests had been fruitful in respect of their money laundering activities but there had been no trace of the couple's mystery visitor. Whoever he was had cleared out long before.

'What, or who, put you on to them?'

Alain relented and, after swearing Lucy to secrecy, agreed to tell her a little more: the Braythwaites had already been on the *Police judiciaire's* radar but the MD had considerably helped them accelerate their investigation. He had, apparently, become uneasy about the large cash payments he was receiving. He was worried he could be being used for money laundering, which indeed he was. He approached an old lawyer friend.

'Maître Aulnay.'

'Perhaps. Who discussed the matter with a friendly policeman.'

'Who just happens to be in the *Police judiciaire.*'

'Perhaps. Who was already aware that certain non-nationals, mistakenly assuming that the Swiss police are simpletons, were trading financial instruments without the appropriate authorisations or adequate capital and that large sums of money were sloshing about without any apparent source. It does get irritating, you know: foreigners think Swiss banking is completely lawless when it's actually more transparent than a few countries I could name in the European Union. Anyway, a full surveillance programme was greatly assisted by the information from a party who could give precise information about an imminent large cash payment on a particular day.'

'The orchestra fee! Of course, so you had to wait until they handed over the money to catch them red-handed on the money laundering charge, so you could then seize all their other property to get the evidence to convict them on all the other crimes.'

'You make it sound almost underhand.'

'On the contrary, I think it's ingenious and I am in total admiration in the efficient pragmatism of the Swiss *Police judiciaire*.'

Alain looked at her cynically.

'This is all just theoretical, you understand, and not to be speculated on with your chums.'

'Ha. I'm not sure I'll be able to pull that off.' She laughed, knowing that the next time she was in The Pub she would be subjected to an interrogation worthy of the Spanish Inquisition.

'Try,' Alain said firmly. 'You are going out with a policeman.'

'Okay, okay, but explain the bit about the MD's timing.'

'It seemed to be imperative for the MD that we "corner" his wealthy benefactress *before* the concert. It would appear his soloist had been imposed upon him and he had a preference for another.'

'Jodie. Apparently, he's been having her rehearse in secret for weeks. She was wonderful, wasn't she?'

'She was. But for me the most beautiful sight of the evening was my girlfriend who cried her eyes out from start to finish out of joy at her friend's good fortune.'

Lucy blushed and gave him a kiss.

'So, does that mean the orchestra didn't get their money?'

'A local resident picked up the bill. Someone called Humphrey Watson.'

'Humphrey was in on it too? Wow!'

'A most helpful gentleman. He and the MD make a formidable team. And *that* you are to keep to yourself.'

'I am looking forward to enjoying tonight's performance from a more comfortable position.'

Alain was drinking a coffee with Lucy on the balcony before donning his parachute.

Lucy, switching to English to find the right words, wagged her finger at him, 'Serves you right for skulking in the shadows.'

Skulking, that's one for Blonnay, he thought.

'You won't forget the tickets, will you?'

'No, I won't. Anyway,' she asked, 'who are the ten tickets for? Your team isn't that big.'

'No, but Jodie's is and I am sure they would like to be there for her.'

She looked at him and felt a huge wave of love flood over her.

'So, with you, me, Mother, Maître Aulnay, Blonnay and Sylvie, that leaves tickets for Poppy, Johnny, Eddie and

Eddie's girlfriend, Émilie, who I believe, is available to join us tonight.'

'You planned the whole thing!'

'I am Swiss, that's what we do. Was I wrong?'

'No, you were absolutely and wonderfully right!'

'You'd better call your friends and let them know.'

Lucy looked at her watch and wondered how early she dared wake them.

'Shouldn't we arrest Charles Sidforth-Sykes?' asked Blonnay as they sat, the following evening, listening to the orchestra tune up.

Alain winked.

'Not until after tonight's performance, apparently he's the strongest baritone they have.'

As the audience filtered in, Lucy caught sight of Anya and her husband. Anya gave her a big wink and an excited thumbs up. The mood in Grondère was jubilant.

The second concert was even better than the first, and, despite the fact that the press had got hold of the story and the local television company had managed to get a camera in, Jodie gave an even more assured performance. Lucy, her emotions under control this time, was able to enjoy the music properly. She sat proudly between Alain and Inspectrice Sylvie Jacquier, who, as soon as the choir had taken their final bow, slipped out the back with Blonnay and discreetly arrested Charles Sidforth-Sykes.

Charles, once he told the police everything he knew about the Braythwaites' dealings, was considered more as a guileless victim than a criminal. He was feeling sorry for himself: letting Henry invest his final reserves had been his last throw of the dice and he had had no idea it was being managed illegally. Charles' history of bad investments and business dealings had finally caught up with him: in short, Charles Sidforth-Sykes was utterly broke.

Twenty-One

Could you understand the meaning of light if there were
no darkness to point the contrast? Day and night, life and
death, love and hatred; since none of these things can
have any being at all apart from the existence of the
other ...
Elizabeth Goudge, Green Dolphin Street

The ever-efficient rumour mill of Grondère ensured that
Lucy didn't have to keep anything to herself with respect
to Humphrey's benevolent gesture. Increasingly
exaggerated stories of unpaid singers and orchestras were
rapidly replaced by tales of Humphrey saving the day.

Johnny cornered him one afternoon, cradling a glass of
wine at his favourite sunny corner table outside Les Deux
Moines.

'Humphrey?' he asked (no one else would have had the
guts). 'Is it true you bailed out the concert?'

'Yes, guilty as charged.'

'That was bloody generous of you.'

'D'you think so? Money well spent as far as I'm
concerned. Best entertainment I've had in years watching
Charles puffing through *Officer Krupke* and Bloody L
bossing everyone around.'

'How did you know we called her that?'

'Everybody knows.'

'Oh.'

'Yes, I made sure of it. I'm going to miss the old girl.'

'Really?'

'Yes, Johnny. During her short time amongst us, BL really
stirred things up around here. Gave us all something to talk
about, someone to laugh at and inadvertently,' he added,
thinking of Poppy's sartorial triumph at the festival, 'she

also smartened some of us up a bit! Overall, great fun! Don't you think?'

'No, I thought she was bloody awful.'

'Indeed she was. In fact, she was the perfect embodiment of awfulness, but you see, we need the dark to appreciate the light. Don't tell me you didn't enjoy Jodie Scott's triumph all the more for BL's downfall?'

Johnny grinned.

'You're right, Humphrey. So, Carla's gone, BL's gone. Who is going to be next to disturb our peace?'

'Trust me,' Humphrey tapped his nose knowingly, 'there'll be someone. And,' he added sagely, 'take my advice, Johnny. Next time, don't sit sulking in the bar. Come and join me in the front row.'

Twenty-Two

To awaken quite alone in a strange town is one of the most pleasant sensations in the world. You are surrounded by adventure.

Freya Stark

The week after the concert, Lucy and Alain left for a long weekend in Wales. With one investigation over and the other stagnant, Alain's team and Lucy had managed to convince him that a break wouldn't hurt and may even have a positive effect on his detecting powers.

Their ultimate object was a festival called *The Big Cwtch* held by Lucy's friend, Bethan, and her family, who ran the adaptive ski charity Ski4All Wales. Lucy had first met Bethan, Jo and the rest of the team when they brought a small group of adaptive skiers out to Grondère. Finding herself temporarily unemployed during the Grand Cour murder investigation, Lucy had volunteered and found herself really appreciating the charity's work. Lucy was curious to see how a small fundraising event had grown into a popular event on the Welsh festival circuit featuring exclusively upcoming Welsh artists which had received all sorts of awards. Alain was curious too.

'It must be a big garden,' he commented as they got into their hire car at Bristol.

'Yes, it must,' smiled Lucy. 'I think it even has a lake in it.'

They stopped at a place called *Gwasanaethau* for a break.

'*Gwasanaethau*, how do you pronounce that?'

'I'm not sure,' she replied.

'Why not? This is your country.'

'No, it's not, and it's not my language either.'

It was only when they had passed a few more *Gwasanaethaus* that they realised it was the Welsh word for service station and laughed at their own ignorance.

'I have to share that one with Blonnay,' Alain laughed. 'He'd be ecstatic surrounded by all this new and wonderful vocabulary.'

Before their visit to the festival, Lucy was taking Alain to visit something Switzerland didn't have – the seaside. She had booked them into a country pub near Pembroke.

She drove as Alain fed the address into his phone: he also had a detailed map on hand as back-up. Lucy's laid-back approach to the outing was proving rather 'un-Swiss'.

'Blonnay is quite jealous, he's never been to Wales.'

'I've only been here once, for a wedding.'

'Really?'

'Yes. To be honest, I have probably visited more of Switzerland now than the UK. I'm really looking forward to discovering a bit more of my own country.'

'You just said it wasn't your country.'

Lucy sighed. 'It's complicated.'

'More complicated than 21 cantons and four different languages?'

Lucy thought about it.

'Yes. Fewer countries, fewer languages (debatable), but a much bigger historical mess.'

'When I think about it, beyond the French-speaking part of Switzerland, the only parts I have visited are the ones I went to during my military service,' he confessed.

'Well, there's an idea,' she laughed. 'Each summer, let's do a bit of Switzerland that you don't know and a bit of Britain that I don't know and eventually, we will both get to know our two countries.'

'That's a great plan, I really like that.'

They both smiled, they were talking about the future and it felt good.

Alain and Lucy spent two glorious days exploring the cliff paths and golden beaches of Pembrokeshire, walking, swimming and jumping waves in little horse-shoe bays. Lucy was also determined that Alain get the full culinary experience, so they had fish and chips, pub steak and kidney suppers and scones at a National Trust café.

'I can't believe we've done so much in just two days,' he laughed as he switched on the maps on his phone.

'Nor me; now it's time to face the music,' she joked, turning onto the main road eastwards.

'I take it you don't know how to pronounce "Crugybar" either,' he teased as he typed in the address.

They arrived in Carmarthenshire at early evening milking time and were held up twice as the cows, ambling towards the milking sheds, took ownership of the country roads.

'This could be Switzerland,' Lucy joked.

'Yes, feels just like home,' Alain agreed.

Dusk was falling as they arrived at the festival. As they turned the corner it made for a magical first impression. Coloured lamps and bunting dangled from the trees above them and skirted the small lake down towards which sloped the main lawns from the house. The reflected lights danced upon the water, fringed with tall reeds and marginals, as festivalgoers paddled to and fro in a variety of watercraft. At one end of the lake stood a large, arched stage and at the other sat a steaming wooden hot tub. Pretty craft stalls edged the lawns with The Wonky Table Bar perched on one high corner and Mia's après-ski bar on the other. An avenue of street food stalls, emitting a fusion of smells, familiar and exotic, led to the camping and activity areas.

As the bands played, children ran happily in and out, amongst picnic blankets and camping chairs, whilst a tall man circulated, flirting with the stall holders and their clients. Costumed actors wore oversized animal heads and posed for selfies with the public. It made for a very enchanting scene.

'I feel like I just walked into *A Midsummer Night's Dream*,' Lucy laughed.

'It does feel magical,' Alain agreed. 'Especially as, when you drive in the car park, you have no inkling that it's here.'

'True.'

As they had arrived, they could never have imagined that all this magical colour and activity lay bosomed between the intertwining rounded hills which sheltered Glanrannel House, Crugybar.

The attractive couple could not remain unnoticed for long themselves: they were soon surrounded by Bethan, Jo, Mia and being introduced to so many people they had no chance of remembering their names. The voice of Bethan's husband, Dave, could be heard at regular intervals marshalling the volunteers down the headsets they were all wearing. It all looked very professional and 'roadie-ish'. Lucy, surprised by the funky outfits they were wearing, realised she had only ever seen them in jeans and ski clothes, the uniform of the mountains in winter. Seeing that the team were frantically busy, Lucy and Alain took themselves off to listen to the music and visit the après-ski bar where Mia made them drink shots from a ski. That evening they gorged on the bearded Californian's heavenly tacos and cuddled up on a blanket together with a bottle of wine, listening to the music: it seemed other-worldly, suspended in time.

The following morning, arriving early in the drizzle, as the campers were beginning to stir, they greeted Dave who was wandering around, soaking wet, organising the day's set up. Munching on their glorious Sloppy Joes breakfast toasties, they admired the stalls as they opened one by one. Lucy found some pretty *Cwtch* jewellery as Christmas presents for Sally and Jodie and later, when the sun came out, they tried out the crafts: Lucy had a go throwing a pot and then watched on as Alain tried his hand at forging.

Bethan crept up behind her.

'He's absolutely lush, your Mr. Darcy.'

Lucy laughed.

'Yes, I'm happy.'

'Good with his hands too.'

'Don't be cheeky.'

'Do you remember what I said to you last March in Grondère?'

Lucy grinned as she recalled the remark.

'You told me, I was capable of great love and that it just needed an almighty spark to ignite it.'

'And,' Bethan concluded, looking pointedly in Alain's direction as he hammered the hot metal on the anvil, 'that you would find the man with the necessary steel to match your flint. I thought it a corny metaphor at the time but right here, right now …'

Jo, who had crept up behind them finished the sentence.

'It seems more like a prophecy.'

Alain, his concentration broken, looked up to see Lucy and her friends groaning and laughing together at some joke. He had no doubt that he was the subject of their mirth but he knew it could not be malicious and was too busy enjoying acquiring this new skill to care. Lucy grinned across at him and his heart swelled with love for this funny, beautiful, unpredictable woman who had changed his life for ever. He grinned back, shook his head in mock despair and bent down to his work again.

As they crossed the Severn and the border back into England the following day, Alain's thoughts had already turned back to his investigation into Maria's murder. It had been a lovely interlude and he did feel that his mind was sharper for having been switched off for a few days. He also had a feeling that things were about to come to a head: he saw it in the form of a big shadow looming over Grondère. But Lucy was looking dreamily out of the window and so he didn't mention it.

Twenty-Three

When someone mattered like that, you didn't lose her at
death. You lost her as you kept on living.
Barbara Kingsolver, Unsheltered

During the flight Tonita caught up on her sleep and
Sebastian worked. He had to try and keep up, if he didn't
want to be ousted before he was ready. Having
disentangled his and Ellen's lives he was struggling to
adapt to single life. He had looked around at the young,
glamourous, intelligent women he encountered every day
in his job, many of whom had been showing decidedly
more interest in him since it had become known he was
newly available, but all he could see were more Ellens who
would not be interested in a man with no ambition left in
him. Until he had worked out what he did want, he needed
to hang on to the only certainty in his life – his job. He
wondered how it was possible that, after all his
endeavours, he could have everything and nothing a man
could want at the same time. If only his mother and sister
hadn't committed that heinous murder and turned his
world upside down.

He stared at the draft sales memorandum in front of him.
It was good but he could still see the shortcomings. He
circled gaps in the facts and struck his red pen through
some misleading statements, knowing that the lawyers
would be doing the same and wondering if his contribution
was actually worth anything. After a while, bored, he
turned to the business plan Sally had sent him. That too
was good but he could also see gaps, oversights and room
for improvement. Maybe he could add value to the
exercise, after all. Grapes, wine, soil … it was all more
tangible. It felt good also to be creating a product and jobs

instead of charging outrageous fees and advising headcount cuts.

'I had a call today from Maja.'

'Maja?'

'The Polish girl who helped me with Słowik.'

Lucy and Alain were sitting enjoying a glass of wine on the terrace, soaking up the early evening sunshine.

'I remember. She didn't know Maria well, did she?'

'No, that's just it, but apparently she was contacted by Maria's best friend who wanted to know what had happened to Słowik. Maja told her I had taken her and she asked if she could meet me.'

'That's the first I've heard of a best friend, but then we could find no trace of Maria's phone and her phone records only showed a few calls with her employer, nothing else. It was as if she rarely used it.'

'Shall I get her to call you? Or Sylvie?'

'No, could you meet her? This case is going nowhere and you might just be able to coax some information out of her. Would you mind?'

It suddenly felt like the onset of autumn. As Lucy walked down to Grondère the following day, the earth smelt damp and fungal and dry leaves fluttered around her legs. Lucy stood still, enjoying the feel of the warm air on her cheeks and contemplating the pleasures of the season to come: collecting blackberries, blueberries, sloes and hazelnuts and mushroom hunting with Poppy.

She came to a halt above the White Snowflake development, watching three giant cranes lifting and shifting huge blocks of reinforced concrete, enormous iron girders and large tubes of plastic whilst the newly-laid foundations dried. Tommy and Eddie were down there somewhere in the thick of all the activity. Construction sites are rarely beautiful but she had to admit that the demolition of the ramshackle holiday huts that had previously occupied the barren spot did not cause her any pangs of regret. She was hopeful that the new complex would be tasteful and provide lots of new jobs for her and her seasonnaire friends.

Lucy was waiting for Lina Lewandowska to appear. On Alain's advice, she had cautiously appointed an outdoor meeting spot with an uphill vantage point from where she could check out the person she was meeting before she showed her face. If Lucy felt something was wrong she had been told to stay out of sight and call Inspectrice Sylvie Jacquier who had been instructed to work from her home in Grondère that morning just in case.

A slim, blond woman eventually appeared and, finding herself alone, looked nervously about.

Słowik recognised her immediately and started wagging her tail furiously and straining at the lead. Lucy let her go and followed her downhill as Słowik barked in recognition and was swept up in the arms of her former mistress's friend.

As Lucy reached them she could hear Lina muttering words of affection in Polish to the little dog. The woman greeted Lucy shyly and Lucy steered her to the terrace of a nearby café.

'Do you want to take Słowik?' Lucy asked: the dog hadn't stopped wagging its tail once.

'I would love to but I cannot have a dog. I am a live-in carer and housekeeper for an elderly lady who won't have animals in the house. It would do her good to have a bit of life around but she prefers to live in a museum filled with precious china and stale air. She sits there all day surrounded by porcelain people. I think they're horrible but Maria loved them!'

'Did you see Maria a lot?'

'Yes, until her awful cousin turned up, we timed our days off so we could go walking together and I could get some fresh air. I used to love coming up here for walks with Maria and Słowik. When Sergei arrived, she couldn't manage it so often, but I always saw her at church.'

'You can come and walk Słowik any time you want, just let me know.'

'I would like that, thank you.'

Lina cried silently as Lucy gave her the sanitised version of Maria's death authorised by the Swiss police. When she had finished, Lucy saw that it was her chance to find out if Lina knew anything that could be useful to the investigation into Maria's murder. Feeling a bit mean, she asked, 'Would it help to talk to me about Maria? What was she like?'

'Oh, she was a sweet girl, we enjoyed sharing our faith together. And we often went shopping and to the cinema. She was very humble but she was fascinated by royalty.'

'Royalty!'

'Yes, she bought all those magazines, you know, that have pictures of members of the European royal families getting married and having babies. I thought she was a bit silly about it myself. That's why she got an Italian greyhound: some fast-talking breeder convinced her it was an aristocratic dog. Personally, I think she'd have been better off with a corgi – they're more hardy.'

Lucy looked down at Słowik, who was looking mildly offended.

'She certainly has the bearing of nobility.'

Słowik seemed happier with this remark and settled at her feet looking suitably haughty.

'Maria didn't like her employer much.'

'Letty Braythwaite?'

'Yes, she liked working at the hotel better but this bossy woman gave her better money and regular hours. She was Polish too, but she didn't like anyone to know. She thought she was better than us, but she came from the same village as Maria.'

'Really? Were they related?'

'No, I don't think so. Maria said she couldn't stand her but the money was good.'

'She's in prison now – for money laundering.'

'Ooh. Good!'

'Why did you see less of Maria when her cousin arrived?'

'He was always hanging around listening in to our conversations, she said she didn't have the time to go walking anymore because she had to help him find a job. I have to confess, I didn't like coming here with Sergei around. He made me feel uneasy. One day, Maria pointed out someone to me in one of her magazines, some aristocrat who had stayed in the hotel, and he snatched the magazine away and told her off for mentioning it.'

'Do you remember who it was?'

'No, I'm sorry. Sergei took the magazine before I could look at it.

'Why did he come here?'

'I don't know. He probably ran out of other people to use, so he thought he could live off Maria for a bit. I heard from some people back home he also had a bit of a shady past but Maria wouldn't hear it, she said that everyone deserved a second chance. She helped him get some work, enough to get a resident permit, but then he stopped going. She did everything for him and he… look what he did for her!'

Lina was angry and upset but Lucy knew Alain needed her to keep digging.

'Do you think he was really the cause of Maria's death?'

'Who else? She was a good girl. She felt bad about stealing a hairbrush.'

'But that makes it even stranger. It explains why someone would kill her cousin, but why would anyone kill Maria?' Lina looked puzzled.

'You're right. She didn't know any of his bad friends. What could she have known?'

She furrowed her brow and concentrated.

'She didn't know anything. She told me once that Sergei never told her anything. He never got any phone calls, no friends, nothing. She thought that was sad, she wanted him to meet people but he wouldn't. The only thing she knew about him was that he was fascinated by anything to do with Sherlock Holmes.'

Lucy's ears pricked up.

'Really, that's strange for a young man.'

'Yes, apparently he knew all the stories, almost by heart. The place where he died, that's where Sherlock Holmes died, you know?'

Lucy replied cautiously, 'Yes, I read it in the paper.'

'Oh. Yes, of course. Apparently, there are even more visitors going there now. People are fascinated by murder.'

'I'm definitely not.'

'No, not me either. But isn't it strange he should die there, just like his hero? She told me he wanted to visit the Falls ever since he arrived: she was supposed to go with him. She sent me a text saying her boss had changed her day off and he was going alone.'

'You have a text from her about that? Did she often text you?'

Lina looked at her suspiciously, 'Yes, who doesn't?'

Lucy realised that she was going to have to tell Lina the truth if she wanted more information.

'Lina, I know that the police never found Maria or Sergei's phones and that their phone records were almost empty. I think your phone will now be of interest to them. I'm going to have to tell them.'

'Lucy, you're scaring me. I don't want to end up like Maria. If someone took her phone, then they know about me.'

'They do, but that was weeks ago. Whoever it was must have decided you didn't have whatever information it was they were looking for.'

'Or I would already be dead too.'

'I can get Sylvie Jacquier to come and see you now, she lives here and she's really kind. In fact, she knew Maria and was very fond of her.'

'Maria mentioned her to me, she said she was kind during the other murder case. Yes, I will speak to her. If I can help find Maria's killer, I will do that.'

'I'm really glad I met you, Lina,' Lucy said after she had put in a call to Sylvie. 'This may sound weird, and I'm sorry you've lost your friend, but I'm glad Maria has someone to cherish her memory.'

Lina nodded her comprehension.

'Wherever I am, a candle for Maria will be burning in the nearest church.'

Minutes later, Sylvie arrived and confiscated Lina's phone.

Later that day, Sylvie sent Lucy an instruction that Lina's number had now been cancelled and that the two women had better not contact each other again until Maria's murderer had been brought to justice. Lucy wondered whether the police considered Lina a risk to her or her a risk to Lina.

'Shit!' Poppy said when Lucy told her. 'This is getting serious!'

Late that afternoon, in Grondère, Sebastian decided to go for a walk to try and clear his head before the trial. He should have been at his computer, managing his deals, but he couldn't settle to anything.

He headed uphill in no particular direction but found himself naturally gravitating towards the path that ran along the old *bisse* above the heights over Grondère where he and Tonita had seen the stag.

Approaching the forest, he saw a man stacking logs by a small chalet: as he got closer he recognised Capitaine Dupertuis. Alain stood up and greeted him warmly. Sebastian was surprised: the policeman had always seemed so prickly before.

'Come and have a coffee,' Alain enjoined, 'Lucy's lost in the mountains somewhere and I could do with a break.'

'I'm just trying to get my head in the right place for tomorrow.'

'Me too. I'm going to go for a flight later.' Alain looked to the skies. 'Thermals should be just about perfect in an hour or so.'

Sebastian looked at the parachute bag at his feet.

'Is that how you unwind? Flying? Seems a bit extreme to me.'

'It's not extreme if you study and respect the elements. But yes, it's one of the ways: I find physical labour also helps clear the head.'

Sebastian, who had never done any physical work in his life, grinned wryly.

'The truth is, until Dad died I never felt the need to clear my head. It was full and busy up here,' he tapped his head jokingly. 'And I liked it that way.'

'I know what you mean. Then suddenly you're alone with noisy demons that come out of nowhere.'

It hadn't occurred to Sebastian that he wasn't the only fatherless man around.

'I'm sorry, was it recently?'

'No, about four years ago, but the sense of loss doesn't go away I'm afraid. You just learn to live with it. Unlike you, at least I got the chance to say goodbye. Afterwards, Mum and I felt the need to move out of familiar surroundings and we both ended up here. Re-building this place helped.'

He showed Sebastian around and then installed him on the terrace beside the cool pool.

'This is stunning!' Sebastian admired the results of Lucy's summer of working on the garden. The planting in the 'flowerfall' had romped away and, despite having nothing in bloom, looked natural and abundant. The planting around the pool had also taken root, the Alpine lady's mantle had spread, forming a springy carpet all around the pool and rocks of various sizes, some in full sun were covered with creeping thymes and others in shade were covered in moss. Dwarf conifers were artistically placed at intervals between the boulders, growing in height and number towards the garden's edges where the whole blended in with the forest behind.

'I've never seen anything like it,' Sebastian continued. 'It's exquisite, like an Alpine Japanese garden.'

'Lucy's work,' Alain said proudly. 'She has spent hours on it. In fact, there is an area a couple of valleys away that is known locally as the Japanese Garden that Lucy said inspired her.'

'Looks totally natural. Wow! She doesn't mind living up here? It's a bit remote, isn't it?'

'You kidding? This is Lucy's natural environment. Her idea of urban living is that down there.'

He pointed to the hamlet of little chalets where Lucy, Tommy and Eddie lived in winter.

'And her idea of a shopping expedition is up there.'

He pointed up towards Old Folk's Rock where he knew Lucy was, at that moment, exploring the undergrowth for ferns to underplant the conifers.

'Ellen, my ex-girlfriend, she could never live anywhere but New York: she came out in a rash if we spent more than a week at our place on Long Island.'

'Long Island! That's supposed to be really nice.'

'It is, but I have to confess, you end up hanging out with exactly the same people as in Manhattan, it's just the scenery that changes.'

Sebastian wasn't even sure he liked the Long Island part of his life any more. He felt slightly envious of Alain: here was a man who knew where he was comfortable and with whom. Sebastian had to admit to himself that he did not.

Alain, sensing Sebastian's discomfort, tried to change the subject. He couldn't resort to the usual male avenue for avoiding heartfelt discussions – a discussion on sport – as he was pretty sure Sebastian would not be able to sustain a conversation on that subject, so he chose another.

'I hear you have inherited a vineyard.'

'Yes. Fortunately there seems to be an army of capable young women doing everything for me. I just need to be around to take the credit.'

'I'm sure that's not true. Your business experience must be of some value. Although I guess it's not really your line of business, is it? It was your father's.'

'Do you know? I'm getting to like it more and more.'

'Really?'

'Yes. Really.'

Alain was now at a loss for words, his capacity for small talk had been exhausted, but then he had an idea.

'You know what? This is probably totally irresponsible the day before your mother's murder trial but, the thermals are about to hit perfection: would you like to come for a flight?'

As Sebastian ran down the slope as fast as he could to stay in tandem with Alain he wondered what on earth he had agreed to but, as the parachute lifted them higher and higher, a sense of complete tranquillity came over him. As they banked left, over the resort, he could see his hotel beneath him, his staff running around parking cars and greeting clients with no idea of who was supervising them from above. The air was warm and gentle on his face and Alain took him low over the bowl of Grondère surprising racing deer and solitary ibex, before lifting again, over the forest where the old *bisse* finished its course and fell over the cliff to the thirsty pastures below and higher still, over Old Folk's Rock, Seal Flat, to the valley beyond. This was no short flight, Alain took his time and great care to show Sebastian all his favourite spots, pointing out mountain lakes, hidden gullies, waterfalls and, one valley further over, the Japanese Garden that Lucy was so fond of. Lifting higher and higher they returned, passing so close to the face of Mont Grondère that Sebastian could see the detail in the rocks, the small crevices encrusted with different coloured lichens and thymes. It was the greatest moment of peace Sebastian had known since his father's death.

By the time they landed, Lucy and Słowik had returned home and were looking at them in amused amazement.

'I leave you alone for an afternoon and this is what you get up to!'

Sebastian turned to Alain.

'That was wonderful, thanks.'

'Are you staying for supper?'

'No thanks, Tonita will be expecting me to join her for supper and tomorrow will also be a difficult day for her. She actually saw him die.'

'Then I'll run you down in the quad,' Alain offered.

By the time he returned, he and Sebastian were firm friends, Lucy had planted her ferns and was covered in mud. She took a dip in the cool pool while he prepared supper. Sebastian would have been welcome to stay but it was better, Alain thought, planning a shared shower after supper, to have the place to themselves at the end of the day.

Tonita had also had an interesting afternoon which she recounted to Sebastian with great glee over dinner.

'I went to have a coffee with Charles this afternoon.'

'Sidforth-Sykes?'

'Indeed.'

'I have to confess, I haven't given him a thought since the funeral. What brought that on?'

'He called and suggested a drink before the trial and I felt a bit guilty for having neglected him since Malcolm died. We used to see him a lot.'

'So, how was it?'

'Cringeworthy.'

'No less?'

'He took my hand and started stroking it, telling me how he had felt for me in my distress and wishing he'd been there for me in my hour of need.'

'Go on.' Sebastian was warming to her narrative.

'Then he started talking about himself and how he'd been taken for a ride by that dreadful Braythwaite couple and went on a diatribe about there being no more integrity in business. This was followed by an interrogation on the White Snowflake project, and then…'

'And then?'

She looked at him wickedly.

'And then, he thrust himself at me, telling me he had always loved me from afar, I was the only woman for him and he knew I felt the same way.'

'And do you?'

'What do you think? I couldn't get out of there fast enough. I told him I was very sorry if he had got that impression but that I couldn't remember having given him the slightest encouragement. I said something lame about "staying friends" and got out fast.'

'Poor Charles.'

'Poor Charles! What about me? I never asked to get pounced on by that blundering idiot. I can't even feel slightly flattered as I'm convinced his declaration was mainly motivated by my shareholding in the White Snowflake consortium. I think he's still smarting about selling his shares to Malcolm at the wrong time. I can't think how I ever found him good company.'

'Dad liked him. He thought Charles was a loveable buffoon, if a poor businessman.'

'Well, he's proved himself to be a buffoon, although I can't quite agree with the "loveable" bit, and as to being a poor businessman, that's spot on, especially if he's allowed himself to be conned by that pair. But yes, you're right, I didn't used to mind him: now I just think he's a bore. In fact, Sebastian, I'm finding a lot of people I used to like don't interest me anymore. I have changed.'

'Me too, it's this place.'

'It's the crazy people too. I've come to the terrible realisation that I'd rather listen to Lucy and Poppy trying to identify some rare flower they've discovered growing in some rocky cranny than listen to people discussing the shades of the latest designer range's nail varnish.'

'Then this is indeed a changed Tonita.'

'I mean, I wouldn't like to go scrambling about all over the hillsides and come back covered in dust like them, but you have to admit, they don't need face powder, they positively glow! I don't know a single woman of Poppy's age in New York who has a complexion as good as hers or a single woman of Lucy's age whose eyes shine like that.'

Sebastian was astounded at this outburst.

'So, what about your business ambitions, are they also undergoing a radical change?'

'I don't think so but I do think it's revitalised my creativity. Haven't you noticed, all my recent work is inspired by nature. In July, I remember Lucy and Poppy ruminating over pictures of some rare sedum Poppy had stumbled across in a sea of scree and all I could think about was what a great ring I could turn it into. I had to run back and draw it immediately.'

Sebastian laughed out loud. 'You need to get Lucy to show you her secret garden, you should get a whole collection out of that.'

Tonita grinned back at him.

'Dad would have loved this: we're turning all countrified.'

'He would have had a good chuckle over Charles' clumsy attempt at seduction as well.'

'Poor Charles.'

'He'll get over it, just you watch: tomorrow at the trial, it'll be as if it never happened.'

'Oh, I wish you hadn't said that word.'

'Trial? Sorry.'

Trial was the word. Not only for the accused but for the witnesses. Sebastian, bound by filial duty to the dead father he had loved and the living mother and sister he hated, sat every day in the courtroom and listened to the factual dissection of his father's murder. He avoided, as much as possible, meeting his mother's pleading glances which just made him nauseous, but he sat there, out of respect to his father, and listened to every word. The French wasn't always easy to follow but many of the witnesses were allowed to give their evidence in English.

At each pause, he rushed out to the foyer to try and conduct his business with New York but he could feel it slipping away from him. Decisions were starting to be taken without referral back to him with the justifiable excuse that he was unobtainable: he could only endorse them. He felt he was chasing after his work rather than directing it.

He watched as Tonita, Lucy and all the other protagonists of that fateful evening filed through the courtroom. The first day heard the evidence of all those present at the head table. The highlights for the press were the brief appearances of the ageing but ageless French film star Aurélie Domboule and Swiss favourite Antoinetta who had been the guest celebrities on the evening of the murder. Aurélie Domboule didn't walk like other human beings: she glided into the courtroom as if she were floating on air. There was an unearthly silence as she gave her brief and accurate responses to the questions about what she had noticed from her privileged position at the centre of the table beside the murder victim. Antoinetta, who was ashamed to admit she had thought the whole thing quite funny until she realised Malcolm had actually died, also held the public enthralled. The two stars came and went swiftly: Lord Shilton didn't hang around either, briefly nodding at Charles and Tonita before heading back to Geneva airport. Prince Anwar had booked into La

Grande Cour for the week, having accepted Tonita's invitation to attend the launch of Malcolm's book. After giving evidence he came and sat at Sebastian's side, in silent support, for the rest of that day's proceedings.

As Sebastian listened, the full extent of the evil of his mother's designs and her deliberate attempt to frame Lucy Wilson shocked him to the core. His greedy, stupid sister had been but a puppet. But how could any mother have turned her own daughter into a murderess? It was verging on Greek tragedy.

On the first evening of the trial, Tonita and Sebastian dined with Prince Anwar, who had been looking curiously at Tonita since she had been introduced in court under her real name Tonita Onion.

'Excuse me for asking, Tonita, but I remember you mentioning in the past that you had grown up in my part of the world. Do you have any connection with a chap called Anthony Onion?'

Tonita looked at him, horrified.

'He is my father,' she replied, with a touch of her old frostiness. He was surprised at her reaction but she recovered quickly.

'Forgive me,' she stammered, 'we are not close. My parents divorced a long time ago.'

'I understand, please forgive me, I didn't mean to intrude.'

He was such a gentleman that he clearly didn't and they left the matter there.

A few days later, though, encountering Sebastian at the hotel swimming pool he quizzed him a little more closely.

'Miss Shalott doesn't seem to want to talk about her father, and yet he is highly placed and respected for a non-national in my country.'

'Indeed?' Sebastian was also curious. 'Do you know him personally? Tonita doesn't seem to even know what he does.'

'I do not know him personally, just by reputation and I cannot discuss what services he provides, but he is considered a loyal servant of the state.'

Ah, thought Sebastian, that backs up Tonita's theory. He knew Tonita thought her father was an arms dealer.

'So, Tonita has no contact with her father?'

'Until recently, she hadn't spoken to him for years. She only accepts limited contact now so that she can have access to her half-brother and sister.'

'Ah, I see. What did he do to earn such wrath? Apart from divorcing her mother?'

He saw Sebastian hesitate.

'I am being too nosey, I apologise, it's just I have recently become a father myself and it saddens me to think such a gulf could ever exist between me and my daughter.'

'Congratulations! I'm happy for you. But, as to the whys, I think you would have to ask Tonita, all I can say is – I think he broke her heart.'

'That is not the role of a father.'

'It is not.'

The trial did not last long. The case against Carla Sturridge and Genna McDonaghue was, as Inspecteur chef adjoint Blonnay had told Sebastian, 'cast iron' and, at the end of the week, the two women cried pathetically as they were led back to complete their lengthy sentences in prison.

At least, Sebastian told himself, they are in Switzerland. I don't need to worry about sending them food parcels.

He was glad to be rid of his responsibilities towards them: now he told himself he could forget about them and get his life back on track. He turned his back on the court and on them, walked down the steps, little thinking that his father had not had his final word.

The book launch had been deliberately timed for autumn, to coincide with the end of the trial and precede the pre ski season lull, when the residents of Grondère would once again disappear to avoid the damp weather and closed resort. It was to take place in Golden Mountain, which combined the ski shop where Tommy worked with a swanky bistro. Golden Mountain was in a modern complex close to the main ski lift: it looked like a smart chalet from the outside but inside it was light and spacious with high ceilings showing exposed pipes and air ducts, giving it more the feeling of a Greenwich Village warehouse conversion than an Alpine restaurant. It was the perfect place to invite all the local dignitaries, the Swiss tourism representatives and press. The book was receiving a lot of attention and the agency marketing it had not hesitated to use Malcolm's murder and the recent trial to whip up media interest. Sebastian had, at Lucy's request, given strict instructions that her involvement was to be treated with discretion. Her name appeared in the book's flyleaf, as its compiler, and she was happy with that.

She stood and watched with admiration as Sebastian and Tonita handled the VIP guests with finesse and dealt deftly with the media questions.

'They're so good at it,' she said to Poppy.

'It's their world,' Poppy agreed. 'Sebastian must deal with much more important people than this all the time. He's done deals for governments and multinational companies. This lot is small fry to him.'

'And yet, he treats everyone as if they were a lord or lady,' Lucy said, in wonderment at his patience.

'He does, the sign of a true gentleman. But don't forget, he has got a book to sell.'

Lucy smiled. 'True. Tonita's a natural too, look at her talking to Councillor Crettize, she's behaving as if he's her best mate.'

'She too must be used to making a sales pitch to sell her jewellery, but yes, she is much more at home in this environment than us.'

'Why is that, then?'

'How long did it take you to get your hands and fingernails clean before you came?'

'Ages, my skin is itching, I had to scrub so hard.'

'There you go then.'

'What does that explain?'

'You're out of your natural environment. Tonita never has to scrub under her fingernails, her hands are always immaculate. We're outdoor people, that's all. We get nervous if we're inside too long.'

'I like to dress up sometimes, look nice, put on a pretty bit of jewellery.'

Lucy had bought a new dress for the occasion and Jodie had helped her put her make-up on.

'Me too, but it's an effort and I enjoy it because it's not every day. But look at her.'

Lucy looked at Tonita and understood.

'Effortless,' she sighed.

'Exactly, effortless. She was born to waft around looking beautiful and being admired in this setting and you …'

Lucy looked at Poppy a little hurt, but Poppy just pointed through the window, at the mountain tops glowing in the early moonlight.

'You were born to waft around looking beautiful and being admired out there.'

'That's a lovely thing to say, Poppy, thank you.'

'Don't mention it. It's true, Lucy. And you don't look so terribly out of place in here either, however much you feel it.'

Lucy almost turned red, blushing at the compliment and Poppy, also feeling a little embarrassed at her display of affection, hurried off to find some more free champagne, the unlimited supply of which she was enjoying immensely.

Lucy didn't notice Tonita sidling up beside her.

'You look lovely. New dress?'

Lucy nodded. Right then, despite the knowledge that her dress probably cost a fraction of Tonita's designer outfit, she felt no difference between them. Their friendship made it irrelevant.

'Lucy, I'd like you to have this. I noticed you don't wear any jewellery except studs in your ears, so I hope you can get some use out of these.'

She handed Lucy a little blue box with a white ribbon and the word 'Tiffany's' printed on the top. Lucy opened it: inside sparkled a pair of gold earrings in the form of a grape vine. It was a modern delicate, intricate design.

'Tonita, it's beautiful, but I can't accept this, it's far too valuable,' she gasped.

'Nonsense,' laughed Tonita. 'Firstly, it didn't cost me anything and secondly, I should be paying you: you inspired the design of my first Tiffany's range.'

'I did?'

'Yes, you and Malcolm and this beautiful book. The photos you sent through, the wonderful descriptions. You achieved what Malcolm had told you he wanted, you captured more than the facts, you caught the light of the sky, the feel of the earth, the scent of harvest and suddenly these designs came to me. I lived and breathed the book for a month until I had perfected the designs and when I saw the prototypes I knew I had something special.'

Lucy looked at the design and had to admit, Tonita's talent blew her away. Deceptively simple, the design caught the structure and irregularity of a grape vine with a bold modernity that could only come from the imagination of a true artist.

She told her so.

'Really? Thanks, Lucy.' Tonita was thrilled at the compliment. It meant more to her than all the rave reviews she had received from the New York design world.

'So, who was that glamorous redheaded woman you were talking with before? She's talking to Prince Anwar now.'

'That,' Tonita replied ominously, 'is Alessandra Rosset. She's the boss of the White Snowflake consortium and we're all terrified of her.'

'I can see why: she looks really intimidating. So, she's the woman that wanted to buy the hotel.'

'The very woman. We're not sure she's given up either.'

'I wouldn't want to work for her.'

'No. Your friend Anya feels the same. But she's been amazing for the consortium, we're lucky to have her.'

'I guess. Did you invite her? It's a bit like inviting the viper into the nest, isn't it?'

'Oh Lucy, she's a business partner, it would have been very rude to exclude her, and possibly even dangerous. Sometimes you have to knowingly invite the viper into the nest so you can keep an eye on it. Besides, the press photos will benefit from her being on them.'

'You have a good business brain.'

'I have scrapped my way up in the world, a bit like her.'

'Is Prince Anwar part of the White Snowflake consortium?'

Tonita grinned, looking over at Alessandra in intense discussion with Prince Anwar.

'As of half an hour ago, no. As for now, I wouldn't bet against it.'

She gave Lucy a wicked look.

'Shall I introduce you? I'm sure she would be interested to meet the book's compiler. Maybe you can work your magic on her, like you did me and turn her into someone Anya would like to work for.'

Lucy laughed. She could see Anya carefully keeping to the other side of the room.

'I think there are some tasks too tall, even for my "magic". Besides, I have just seen someone very important arrive.'

Tonita saw who Lucy was referring to, gave her a hug and then headed back to her guests.

Lucy felt her heart get that warm, fuzzy feeling as she saw Alain arrive, look for her, and smile as he spotted her. It was, she realised, very special when someone looked for you in a crowd. She watched him make his polite hellos to Sebastian and then Tonita before heading over. She immediately showed him Tonita's gift.

Touching the earrings in admiration, Alain felt a surge of energy and imagined he saw Tonita bathed in the light of stained glass and surrounded by giant stone columns; suddenly the image turned dark, the light disappeared, the columns turned into tall trees, Lucy had taken Tonita's place and he got the feeling she was in terrible danger.

'What is it? What's wrong?' she asked.

He gave her a strained look. Lucy knew that once before, when they had first met, Alain had had a glimpse into the future and it had spooked them both.

'You saw something, didn't you?'

He nodded. 'Not here. I'll tell you later.'

At that moment anyway, Anne Dupertuis and Jacques Aulnay arrived and came straight over to congratulate Lucy. She turned the glossy pages of the book with them and explained how she had put it together to respect Malcolm's concept. Alain looked on proudly, it had clearly been a labour of love for Malcolm to conceive it and for Lucy to complete what he started.

———————

Later, back at Alain's chalet, Lucy had not forgotten: she asked him to tell her exactly what he had seen. Alain reflected on the relative pros and cons of telling her. He wanted to protect her but his girlfriend was no shrinking violet and he knew that she would not appreciate being treated like one. More importantly, somewhere in there was a warning. He wisely decided that she was entitled to total honesty.

'That's weird, so you saw Tonita in a cathedral and me in danger in the forest?'

'I'd put it down to my imagination but it's not the first time: when we found Słowik I saw something similar.'

'Alain, anyone less likely to have mystic seeings, I cannot imagine.'

'It never happened till I met you.'

'I'm not sure if that's a good or a bad thing, but it was right last time, so it must mean something, though what, I can't imagine.'

'I don't suppose I can ask you to stay away from forests.'

'No, but I promise, I will take it as a warning and I will be on my guard. No clues, I guess, as to what this danger might be?'

Alain shrugged his shoulders. 'No, that would be too helpful, wouldn't it?'

She grinned.

'You poor old thing. Did you have a nice evening apart from that?'

'Actually, not really. It was a bit awkward for me, I'm not good at small talk. I hope it didn't show too much.'

'Your mum and I are probably the only ones who noticed.'

'By the way,' he asked, leading her into the empty rooms that he had not yet refurbished in the lower part of the chalet. 'What is all this?' he asked, scratching his head. 'Are you practising witchcraft?'

'Ah, yes, I meant to tell you, but I clean forgot.'

As summer had moved into autumn, Lucy had been honing her foraging skills. Already, in the spring, Poppy had shared her secret spots for morel and bolete mushrooms: now it was chanterelle mushrooms. It was rare for someone to share such knowledge, acquired over decades, but Poppy laughingly joked that she was investing in her future and expected Lucy to keep her supplied when she could no longer make it up the mountain.

Lucy had stored jars of pickled mushrooms and hung some to dry, as well as little bundles of herbs and flowers, in an unused room.

'Don't worry, I'll clear it all out before winter; you don't need to start worrying until you find pickled toads,' she answered solemnly.

'I'll keep that in mind. So, what's in that big *bonbonne*?' He pointed to a vast demijohn sitting in one corner.

'That,' she tapped her nose, 'is still empty. It's waiting for the ripening of the magical fruits of the blackthorn bush so that I can steep them in the silver solution from the aromatic juniper bush to create sloe gin, one of the essential ingredients for the Charlie Chaplin.'

'Ah,' he replied. 'None the wiser.'

'Are you really a detective?' she asked. 'You do remember I worked in a bar when I first came here?'

'Ah, one of your magical cocktails.'

'Exactly, one of my favourites.'

'Could you not just make apricot jam like most people in Valais?'

'Nah, Tommy makes the best apricot jam, but thanks, you've reminded me I need some apricot brandy for my cocktail.'

'I do believe Tommy's the only sane member of that household.'

'That's just because you haven't really got to know him yet, but thanks anyway.'

'I have just discovered I'm living with a white witch.'

'Is it an arrestable offence?'

'Probably, but I'm already bewitched.'

In a tight embrace, they closed the room behind them and made for the first comfortable surface they could find.

Twenty-Four

Nothing puts things in perspective as quickly as a mountain.
Josephine Tey, The Daughter of Time

Lucy woke up hot and sweaty; bright rays of sunshine pierced the slatted blinds. She reached for Alain but he was long gone. The clock showed it was already 9am. Lucy could not believe it, she never slept this late. And then she remembered how much champagne she had drunk the night before and how long she had spent making love to her beautiful man when they got home, smiled and turned over. She could allow herself a lie-in for once.

Eventually Słowik came to remind her she had walking duties and, after her usual cup of tea, she made up a picnic and they headed out. Normally she would also be collecting Alain's parachute but he had left a note to say it had failed his pre-flight check and so he had taken the quad. This meant she had the whole day to wander the hills.

The perfume of heated pine needles on the forest floor made her think of the south of France. It was a long time since she'd been to the Mediterranean coast, maybe next summer she could persuade Alain to have a holiday there. Silence reigned as they went deeper into the forest, where Lucy quickly became engrossed in inspecting seed heads and scrabbling around for any plants she didn't recognise, pleased to note that these were becoming fewer and fewer. In silent companionship, Słowik snuffled around in the undergrowth, never letting Lucy far from sight: after chasing that unfriendly and noisy marmot, she didn't want to run into any more strange creatures.

Lucy reflected on how much she had got used to walking with a dog; she loved to walk alone but now it seemed somehow selfish. She felt it gave her walk more purpose and the company of dog was ideal because it didn't chatter. But although she loved having a little shadow by her side, she didn't feel that she and Słowik had ever really connected. They rubbed along together all right but it was more like a marriage of convenience than of true love.

She could hear blackbirds turning over leaves in the undergrowth and great tits and chaffinches fluttered in amongst the branches above. The forest occupants were busily preparing for winter.

After a while Lucy decided to change microclimate and head higher. As she strode along purposefully, Słowik started growling gently in the depths of her throat.

'What is it, Słowik, spotted a marmot?'

Lucy stopped to listen.

In the distance, she saw another walker on the path a way behind them. There was nothing unusual in this but something told her this walker was the cause of Słowik's distress, the easterly wind was blowing towards them so the greyhound would have picked up his scent. She stroked the little dog's back and her shackles really were raised.

Where she would normally have shaken off her apprehension, Alain's vision made her cautious: at the next bend in the path she put on a sprint. Her mind racing, she peeled off her bright-coloured shell jacket and shoved it in her backpack: she would be less visible in her grey T-shirt. She didn't have much time to work out a plan but, from her weeks spent exploring the forest over the summer, she knew that directly ahead lay the end of the *bisse* where the waters tumbled over the cliffs to the pastures hundreds of metres below – a dead end; the paths downwards led into a hollow from which there was no exit, and so, her only real option was uphill. Thinking hard, she visualised the path ahead and recalled a small path nearby edged by some large boulders she could hide behind. When she came to the spot she reached down to pick up Słowik, but Słowik slipped free and ran onwards.

'Come here Słowik.' She whispered frantically, moving up the path hoping that the dog would follow.

Słowik advanced ten metres, crouched in the middle of the path and produced a little poo.

'Oh no, Słowik, this is not the time,' she groaned. Normally Lucy conscientiously picked up Słowik's stools but this time she could not take the risk, Słowik was losing her precious time.

Słowik briefly inspected her work and then ran back and leaped into Lucy's arms.

Darting up the side path, stopping any waving branches disturbed by her passing, Lucy paused behind a protruding rock and held Słowik's jaw just in time to see the man pass. He had also picked up speed: he paused briefly and looked at the path but then he caught sight of Słowik's offering ten metres further on and continued on.

Lucy's heart stopped: that had been close. If it hadn't been for Słowik's laying a false clue, he might have seen her. If she didn't know better she'd have said Słowik did that deliberately. Lucy's heart had stopped for another reason: from that distance and that angle there was no mistaking it, she had just recognised the man from the Reichenbach Falls, her Sherlock Holmes, only her Sherlock Holmes seemed to have turned to the dark side: she knew he meant her harm.

She ran as fast as she could up the narrow track, using her local knowledge to switch paths and disguise her trajectory. When she thought she was out of earshot she dialled Alain.

'Oh, please be there!' she prayed.

He was. She never called him at work and so he answered. She gasped what was happening down the phone as she ran and he, his throat dry, relayed the information to his colleagues.'

To his relief neither of them took the matter lightly.

'We need to call a helicopter,' Blonnay said, 'there's no help for her up on that mountain.'

Sylvie Jacquier called the procureur.

Whilst Alain, distraught, talked to Lucy, the procureur joined them in the office and asked to be informed as to what was going on.

'Hold the line, Lucy. Stay on the line.'

He held the line open so Lucy could hear the conversation.

'So, Mlle Wilson is being pursued through the forest by Sherlock Holmes?'

'The man she recognises as Sherlock Holmes from the Reichenbach Falls.'

'She has identified the murderer?'

'She says it's him.'

Alain was shaking.

'So why have you not called a helicopter?'

'I can't call a helicopter on the hunch of my girlfriend.'

'We cannot punish her for being your girlfriend. In fact, I believe your fear of showing favouritism is clouding your judgement. We failed to believe Mlle Wilson in the past. She has proved herself a reliable witness and I would not like to be in your shoes if Herr Schmutz found out that you had not done everything in your power to protect his only witness. Blonnay, call a helicopter immediately.'

Blonnay needed no second invitation.

Alain returned to the phone.

'Lucy,'

'Shhh,' she hissed back. 'What?'

'Did you hear that?'

'No, I'm a bit busy right now.'

'There's a helicopter on the way.'

'Crikey.'

'Where are you? Can you get to Seal Flat?'

'Yes, I'm just going up and up. I think he's worked that out and is tracking me. Słowik keeps growling.'

'Can you switch on the localiser on the phone?'

'How do I do that?'

'I'm going to put Blonnay on.'

'Okay.'

Blonnay instructed Lucy how to switch her localiser on.

'Thanks,' she told him. 'Can you lot shut up now? I need to get a sprint on.'

Alain Dupertuis' heart was beating so hard he could hardly think. The whole team spent a tense fifteen minutes watching the small dot on his phone screen as Lucy progressed up towards Old Folk's Rock and Seal Flat.

As Lucy approached Seal Flat she realised that if she left the cover of the forest she would be in the open for a good ten minutes before she reached it. She would be visible to anyone following her before she could reach the spot where the helicopter could land. She decided not to chance it until she could hear the helicopter approach.

What to do? she asked herself, panicked.

She decided to hug the edge of the forest and approach the landing spot crab-like.

'What the hell is she doing?' asked Alain to his colleagues as he saw her moving sideways instead of directly towards her pick-up point.

'She's staying under cover,' Inspectrice Jacquier surmised. 'She must be terrified.'

Alain glared at her.

'Sorry,' she apologised, 'not helpful.'

'No. Where is that helicopter?'

'Five minutes away. She's going to have to break cover.'

The detective texted Lucy desperately.

'Move up, helicopter ETA 5 mins.'

They watched as Lucy's little dot obeyed the command and headed upwards again.

Lucy was by now gasping for breath. Fear seemed to be shrinking her lungs.

As she approached the open, she stopped and forced herself to take some deep breaths. She listened carefully. The little dog also cocked its ears alertly in the direction of the steep slope behind them. If Lucy's breathing was hindered by fear, her sense of hearing seemed more acute. She was sure she could hear someone moving in the undergrowth and she could tell that while she was slowing, he was steadily gaining.

The rotating blades of the approaching helicopter was a more welcome sound to her nervous ears. Suddenly Lucy no longer felt scared, her sense of adventure kicked in. She looked at her pretty companion watching her, waiting for her next command and grinned.

'Ready?' she whispered. 'Charge!'

Lucy burst into the open and ran for all her life was worth towards Seal Flat with Słowik on her heels. The helicopter suddenly whizzed over the treetops, so close it blew her hair skywards. She pushed it away from her face and raced on, hoping that anyone hidden by the tree canopy would think twice before showing themselves now. Feeling less threatened, she sprinted with every last bit of energy she possessed as the helicopter, having circled and surveyed the site, hovered above and descended.

Lucy flattened herself against the steep cliff of Old Folk's Rock as the force of the helicopter blades created a micro tornado around her. As she clung to the granite monolith that loomed above her she saw a shadow lingering at the forest edge. As the helicopter landed and the co-pilot opened the door and beckoned her to run towards them, she saw the man skulk back into the darkness.

As the helicopter took to the skies she heard the pilot confirming over his radio that he had also seen her pursuer retreating back into the forest, taking the secret of his identity with him.

Lucy had never been in a helicopter before; the relief at being rescued and the adrenaline of outsmarting her pursuer soon evaporated in the excitement of finding herself in the wonderful machine. She jammed her face to the glass and watched the mountains rush past below, loving every vibration and surge of power as it ducked and dived towards the valley below.

———————————

Little imagining that Lucy was the subject of such drama, Johnny watched the helicopter land and take off from beyond Old Folk's Rock. He and Louie had been on a hike in the valley beyond and Johnny had been enjoying a quiet joint and a sunbathe in a secret spot. Their peaceful moment had been disturbed by all the noise and so they set off home for Grondère. As they wandered through the forest along the old *bisse* they crossed two sets of local police officers with search dogs. Both stopped to ask Johnny who he was and what he was doing there. The dogs sniffed interestedly at his backpack and he was made to open it. The remnants of his afternoon's pleasure were identified and replaced. They clearly were not interested in that, in fact they seemed relieved to find it. He was mystified: in all his forty or more years in Grondère he had never seen policemen patrolling the mountain. He scratched his head and carried on. Spotting Słowik's poop in the middle of the path, he allowed himself a rant.

'Look at that, Louie. That's appalling: too posh to scoop!' He pulled out a poop bag and bent down to remove the offending pollution.

Louie had a quick sniff, identified its producer, and disappeared. Louie often disappeared, pursuing foul smells and uncatchable wildlife, he was, after all, a Jack Russell, so at first Johnny paid no attention. After a while, Louie failed to reappear as usual and Johnny knew something was up. He back-tracked until he heard scuffling sounds and climbed upwards to find Louie struggling to drag a heavy object from beneath a tree stump with his teeth.

'What have you got now? Fuck!'

What Louie had hold of was a huge revolver with a silencer on the end. His teeth were on the trigger.

Terrified Louie was going to set off the gun and blow them both to pieces, Johnny commanded Louie with a sternness that Louie had never heard before.

'Drop!'

Louie was so shocked, he dropped it. It went off! The bullet whizzed past Johnny's foot and straight into the eye of a wooden sculptured owl that adorned the track.

'Fuck!' said Johnny again. 'We need to get out of here and we can't leave this lying around: any idiot can set it off – as you've just demonstrated!' he told Louie who had the grace to look a little sheepish.

He looked around for the police officers he had met earlier but they were nowhere to be seen.

'Typical,' he said to Louie, 'buzzing around like flies on shit when you don't want them and, when, for the first time in your life, you actually want a copper, not a bugger in sight!'

Nervously he picked up the gun and placed it in his backpack, facing outwards and carried it gingerly in front of him all the way down to Grondère. Johnny had never walked so fast in his entire life. All the way down the track he wondered who, in Grondère, would have possession of such a weapon and why they would have abandoned it in the middle of the forest. He thought of poor Maria, the helicopter and the policemen: there had to be a connection. Covered in sweat he entered the local police station. Johnny didn't like police stations. He looked at Adjutant Corthay who, with enough on his plate coordinating fifty men searching the forest, looked at Johnny as if he was mad.

Five seconds later Johnny had all Adjutant Corthay's attention.

Five minutes later, having been allowed a glass of water only, Johnny and Louie were on the back of a quad heading back up the mountain to show the search teams exactly where they had found the gun.

Louie hopped off the quad and immediately went to the stump under which he had found the gun, pointed with his nose and then, job done, trotted back to Johnny and hopped on the quad.

There was a lot of shouting and confusion as the police dogs sniffed around and set off in various directions and the search recommenced. Johnny looked at his little companion and grinned wryly.

'You clever little bastard,' he chuckled, tickling him under the chin, 'I could swear you're looking smug!'

Louie looked most affronted, he was no bastard, he had a very fine pedigree and he had just proved to all that his acute sense of smell was stratospherically superior to those upstart police puppies. The pair were driven back down again where Johnny was asked to return to the station to speak to the *Police judiciaire* who were on their way up from Savigny.

'I'm not talking to anyone until I've had a cup of tea,' Johnny replied. 'And none of that weak Swiss stuff.'

The policewoman driving the quad agreed to take Johnny back to his place so he could have a quick shower and pick up his own supply of tea bags. Johnny had another reason

for stopping off at his flat, he wanted to get rid of his
backpack: he didn't want the distinctive odours of its
contents wafting around a police station.

———————————————

The phone call informing them of the discovery of the gun
sent shudders around the police station in Savigny. They
realised how close it had been for Lucy. It also sealed her
fate.

'Where are we going to put them?' asked Capitaine
Dupertuis whose professional instincts had been restored
to him as soon as he knew his girlfriend was safely in the
custody of the Swiss mountain rescue services.

'Where do you hide anything in Switzerland?' laughed
Herr Schmutz, speaking from his office in Bern. 'At the
top of a mountain, of course!'

The 'them' being referred to was Lucy and Poppy who
were now, in respect of both murder investigations,
considered as witnesses in danger of their lives. Poppy
may not have actually seen anything but it was probable
that both of them had been identified by the murderer and
so they were now being placed under the protection of the
Bern *Kriminalpolizei*.

Adjutant Corthay, the head of the *Police municipale* in
Grondère had been dispatched to collect Poppy and the
two women would be the responsibility of Herr Schmutz
from then on. Poppy had called Sally and asked her to put
together a bag of essentials for Lucy and meet her in the
Grande Place.

'What on earth is going on?' asked Sally, phone to her ear,
as she hunted around for some warm clothes for Lucy.

'I'm not sure, I've just been told to get ready to be away
for a few days. You're not to talk to anyone. As far as

everyone's concerned, we're off for a final hike before the winter.'

Lucy's helicopter had to stop at its base for re-fuelling. By the time it took off again and Lucy landed at the military airbase close to Savigny, Alain and the procureur were there to meet her. The procureur tactfully turned away as Alain ran towards Lucy who was buzzing, hopping up and down with the excitement of her helicopter ride. He hugged her tightly.

'I was so scared, I thought I was going to lose you.'

'I was pretty terrified,' she confessed. 'But wowee! A helicopter, I've never been in one before! I didn't know you wielded such power!' she teased.

He looked at her; she was buzzing with endorphins. It was a shame to bring her back down to earth but he had to put her in the picture.

'Lucy, listen to me. It wasn't me who called the helicopter, it was the procureur.'

'The procureur? Why?'

'You are the only witness who can identify the Reichenbach Falls murderer. Your life is in danger and you are now in protective custody. We found a gun, we're pretty sure it's the gun that killed Maria: that guy meant to kill you, Lucy.'

'Shit!'

Alain watched with sadness as Lucy's bubble burst and she realised she had lost her freedom to roam the Alps.

The procureur started coming towards them; Alain took Lucy's hands and looked straight into her eyes.

'I promise you, *mon amour*, when this is all over, next winter I will personally pay for you, Poppy and all your dotty friends to go heli-skiing.'

'Deal!' she smiled and then frowned. 'Poppy too?'

'Yes. I'm afraid so.'

'Ah well,' she smiled at him encouragingly. 'At least I'm not going into solitary confinement.'

Alain didn't think he could have loved her more than he did already but this little dynamo never ceased to astound him. His heart burst with pride at her ability to withstand life's setbacks with such equanimity.

'Where am I going?'

'I do not know,' he replied. 'The fewer people who know, the better. I have been told that the views are outstanding.'

He kissed her and led her towards the procureur and the representatives of the Bern *Kriminalpolizei* who were to take her into hiding.

'You will get this sorted quickly won't you? My exams are in November.'

'I'll do my best.'

'Stay safe,' she warned him jokingly.

'I promise.'

Lucy and Poppy sat with their Swiss German protection officer in a small uncomfortable waiting room in a military airport. The high windows let in a little light but ensured no one could look in: it seemed that the Bern *Kriminalpolizei* were not taking any chances that the two women might be seen.

Their mobile phones had been confiscated but they had been issued with replacement numbers and allowed to call their close friends and family with a fictional excuse for a prolonged absence. Fortunately, with the pair being regular hikers, no one suspected there was any other reason for their disappearance. Słowik had been taken away by Alain: apparently their destination was not suitable for dogs.

'Sounds ominous,' grimaced Poppy. 'Where do you think they're taking us? I was told, no computer.'

'I suspect it's somewhere quite high, Alain said the views were good.'

'Bugger!' Poppy exclaimed. 'It's truffle-hunting time. I was due to leave for Italy the day after tomorrow.'

Lucy was looked at her apologetically as the buzz of an approaching helicopter came within her hearing for the second time that day. Ignoring the disapproving looks of Herr Anderegg she stood on a chair to look out of the window.

'*Air Glacier*. Do you think that's for us?'

The helicopter took off with a big swoop over the airfield and climbed high. The green flatlands of the Rhône Valley passed below in a blur: this was clearly no sight-seeing trip. Patterned vineyards and bronzing forests on the mountainsides raced past in a flash of gold in the late afternoon sunlight. Heading north and east they climbed rapidly towards the Bernese Alps. No man-made features were distinguishable, only craggy mountains, crowned with snow, and glaciers and shining lakes in between. Then, as they descended, they began to pick out the detail of the rocky formations, the folds and layers, the peaks and fault lines and even climbers and walkers against the snowy gullies. They were approaching the three peaks they had walked below in June, but then they suddenly swerved down to their left. They were heading straight for the steep and sinister Lestersaarhorn: its dark walls loomed ever closer.

As their helicopter landed on the tiny pad attached to the mountain refuge and they realised just how high they were going to be staying, the two women looked at each other in wonder.

'Amazing!' shouted Lucy.

'You have to admit, there's a certain irony in this!' Poppy shouted back. 'In June we decided to stay low to avoid hiking on snow, and now we've been brought back to see the high bits.'

The lonely, lightning rod mountain, Lucy thought inwardly, I knew it was calling me.

Their protection officer led them towards the shelter of the mountain refuge so that the helicopter could take off again without blowing anyone off the mountain. The sun was due to set and the helicopter team clearly didn't want to hang around. They stood and watched as it became a smaller and smaller dot on the horizon.

Lucy grinned at Poppy.

'Definitely no truffles here. What an adventure!'

'My life has been nothing but, since you came into it!' teased Poppy.

They scrambled up to the refuge where they were shown to a small cosy room with two single beds.

They had been told to keep a low profile, not to give their real names, not to talk about themselves, and to avoid any alpinists who might be staying at the refuge. The refuge hosts had clearly been given the same instructions and they told the two women they would come and get them for supper when everyone else was in bed. In the meantime, the woman said she would bring them some coffee and biscuits.

'Not exactly a low-profile arrival, was it?' Poppy laughed. 'I heard the pilot saying something about emergency repairs to the generator over the radio.'

'More like an emergency inconvenience, these places usually close about now. Although when I think about it, that probably suits the police. Fewer alpinists for us to run into.'

'I guess.'

The women began to unpack the small bags they had brought with them. Poppy had brought a big supply of tea bags.

'Bugger!' she exclaimed. 'Forgot the Marmite.'

Lucy rummaged through her bag, wondering what Sally had managed to find for her. She was glad to find some warm layers, her pyjamas and lots of clean knickers, her toothbrush and pills. Sally had also included her *Flora Helvetica*, her study materials for the mid-mountain guide course and her poetry anthology. There was alas, no Marmite.

'This is nothing short of an international calamity,' Lucy declared.

The refuge guardian arrived with the coffee and asked what was causing them such distress. She laughed when they told her.

'That disgusting stuff, we have that,' she reassured them. 'One or two of the British climbers always forget a pot each summer. We normally end up throwing it away, which is a shame, we don't like waste up here.'

'Ah,' smiled Poppy, gratefully taking her cup of coffee. 'All is right with the world then.'

The alpinists were all in bed and snoring by 9pm and the guardian came to release them for supper. In the hosts' own sitting room, they gratefully supped their vegetable broth and chunks of bread and cheese. It was their first chance to get to know their hosts, Herr and Frau Bachmann.

Over dinner Lucy also asked their protection officer, Herr Anderegg, if she could have access to a computer without internet so she could at least write. He promised to do what he could.

Frau Bachmann told them that the four alpinists staying that night had all arrived after the helicopter so, although they had seen it, no one had seen them and no one knew they were there. She also said that bookings were low for the next few days and that after that the refuge would officially be closed: they would then stay for a couple of weeks for the annual clean before closing up. As soon as bad weather was forecast, the police, if they hadn't caught their man, would have to find another bolt-hole for them.

Poppy and Lucy sincerely hoped that their residence at the top of the Lesteraarhorn would be over long before then.

After dinner, encouraged by the loud snores coming from the dormitory, the two friends explored their mountain eyrie.

'I feel a bit Rapunzel-ish,' Lucy declared, looking over the drop from the terrace.

'Well, start growing your hair now,' Poppy joked, looking at the information board. 'It's currently 3,048m too short.'

They gasped as they looked at the scene that greeted them. Alain hadn't been joking about the view. For 360 degrees, all they could see were the white and grey peaks of the Alps and above, a blanket of stars was beginning to envelope them.

'It's so beautiful!' Lucy sighed. 'Ohmigod, I have never seen so many stars: it feels as if we could almost touch them.'

Poppy was also rooted to the spot. She had been wandering the Alps for forty years but she had never seen such a glorious night sky.

'Thank goodness I was allowed to bring my camera and equipment. I shall be getting in some practice at time-lapse night skies.'

Lucy smiled. Poppy was taking her imprisonment well and had already thought of how she was going to fill her time. Lucy, it was clear, would have no excuse for not studying for her exams.

Laying her head on the pillow that night, Lucy wondered how Alain and his team were getting on. Much as she loved the mountains, she did not want to live out her days locked in a tower at the top of one.

'You have to admit,' yawned Poppy as she turned out the light, 'it's an outstanding hiding place.'

Lucy murmured her agreement as she drifted off.

'Ingenious.'

The following morning, when the climbers were well out of sight, Frau Bachmann sat Lucy and Poppy down at the window of the dining room with mugs of milky coffee, advising them not to take their eyes from the window for an instant. She put a pie into the oven and then joined them for this mysterious vigil. A few minutes after she had joined them a huge shape filled the sky in front of them as an enormous bird glided by.

'A bearded vulture!' Lucy gasped, in wonder.

Poppy couldn't speak – to see this majestic bird so close was a true privilege. It cruised over the rocky terraces, looking for finished carrion and then plunged lower, out of sight.

'My camera,' she moaned, 'I can't believe I missed it.' Her camera sat idle on the window ledge beside her.

'That's a first.' Lucy looked surprised. 'Even when we saw the golden oriole you managed to grab your camera.'

'She will be back,' Frau Bachmann consoled Poppy. 'Most days, about this time, she comes to see what we're up to. Sometimes we see the male or the juvenile but we seem to be on the female's regular flight track.'

'You are kidding?'

'No, the nest's 500m directly below. We've had all the VIPs of the Swiss bird world up here this summer,' she pulled a face. 'Once we told them we had a pair, they arrived en masse, rappelled down to the nest, counting eggs, weighing and tagging the chick. I almost wish we hadn't told them.'

'Why didn't you tell them straight away?'

'I don't know, maybe it's selfishness, but I think it felt like a violation of their privacy. It's a young couple and this is their first breeding year.'

'I understand what you mean. Like, by tagging them and spying on them, we're taking away their wildness, making them tame.'

'Exactly. Man always has to interfere.'

'So how many chicks were there?'

'Oh, just one. They always lay two eggs, but the second is just an insurance policy: the largest chick always eats the smaller one. The parents can't feed two chicks.'

Lucy pulled a face. 'That's a bit grim.'

Twenty-Five

Happiness often sneaks in through a door you didn't know you left open.
Joyce Grenfell on John Barrymore

Jodie and Sally were in the small flat they had shared for three seasons, packing their belongings.

'It's the end of an era,' Jodie sighed.

'I will miss you,' Sally laughed. 'But let's be honest, we haven't been using this place much recently.'

Jodie was moving to Lausanne to study voice at the *Haute École de Musique de Lausanne* and Sally was moving into the little chalet with Tommy, Eddie and Lucy.

'It's probably just as well you weren't around much when I was having all those singing lessons. I'd never have been able to keep it a secret.'

'We thought you were having an affair with Gluey Hughey. So, did you actually know BL wasn't going to perform?'

'No, I was told I was being put forward for an audition for the *Haute École*. But I was under strict orders to tell no one. As the concert approached, the lessons intensified and I just knew there was more to it. You remember that moment when the MD walked in and told us BL would not be turning up and sent me out to warm up my voice with the répétiteur? I realised it had been meticulously planned, because I was *so* ready.'

Sally laughed.

'Tommy begged to be the one to make the announcement and Lucy, did you see her? She blubbed all the way through.'

'You've all been so lovely. I can come back and see you at weekends, can't I?'

'Of course. It's going to be very cosy in our little chalet. It's only meant for three!'

The job done, they lifted their bags into Eddie's van and wandered down the road to hand in their keys.

'I don't know what's got into Tommy recently, he seems a bit down.

'Have you asked him?'

'No, I'm scared of the answer.'

'Do you think he's feeling a bit left out?'

'I don't think he's the jealous type: I'm worried he's homesick for his beloved West Country.'

'He is a bit of a home bird, isn't he? Don't worry, it'll wear off once the ski season arrives.'

As he dropped Sally off at the vineyard, Tommy watched her scamper into her new job with enthusiasm written in every movement of her body and felt envious. He immediately felt guilty but he couldn't deny the surge of feeling.

Open your eyes, look around you and remember how lucky you are to be living the dream! he told himself sharply. It was a glorious autumn day and he decided to walk off his negativity.

Pulling into the muddy car park of a deserted sawmill he headed upstream, crossed some fields and headed for the woodlands beyond. It wasn't a spot he knew very well but it looked pretty.

The truth was, Tommy was feeling a little left out, but mostly he was facing the same dilemma many seasonal workers face as they get older. How much longer do you want to do this? How much longer can you do this and shouldn't you be making serious plans for your future? The nature of the work in a ski resort is, by definition, transitory, but being a seasonnnaire is a hard living and finding a permanent well-paid job as a foreigner even harder. Tommy knew his best chance of making a decent living was back in the UK.

Tommy loved the West Country of England where he had grown up. He had never planned to leave it permanently: his plan had been to do a few years in Grondère to get in some serious skiing and then return to set up his own painting/decorating business. He had been saving up to set up his business and, since he and Sally had got together, had imagined her going with him back to England. Now that she had landed her dream job there was no way he could contemplate asking her to give that up for an uncertain future in the UK.

The choice wasn't so clear for him now either: Tommy found himself torn between his love for homeland and the Alps. The mountains have a way of drawing you in and holding you and Tommy was just as attached to them as Lucy and Poppy were.

As he walked he had to acknowledge to himself that he had only himself to blame for this predicament. He had never spoken of his plans to Sally and he could not expect her to sacrifice her current career prospects. But where does that leave me, he wondered.

Tommy worked in a ski shop in winter and on the building sites in summer. It was a wonderful arrangement in the short-term but he hadn't bargained on doing that forever. Even as he approached his thirties, he could feel his body beginning to complain under the strain he was putting on it.

As he walked, he didn't realise that he had come close to a farmyard where a young man was moving bales of hay with a tractor.

'Hey, Tommy!'

Tommy turned to see who on earth in this unknown spot could possibly have recognised him.

'Tommy. It's me Christophe! Don't you recognise me?'

Wearing the traditional green overalls and felt hat of the Swiss farmer, it did take Tommy a few seconds to recognise his former construction site co-worker sitting on the tractor. Replying in his hesitant French, he apologised. 'Christophe, sorry, I didn't recognise you out of Grondère.'

'What are you doing down here?'

'Just having a little stroll.'

'You looked deep in thought.'

Tommy laughed. 'Yes, not like me. Is this your place?'

'For now, it is, but for how much longer, I'm not sure.'

'That's not good. I was just about to say how lucky you were and ask whether you ever needed a hand. I used to help out on a farm in my summer holidays.'

'You got a minute?'

'Yes.'

'Hop on then, I'm just off to lunch with my uncle. He owns the next farm along.'

Tommy hopped on the tractor and allowed himself to be carried along by the spontaneity of the moment. As they trundled over the rough farm tracks, he happily sat beside his renewed acquaintance admiring the neat fields and happy cows. Tommy was very fond of the black Herens cows and Christophe's looked particularly fat and glossy after their summer in the mountains.

'I still have a herd up there,' Christophe told him. 'I would have left them all up but there's only me and so I can't wait for the *désalpe*, I have to bring them down in dribs and drabs.'

Plates of cold meats and cheese fresh from the farm dairy were already set out on a long table in his uncle's orchard. The table had been assembled from old tree trunks and lay under the shade of ancient gnarled apple and apricot trees, their trunks blackened with age and the leaves above turning red and gold. Lunch turned out to be a long affair, Christophe had much to discuss with his uncle. Tommy, only listening with half an ear, tucked in and allowed himself one generous glass of *Fendant* before switching to the freshly pressed cloudy apple juice that reminded him of home. By the time Christophe's aunt brought out a huge dish of *spaghetti puttanesca*, Tommy became aware of a story unfolding.

Christophe and his brother had inherited the family farm young. It had been their father's wish that his two sons run the farm together. Christophe had been happy to comply with this wish and had duly been to agricultural college to learn the trade. His younger brother, it seemed, had had different plans. When their parents had died within a year of one another, Christophe, who had been making a good salary to subsidise the farm working on the construction sites in Grondère, had dutifully applied himself to keeping the farm going. His brother had quit Switzerland straight after his father's funeral to 'go and find himself' abroad. He had since found himself a bride in Thailand and was now demanding the farm be sold so that he could have his share to finance his father-in-law's floundering hotel business into which it seemed he was putting much more effort than he had ever put into the family farm.

Both sensing disaster looming, Christophe and his uncle had come to the conclusion that the sooner the younger brother could be cut adrift the better. Christophe needed to find a partner or a buyer quickly. Tommy realised that his spontaneous free lunch invitation may have had an ulterior motive: Christophe and his family were now looking at him with considerable interest.

By the time he was due to pick Sally up from work, Tommy had a whole business plan before him. Christophe had shown him round the farm and the modern little chalet that had been built for the errant brother. Tommy could see him and Sally there, it would certainly be much more convenient for her new job, and, they wouldn't need to plant their dreamed-of apricot tree, it already had a little orchard with apple and apricot trees.

He would need to go through the figures carefully and check that the farm really was a viable proposition. He couldn't buy it outright and, besides, he didn't have the necessary knowledge to run it alone, but he could find enough to enter into partnership with Christophe. Their joint idea was that he would handle maintenance of machines and infrastructure and eventually assume the administrative tasks, leaving Christophe free to work the farm. But Tommy was not the impetuous type: he promised Christophe a decision within a week but he knew in his heart that this was where his path lay. For the first time in weeks he was feeling his own happy self again.

Tommy drove to pick up Sally full of enthusiasm, ideas and with a much lighter heart.

He had so much to tell her and this time he would leave nothing out!

Twenty-Six

*I have found a dream of beauty at which one might look
all one's life and sigh.*
Isabella Bird, *Adventures in the Rocky Mountains*

Alain and his team were worried. Search teams had trawled through the forest beneath Old Folk's Rock and Grondère all afternoon but 'Sherlock Holmes' had eluded them. They left the office and went for a beer in Grondère.
'We need a lucky break,' Alain said. 'He knows we're on to him now.'
'How are we ever going to identify him?'
'The British police are sending a "rogues gallery" for Lucy to go through with the officer from Bern but it's a long shot.'
'Neither the British or Polish police have been able to identify Blonnay's photofit of the guy who bought the deerstalker in Edinburgh. Mlle Wilson has said she thinks it could be him, but that doesn't help if we don't have a name,' sighed Sylvie Jacquier.
'Any other ideas?'
Blonnay spoke next. He was a little anxious as to how Capitaine Dupertuis might react to his next suggestion.
'Whoever this man is, to know that Mlle Wilson goes hiking alone, means he has been watching her for a while.'
'Yes?' Alain realised what he was going to say.
'So, he has also been watching you. Didn't you say there was something wrong with your parachute this morning?'
'You're right, I'd better stay down here for a few days. I don't want to put my mother in danger. Słowik had better stay here too. I don't want her leading anyone to my mother's door.'

The Grondère murder team received a phone call from the Polish catholic church in Savigny. Alain got the feeling it was important and so he agreed to go and see the priest that day.

'I was distressed to hear about Maria. She was a good woman and a good catholic.'

'My colleague was upset too; she was very helpful to us in another enquiry.'

'Ah, yes. Her former employer.'

'You know about that?'

'I visit Switzerland at intervals to take confession and give communion. It is a post I share with other fathers and so I visit here every six months. The affair was much in the news on my last visit. I naturally took an interest because I knew Maria worked there. It is because I only visit every six months that I have contacted you now. I apologise if my delay has had a negative impact on your investigation.'

'You have something of importance to tell me.'

The priest nodded.

'But you are bound by the confessional?'

'In respect of what Maria confessed, I am of course, bound to secrecy. However, I can tell you that the last time I saw Maria she came here with a man. When Maria left the confession box I knew that I was not the only one who had heard Maria's confession. He had an unpleasant smile on his face that told me he had learned of something greatly to his interest.'

'If I told you that I believe I know what Maria confessed to you, would you be able to confirm it?'

'I could not.'

'Ah. Then we are at an impasse.'

'We are.'

'Can you identify the man?'

'I can, it was the man who has been identified as the victim of the Reichenbach Falls murder.'

'Her cousin, Sergei Kowalski.'

'Yes. I am sorry, I cannot tell you more, except that *he* never came to confession. I hope it is of some use.'

'Thank you, Father. It is. You may have helped us identify the motive, if not the perpetrator of Maria's murder.'

'Did the poor child suffer?'

'I think she must have been terrified. Her last gesture was to reach for her picture of the Virgin Mary.'

'Then I know she was not alone. Thank you for telling me that.'

Alain, seeing the old man close to tears, took his leave and headed back to report to his team. It was clear they could no longer dismiss the Lord Shilton avenue of enquiry. The date of poor Maria's confession was conclusive: she had not then started to work for the Braythwaites: there was only one piece of information that Maria could have confessed to that could have been of value to anyone of a criminal disposition, the fact that she stole Malcolm McDonaghue's hairbrush so that the current Lord Shilton could check it for DNA. How on earth that information could lead to her murder was the mystery.

'We need to contact the British police. Lord Shilton may be in danger.'

'We are too late.'

'What?'

'Look at this.'

That morning's editions of the British papers carried reports of the accidental death of Lord Shilton at a shoot.

'Oh no. I have an awful feeling that was no accident.'

'I'll contact the British police straight away, but just read the end of this.'

Alain and Sylvie looked at the newspaper report: it said that there was no heir to the estate but that it was believed that the previous Lord Shilton had illegitimate offspring whose claims may now be considered.

'You don't think that Sebastian McDonaghue could have found out?'

'No idea. We need to check up on his movements.'

'We also need to tell him what we know. If he isn't behind this, he could be in serious danger.'

'You can't really think he's in any way implicated with Lord Shilton's death, or the other two?'

'Maybe he's behind the whole thing and this Sherlock Holmes character is his hired hitman.'

'We cannot rule it out: if he knew, why not?'

'I hadn't thought of it for a minute. Murderous tendencies aren't known to be hereditary, are they?' Blonnay was clearly thinking of Carla when he asked this question. 'If they were, there's not just his maternal line to consider in that case, the English aristocracy are historically a bloodthirsty lot.'

Blonnay's phone rang. It was DI Ferguson: Scotland Yard, it would appear, were already on their way to Leicestershire to liaise with the local police and check out just how accidental Lord Shilton's death really was.

Alain knew from Maître Aulnay that he was expecting to see Sebastian McDonaghue in the next day or so. Sebastian's movements were easy to verify. Airport records concurred with his own assertion that he had returned briefly to New York after the book launch and had arrived back in Switzerland, at Zurich Airport that morning. He told them over the phone that he had returned briefly with Miss Shalott to wrap up his father's estate and sign some papers. He would be happy to meet them as soon as they could get to La Grande Cour.

'I guess what we need to determine, is whether he is a risk or at risk,' Alain told his team. 'My gut instincts tell me he's a good guy.'

'But we're Swiss, we don't go on gut instincts, we go on evidence,' Blonnay reminded him.

'Exactly, so where do we get that in a hurry?'

Sylvie Jacquier found the answer.

'It's easy – he's a good guy,' she said.

They both looked at her.

'Pure deduction, my dear colleagues. If Sebastian McDonaghue knew he was possibly a Lord, then he found out the same way we did, directly or indirectly through Maria's information. But, unlike whoever our murderer is, he would also realise that everyone involved into the investigation into his father's murder had the same information and *we'd* all have to be killed too. That would be way too visible: the person behind these killings thinks that the only people in the know were Maria, her cousin and Lord Shilton. The whole strategy relies on a small number of unrelated and different deaths, hence the different methods. He has no need to kill Sebastian because he's pretty sure he doesn't know. That's what he had to get out of Maria when he beat her up. We now know that brave young woman didn't give us away. The trouble is, he now knows he's been recognised: he has some interest in the Shilton title and he can't come out of hiding until Mlle Wilson and Mme Smythe have been eliminated. If he thinks Sebastian knows, then he'll get rid of him too.'

They looked at her with admiration.

'Besides,' she added, 'my *Swiss* female intuition (the best evidence out there) tells me that if Sebastian McDonaghue knew, he'd just call in some hot-shot lawyers and make us all give evidence in court.'

There was silence for a moment. Blonnay was the first to speak.

'Can I tell him, oh can I get to tell McDonaghue that he's a lord?'

'You big kid, Blonnay. Why on earth should it matter who tells him?'

'Because I've been itching to tell him and practising how in my head since we found out.'

Alain laughed out loud.

'You are bizarre, but yes, I have no urgent desire to tell him. I'm going to leave it to you two to finally assess his reaction. If you determine he's guilty, arrest him. If innocent, he has to be persuaded to go into protective custody.'

'I don't fancy telling him that,' grimaced Sylvie.

'Nor me,' shrugged Blonnay. 'Can't you come and do that bit?'

'Somebody has to stay here and as you're so fixed, Blonnay, on annointing Sebastian McDonaghue a lord, you're going to have to take the flack too.'

'Herr Schmutz wants us to send a French and English-speaking officer with them,' Capitaine Dupertuis said after his call to arrange the evacuation of Sebastian and Tonita. He looked at Sylvie.

'Oh, come on,' she protested sulkily. 'You're not sending me on baby-sitting duty when there's so much to do here.'

Alain could sense a feminist protest building.

'Inspectrice Jacquier, we don't know who this guy is, where he is or what he's up to. I am sending you because you're the best shot in the force and, frankly, I cannot think of a greater compliment to pay you than entrusting to you the life of the woman I love. To say nothing of the most wealthy and influential man in Grondère and perhaps even a British aristocrat. Any objections?'

'No,' she replied, knowing that he was right. If it did come to violence, she was much more suited to the task than him or that softy, Blonnay.

'Thank you.'

'Ludicrous!' Sebastian exclaimed.

Inspecteur chef adjoint Blonnay carefully noted down this glorious reaction to his carefully worded revelation in his vocabulary notebook before replying. He had to write it phonetically as he felt it probably wasn't the right moment to ask for its correct spelling.

Sebastian always felt slightly uncomfortable whenever Blonnay appeared. He never seemed to bring good news and Sebastian could never quite make out if he was an authentic nerd or just faking it. If it wasn't for the presence of Inspectrice Jacquier he would, at that precise moment in time, have considered him a complete lunatic.

'Ludicrous it also seemed to us, Monsieur McDonaghue,' Blonnay replied. 'Which is why we have probably not followed this avenue of inquiry as thoroughly as we might, up till now.'

He has been rehearsing that line, Sylvie Jacquier thought to herself.

Sebastian was almost laughing in disbelief.

'So, let me get this straight. Maria stole Dad's hairbrush for Lord Shilton and she's dead. He did a DNA test which proved Dad was the illegitimate son of the previous Lord Shilton?'

'Correct.'

'And now *that* Lord Shilton is dead too, you think, despite the fact it was reported to be an accident that it wasn't, and that whoever did it might now come after me?'

'Yes.'

He looked at the pan expression on Blonnay's face and began to realise that he was in earnest.

'And this all came out in the investigation into Dad's murder and nobody thought to inform me?'

'Our investigation was into a murder not into the extra-marital dalliances of the British aristocracy.'

Oh, that was a good one, thought Sylvie: he really has wanted to do this for ages.

'And now you want to whisk me away to a secret location while you find out who killed Maria.'

'Yes. We already have two bodies, three if we are right about Lord Shilton. Mlle Wilson was stalked by a professional killer and we would like to make sure we do not lose you. To say nothing of the reputation of Switzerland as a safe tourist destination.'

The speech was compelling.

'Shit,' Sebastian said slowly. 'You really are serious, aren't you?'

'I have a helicopter arriving in ten minutes. I would like you to agree to be taken into hiding with Mlle Wilson and Mme Smythe.'

'Sounds like a real party,' Sebastian sighed sardonically.

To this Blonnay had no response except to look at his watch.

'Ten minutes?'

'Nine. Please pack a small bag but with warm clothes.'

Sebastian ran to his room, rustled up some belongings and called for Tonita and his sommelier.

Tonita watched him pack as he explained what was happening.

'I'm coming too,' she shouted as she ran to her room to grab a bag. 'I'm not missing out.'

They took the lift down to reception together as they heard the helicopter overhead.

'I can't believe Mlle Shalott managed to get a bag together in five minutes,' Sylvie gasped.

'No, now you mention it, most impressive. She must have some Swiss blood in her.'

They escorted Sebastian and Tonita to an awaiting vehicle with dark glass as the sommelier loaded two boxes into the boot.

'What's in there?' asked Blonnay sharply.

'Twenty-four bottles of the best wines from my father's private cellar.'

'Ah,' Blonnay grinned in admiration at Sebastian's resourceful thinking. 'Very wise.'

As Sylvie jumped in beside them, he commented wryly, 'Where they're going, they'll be glad of those. Shame you'll be on duty.'

Twenty-Seven

*Avoiding danger is no safer in the long run than outright
exposure. Life is either a daring adventure, or nothing.*
          Helen Keller, Let Us Have Faith

The helicopter dropped Tonita, Sebastian and Inspectrice
Jacquier at the Lesteraarhorn refuge mid-afternoon. The
police officer quickly hustled her charges indoors to
ensure no late-season climbers saw them.

Shortly after their arrival Sebastian called his office to
explain his prolonged absence. He had insisted on keeping
his phone, much to the reluctance of Herr Schmutz and
Inspectrice Jacquier. They had only agreed because he
refused to go otherwise and also because they knew that
the refuge would soon close and they would not be there
much longer than a week anyway. Sebastian had also
brought his portable computer in order to stay in touch
with his office. He would not, as it turned out, be needing
it.

Gusts of wind blew snatches of his end of the conversation
to the others, listening avidly, as he stomped up and down
on the deck looking more and more agitated. His boss
clearly wasn't taking the news well.

'I'm afraid that's the way it is, Sam,' they heard him say.

'I've trained these guys up, there's isn't one of them that
couldn't step into my shoes. In fact, most of them are
desperate to. Ryan Sharp, he's more than ready.

'Yes, I know he's a cocky bastard, but he's good.'

Then there was a pause.

'Sam, you have no sense of proportion. I'm no good to you
dead. How do I explain someone's out to kill me?

'I don't care anymore?

'You know what, you're right, you do need someone
who's 100% committed and that's just not me anymore.

'Let's make this easy for both of us… I resign, immediate effect!

'Mean it? Yes, I do. Ask my secretary to clear out my office, send out the usual memo about "wanting to devote more time with my family and charitable causes" and I'll collect my boxes when I get out of here.

'No, Sam. No hard feelings, we all knew this was coming. I'll buy you a drink when I get back to New York. Good luck.'

He ended his call, and pounded up and down for a good ten minutes before coming back inside where Poppy, impressed, handed him a tumbler of cognac and a congratulatory smile. She had never heard a Wall Street 'fuck-it-all' speech before and she had thoroughly enjoyed it.

'That was stupendous! Are you okay?' she asked.

Sebastian looked at them all and a broad grin spread across his face.'

'Never better!'

Tonita hardly recognised him, she had never seen him looking so positive and bursting with energy.

'You're not going to regret that, are you?' she asked,

'Never. To be honest, it's not really spontaneous. I would rather have resigned to Sam's face and respected the formalities but I cannot do that from the top of a mountain.'

'I think the mountain air suits you,' Poppy asserted.

'Thank you, Poppy. It's certainly cooler than I'm used to, but right now I wouldn't swap it for all the hot air of a Manhattan boardroom. Lucy Wilson, will you stop looking at me like that? Your eyes are positively popping out of your head.'

'Sorry,' she laughed. 'Shall I show you around?'

The refuge was now officially closed, so they could move around at their leisure. Over the next few days they settled into a routine. In the mornings, Poppy and Lucy put on their rubber gloves and helped the guardians scrub the refuge from top to bottom. They washed, ironed and aired bedding, emptied cupboards and sealed supplies. They cleaned windows and helped prepare the meals for the band of eight.

Nobody expected Tonita to help with the cleaning – she hadn't changed that much. It never occurred to her either. During this intensive scrubbing activity, she took herself off to quiet corners where she drew, designed and sketched.

Each morning they all gathered for coffee in front of the window, even Herr Anderegg who was adapting to this strange crew, and watched the daily flypast of the bearded vulture, who by now had been christened Mildred by Poppy and Lucy. Tonita did some beautiful sketches of it.

'Although,' she confessed, 'stunning as it is, it's hard to see how I could incorporate it in my jewellery designs.'

'You are an artist, it's okay to just draw for art's sake,' Poppy reprimanded her.

'You are right, Poppy. I am too focused on art for money's sake. I feel duly chastised,' Tonita winked.

Sebastian looked on in amazement; Tonita would not have tolerated such a criticism, however well meant, as recently as six months earlier.

'Isn't it going to migrate?' she asked.

'No,' Frau Bachmann explained. 'She and her partner will weather out the winter here in the mountains, unlike us.'

In the afternoons, Lucy locked herself away to study and Poppy clambered around the surrounding rocky terrain with her camera.

Sebastian sat most of the time in front of his computer, informing friends and former colleagues that he had retired from banking and drawing up an action plan for his Swiss business interests. He was beginning to realise that it was more than enough to occupy him and was much more interesting.

In the evenings, they dedicated themselves to depleting all the remaining supplies in the refuge and consuming the good wines that Sebastian had brought. One evening, relishing every sip of a particularly delicious red, Poppy thanked Sebastian for sharing such wonders with them.

'All Dad's good taste,' he admitted. 'What a shame he's not here to see it being appreciated.'

Nobody had the indelicacy to point out that if Malcolm had still been alive, they wouldn't be stuck on top of a mountain tucking into his best wines.

'So how come we never see your father in Grondère?' Poppy asked Tonita.

Tonita explained to them the reasons for her estrangement with her father.

'He left my mother to fight breast cancer alone and when he divorced her, because they lived abroad, he was able to dodge paying her any kind of settlement: she was left penniless.'

'So, you came back to Europe?'

'I was already working in Amsterdam at the time, so I brought her over to join me and made sure she got the best treatment I could afford. It was an awful time, trying to get my career off the ground and see her through it.'

'Sounds tough.'

'It definitely hardened me. I think after that I became as ruthless as he is.'

'I can see why,' Poppy exclaimed.

'Malcolm's death made me have a re-think about the children but I'll never forgive him and certainly not invite him to Grondère.'

'But he came to Grondère last February half-term with the children, didn't he? When I had them to teach for a couple of days?' Lucy asked.

'He booked the whole family into the hotel without telling me. His plan was to get me to agree to look after Ruby and Leo, especially as they were starting boarding school in the UK. In a way, he got what he wanted, having met the children it was hard not to get attached to them.'

'You're protecting them, aren't you?' Lucy ascertained.

'Yes, one day, he'll let them down too, and I'll be there.'

'So, you're not the bad person you always make yourself out to be, Tonita: you looked after your mother and now you're looking out for Ruby and Leo.'

'Thank you, Lucy. I've not looked at myself in a positive light like that for a long time.'

'So, what does he do, in Saudi Arabia, your wicked father?'

'Do you know, I have no idea. Mum never knew either, he always said he worked in banking but Mum said she was never invited to any work functions, never met any of his colleagues: she suspected him of being an arms trader.'

'He told Dad he was something in banking,' Sebastian offered. 'But I have to confess, I've done some asking around and no one I know knows him, not even my Arabian contacts. But,' he added, 'that's not unusual, it's a pretty opaque environment.'

They all looked at him astonished.

'You checked up on my father?'

'Dad asked me to do a little research. After the half-term episode, he was concerned your dad was up to something. But I never got much further than asking around, other events took over.'

They all looked sad: he was, they knew, referring to Malcolm's murder.

'Whatever crimes your father has committed,' Poppy commented, 'it's good that you are not punishing his children for them. They are delightful young people.'

'They are, aren't they?' Tonita said proudly. 'And I think they like me too.'

'Maybe your dad's learnt from his mistakes, and wants to make it up to you.'

Tonita looked at Lucy skeptically.

'He's certainly a more attentive father second time round but I'm afraid it's too late for me. I know it seems hard, but I have not got it in me to forgive.'

'I understand, Tonita. I think it is easier to forgive someone who has hurt you than someone who has hurt someone you love,' Poppy concluded.

Lucy knew that Poppy was thinking about Carla Sturridge.

Winter was approaching on the Lesteraarhorn and outdoor occupations became more and more impossible. Lucy and Poppy curled up by the windows to read whatever reading material was available. Poppy became an expert on the history of alpine climbing and could name every peak visible from their mountain eyrie. Lucy leafed through her poetry anthology and Tonita also dipped in and out of it but inevitably the occupants of the hut often had time to do nothing other than sit over a cup of coffee and chat.

The bond between Tonita, Poppy and Lucy, the foundations of which had been laid that summer, was growing daily.

'I'm missing autumn in Grondère,' Lucy admitted.

'Me too,' Poppy agreed. 'My life is rhythmed by seasonal rituals and I feel all out of sync.'

'What are your rituals?' Tonita asked.

'Oh, at this time of year, it's jam and chutney making, collecting and drying mushrooms and herbs, making pumpkin soup, sloe gin.'

'Yes, I hope we can get back in time for the sloes.' Tonita groaned.

'You two, you're a pair of country bumpkins!'

'Mountain bumpkins please!' laughed Poppy in mock offence. 'But it's true, I can't imagine you worrying about finding time to get your Christmas cake made.'

'Yes, tell us Tonita, what are you missing? What do your autumn rituals consist of?'

Tonita pretended deep concentration.

'Ooh, just about now, I should be wandering down Fifth Avenue, foraging for the most beautiful outfits for the winter.'

Lucy and Poppy groaned in their turn.

'Never underestimate the joy of a pair of new leather boots,' she teased, 'a well-cut coat, or a dress you know will turn heads.'

'You do always look gorgeous, I'll give you that,' Lucy asserted and Poppy concurred.

'You turn heads, Tonita, whatever you wear.'

Tonita blushed, she wasn't used to receiving genuine compliments from other women. It was a new experience for her.

'It's just because we're poor, really Tonita. If I had lots of money, I'd … I'd …'

Lucy and Tonita turned on her and looked.

'What would you do Poppy, if you had a lot of money?'

'There's a young artist whose stuff I like. If I could have one of his landscapes to sit and admire on a grisly day like this, that would do for me.'

'I approve!' said Tonita.

'Of course you do, you're an artist,' teased Sebastian.

'And you Lucy, what about you? What luxury would you buy if you could?'

'I've already had those beautiful earrings from Tonita: that'll do for me. Although, I have to say, I do dream of having my own little mountain home with a window seat so I could curl up and read and look out at the cold on a grisly day like this.'

She was getting to know Tonita and realised that if she declared a desire for anything material, Tonita was likely to go out and buy it for her and she knew she couldn't buy her anything in return. Tonita had, however, quietly made a note in her memory of both wishes.

Tonita, like Poppy, was captivated by the night skies, and, despite the cold, on the clear nights, she stayed outside drawing until her fingers were too cold to function. Sebastian also spent inordinate amounts of time watching Tonita when he thought no one was watching him. Sometimes he would sigh sadly at the thought of what had happened to him. Seven months ago he had been totally in control of his life: a successful investment banker, a stable relationship and a great life in New York. Now here he was, unemployed, single, some spurious claim to being a lord, with a hotel, a vineyard and a yearning for the mountains. To top it all, here he was, mooning over his father's rather prickly former fiancée.

This is all your fault, Dad, he muttered under his breath. Once again, he imagined his father's laughter and humphed in reply.

Lucy and Poppy watched all this with relish and gave each other knowing looks.

'When are they going to work it out?' Lucy asked her friend.

'I wish they'd get on with it, it's beginning to feel like a pressure cooker in here.'

'Ah, l'amour …' added Frau Bachmann, who had also become aware of the growing tension.

Together they giggled and kept watch.

'It's stunning,' commented Lucy one evening as she joined Tonita under the stars, handing her a mug of hot chocolate and a hot water bottle to warm her hands.

'Thank you,' smiled Tonita. 'I think I have discovered just the right theme for the next Tiffany's collection.'

On a long sheet of parchment, she had done a 360-degree panorama of the surrounding peaks. Then she showed Lucy a more modern and graphic design of the same scene, and joined the two ends together to show Lucy how it would form a ring or bangle.

'With a few diamonds dotted around for stars, I think it could work quite well.'

'It'll be beautiful,' Lucy agreed. 'I don't know how you can imagine such things.'

'I don't know either,' mused Tonita. 'I never really think about it, it just happens.'

'It's called *a gift*.' Sebastian spoke softly from over their shoulders. They hadn't heard him coming. Sensing a declaration coming on, Lucy beat a hasty retreat.

Tonita, also sensing a change of mood, bent over her drawing but couldn't concentrate.

'I'm not quite sure if this is appropriate,' he began.

She stopped looking at her drawing and looked at him straight.

'I'm not sure how this happened, Tonita, but I'm in love with you. I'm sure you think I'm really sick, hitting on my dad's fiancée and I don't expect you to reciprocate but I can't keep it to myself any longer. So there it is. I hope it won't create any awkwardness between us.'

Tonita turned away from him to conceal her huge smile but still she didn't reply. She was enjoying Seb's discomfort too much.

'You're not mad at me, for spoiling everything, are you? We can still be friends, can't we?'

Tonita finally turned and smiled. Her eyes were full of love and she needed no words to express her feelings.

'Really?' he asked. 'Really?'

Tonita nodded.

'Yes, really!' replied Poppy as she plonked two glasses of champagne beside them.

'Now give her a kiss and we can all celebrate.'

She walked off, adding, ''bout bloody time!' as she closed the door behind her.

They looked towards the refuge and saw that they had an audience. Their six spectators raised their glasses and laughed.

'There's more privacy on Fifth Avenue than on the top of of this mountain,' he protested.

'They're just happy for us. Genuinely happy. I like it.'

They clinked glasses and kissed. A cheer emanated from inside but they ignored it and carried on.

Twenty-Eight

You don't fear for your life in the middle of a storm, you can't really afford to.

Ellen MacArthur

The next morning Sebastian sat staring into his coffee, wondering where on earth life was taking him. He surfed the pages of the newspapers, starting with the serious broadsheets and finishing with the tabloids, scanning without much interest until an item in the gossip column caught his eye: a claim to the Shilton title had been lodged. The article gave a brief outline of the man believed to be the next in line and his photo.

'Well, I think my claim takes priority over his,' he laughed, as he read it. 'His father was born after mine and I'm five years older than him.'

'Maybe that's why he's trying to kill you,' whispered Lucy as she looked over his shoulder.

'Are you sure, Lucy?' asked Inspectrice Jacquier, coming over as she heard the words.

'That's him, that's my Sherlock Holmes,' confirmed Lucy, shuddering as she did so. 'It matches that photofit you showed me too.'

Inspectrice Jacquier decided that this warranted her also breaking the communication ban and called her team.

Blonnay had also just picked up on the report and seen that the photograph was a good match to the photofit obtained by the Scottish police from the deerstalker salesman. The same officers were on their way back to the shop with the photo from the newspaper to see if he could positively identify him, but Blonnay and Dupertuis knew it was just a question of evidence: they knew this was their man.

The information began flying in from all directions. It did not make for pleasant reading. The British police confirmed that Jakub Kamiński, of Polish descent had recently lodged a request for British nationality on the grounds of his British mother. He had furnished DNA evidence in respect of his claim to the Shilton title and it all seemed valid. They had very little more information on him other than him being a frequent visitor to the UK. The Polish on the other hand, had lots.

'Phwee!' whistled Blonnay as he looked at the file. 'This guy's army.'

'More than that, he's JW Grom.'

'Shit!'

Jakub Kamiński had, until two years previously, been a high-ranking officer in the elite Polish special forces, the Polish equivalent of the SAS. Since his retirement from the force he had been a consultant on cyber security.

At this moment, a sense of panic overcame them all. Herr Schmutz who had been simultaneously reading the same information, called.

'I'm getting them out of there, now! The helicopter's on its way. I should never have agreed to Herr McDonaghue keeping his phone and computer.'

'You weren't to know what we were dealing with.'

'No. This guy's in a totally different league. It makes Fraulein Wilson's escape appear miraculous.'

'Where are you going to put them now?'

'I think it's better that you don't know. I need to call my colleague to organise the evacuation.'

'What do you think that means?' Capitaine Dupertuis asked his colleague as they sat there feeling useless.

'He likes extremes, from the top of a mountain, he'll probably put them underground now. My guess would be the cheese cellars in Fribourg.'

'Christ!'

'Quite. Imagine, living in that pong of ammonia!'

It didn't bear thinking about, poor Lucy, surely even she couldn't stay positive in such an environment.

'I think it also looks like you had a lucky escape,' Blonnay grimaced at him.

Alain nodded.

'You were right to be suspicious. Those cords on my parachute were definitely not frayed the last time I used it. I'll wait until this is all over and get it properly checked out before I use it again.'

Neither of them said what they were really thinking: if they didn't get Lucy back safely, that could be never.

―――――――――――――――

The call to evacuate came as no surprise. The small helicopter that could land on the Lesteraarhorn pad could only carry four so it was agreed that Sebastian, Tonita, Herr Anderegg and Lucy would be airlifted out. Lucy tried to protest but her pleas fell on deaf ears.

'Lucy, you are the only person who can testify against him. We have to get you out of here. Also, I'm sorry but you have no climbing experience; you would slow us down. If that guy's out there, taking shots at us, it's no time for climbing lessons,' Sylvie Jacquier told her firmly. 'I am sure Lucy, that you do not want to put the lives of your friends at risk.'

To this, Lucy had no reply.

The refuge was shuttered up and all entrances locked bar the main door. Here they all gathered and waited for the helicopter.

They didn't wait long and the four passengers ran out to clamber in. Lucy, looking like she had forgotten something, ran back.

'Lucy, I've told you, you have to go, now.'

'He's here, Sylvie, I've seen him, just opposite under a ledge.'

'Get back in the helicopter and tell the pilot to hold it until I give the sign it's safe to take off. If the sign doesn't come, you are all to evacuate the helicopter and return to the refuge. *Now*!' she urged calmly. She didn't feel calm: her heart was thumping.

Lucy ran back to the helicopter and got in. The machine sat on the pad, propellers turning.

Sylvie had no time to think. She saw instantly, they were trapped. Jakub Kamiński's plan was perfect, all he had to do was take out the helicopter to get rid of Lucy and his rival. One perfectly aimed shot and the helicopter would smash into millions of tiny pieces on the rocks below, making it almost impossible to identify the cause of the crash. Pure luck and Lucy's sharp eyes had at least given them a chance.

She handed her phone to the guardians who looked calm but frightened.

'Lock yourselves and Poppy in. If I fail, lock everyone in and call this number,' she commanded.

Sylvie took a good look at Jakub Kamiński as he crouched against the cliff waiting for the helicopter to take off. He had clearly not worked out he had been spotted. Lucy had successfully concealed her discovery of him, but he was well entrenched, there was no way she could get a clear shot.

'Damn,' she cursed.

'You need a decoy,' Poppy commented over her shoulder. 'I'm up for it.'

'I'm sorry, Poppy. It's very brave of you, but I cannot allow you to put yourself in the line of fire.'

'I wasn't asking your permission, Sylvie. I'm just telling you for your information that I am heading over to the other side of the deck to get some shots of the helicopter taking off. If your target has to move to see where I'm going, then I expect you to take advantage of the situation.'

And with that Poppy scrambled off, ostentatiously waving to the occupants of the helicopter on her way and pointing to her camera to show what she was up to.

Inspectrice Jacquier sighed, these incomers, they had no respect for authority. But she could not deny the logic of Poppy's plan, she could only hope that Poppy didn't end up getting them all killed.

She watched Poppy scramble over the rocks in front of the refuge, directly opposite the hitman. As she disappeared round the cliff edge the hitman edged slightly towards the skyline to keep her in his sights. The policewoman profited from the diversion to creep round and get a better sightline.

She heard Poppy whistle loudly and, at that very moment, Mildred, the bearded vulture, disturbed by the prolonged noise and currents created by the helicopter, appeared above the cliff, squawking loudly in protest. She dived towards the stranger, who, thrown off balance by this attack from unexpected quarters, had to move to steady himself.

She only had one chance but Sylvie Jacquier's hand did not tremble: one shot was all she needed. She aimed, fired and hit her target directly in the forehead. He slowly keeled forwards and somersaulted over the cliff edge and into oblivion. Mildred followed him down: now here was carrion worth keeping track of.

'That,' shouted Sylvie, shaking in fury, 'that was for Maria!'

The occupants of the helicopter took the falling body as the sign that Sylvie had promised. The door of the helicopter opened, Lucy ran out and the machine lingered no longer. Within seconds it had taken to the skies, carrying the future Lord and Lady Shilton with it.

Lucy and Poppy, running from different directions, reached Sylvie, now trembling with the realisation of what she had just done and the relief it was all over, and hugged her tight.

'I've never shot at a live target before,' Sylvie admitted. 'I just killed a man.'

'You didn't kill a man, you killed a monster,' corrected Lucy. 'He killed three people in cold blood, Sylvie, and he wouldn't have hesitated to kill all eight of us. You *saved* our lives.'

Poppy smiled at her.

'You're a bloody good shot.'

'The pilot was impressed!' agreed Lucy. 'He was convinced we were all for it. Wasn't Mildred awesome too? You'd almost think she was on our side.'

Sylvie gave Lucy a wry look. 'Capitaine Dupertuis will be wondering, Lucy, why you aren't in the helicopter.'

Lucy grinned.

'No danger of Sherlock Homes taking pot shots at me now. I'm not being done out of that climb down.'

Sylvie looked at Lucy with increasing appreciation. Could nothing dent this woman's enthusiasm for the mountains? Alain Dupertuis had chosen a real live wire.

Poppy hugged her tight.

'You are a total hero, Sylvie.'

'You should have been a policewoman, Poppy.'

'No fear!' grimaced Poppy. 'Too much discipline for me.'

Sylvie had to acknowledge that this was probably right.

They headed back to the refuge to collect their backpacks and prepare themselves for the climb down with the guardians.

Alain met Lucy, Poppy, Sylvie and Herr and Frau Bachmann at the foot of the Lesteraarhorn and accompanied them to Bern for their debriefing with Herr Schmutz.

They signed their statements and were given a good warning about not talking to the press. They were told that press accounts might not perfectly match their own knowledge but this was for their own protection and they should on no account discuss the matter with anyone else. They assured Herr Schmutz that they were the last people likely to sell their stories to the media and that he could count on their discretion. Somehow, despite their lack of regard for rules and regulations, he knew they were reliable and also intelligent enough to realise that the fastest way to get their lives back to normal was to lie low.

'What was that all about?' Lucy asked on the way out.

Alain grimaced. Poppy answered for him.

'It means, Lucy, that the press are going to be given as little information as possible to put them off the scent and avoid the police having to answer any difficult questions.'

'Ah.'

Alain shook his head despairingly, he wondered if Poppy wasn't a better detective than he was.

'They'll have to do a bloody good job of watering down that story,' Poppy added. 'Losing one Lord Shilton is unfortunate, losing two begins to look like carelessness.'

Lucy laughed and Alain, who hadn't got the joke, just looked baffled. Alain, however, had his own ace card to play. After a few moments, Lucy realised that they were heading directly for the Federal Palace. She looked at him with a big grin.

'Nooo!'

'Yes,' he grinned back. 'Herr Schmutz, having heard from his officer, Herr Anderegg, of your fascination with Swiss politics has arranged for you to have a private tour of the building.'

For the next hour, oblivious to how incongruous they looked in their walking boots and mountain clothes, Lucy and Poppy were guided like VIPs around the seat of Switzerland's government.

The hour-long visit was over in a flash. The palace was built of solid stone and its carpeted stairs and floors made it feel almost like a luxurious mansion house. Walking through both chambers and the circular gallery where political plots and intrigue played out, Lucy remembered the discussions she used to have with Danny before the avalanche took him: she missed their chats. Architectural secrets and details of the palace added to its charm, and the St Gall embroidered lace panels in the long windows of the State Chamber were a quirky reminder of Switzerland's attachment to her traditions.

'It was lovely,' she sighed as they left. 'Please thank Herr Schmutz for me.'

'I might,' he joked. 'But you ought to know that he has asked if, in return, you two could stay out of his canton for a while. When I told him you were planning to do the tour of Mont Blanc next summer, he put his hand to his head and said, 'God help the French.'

Twenty-Nine

I have come to the conclusion, after many years of sometimes sad experience, that you cannot come to any conclusion at all.
Vita Sackville-West, In Your Garden Again

When they got back to the chalet, Lucy realised that Słowik was missing.

'Oh, well when I went to meet the helicopter that you were supposed to be in, Słowik greeted Tonita like an old friend. Tonita agreed to take her back to La Grande Cour with her and said you can pick her up when you're ready.'

The next day, Lucy texted Tonita and walked down to the resort to pick up the little dog.

Tonita had plenty of her own news. She and Sebastian had decided to marry quickly because they had realised that they both wanted to have children as soon as possible and Tonita was approaching her forties. Sebastian's claim to the Lord Shilton title seemed to be uncontested and, if it succeeded, they would be moving to England.

'And it'll hopefully mean,' Tonita added, 'that Ruby and Leo can come to me more often.'

Tonita looked happier than Lucy had ever seen her and they chatted on for so long that Sebastian had to come and remind Tonita that they had a meeting with Maître Aulnay. Lucy thanked Tonita for looking after Słowik and called the little dog, but the little dog refused to leave Tonita's side.

'That's odd,' said Tonita. 'I promise, I haven't been spoiling her.'

'How have you been communicating with her? I never gave you the commands in Polish.'

'But Słowik understands English perfectly.'

'What?'

'Look,' Tonita issued the standard series of commands in English. Słowik obediently sat, fetched and walked to heel as Lucy watched on, stupefied.

'Well she clearly prefers you: even in Polish she ignores me. She isn't actually mine, Alain just asked me to look after her until the case was over. I've not had her chip changed or anything.'

'So, could I keep her?'

'Do you want her?'

'Actually, yes, we've become great friends. Would you mind? If it all works out, I'd love to take her to Leicestershire with me.'

'I wouldn't mind at all: I know she saved my life but we never really clicked and it would certainly resolve the problem about her not liking the cold. Poppy always said she was an odd choice of dog for a ski resort. I've got Maria's papers for her, I'll drop them off next time I'm passing.'

'Bye Słowik.'

But the little Italian greyhound trotted off at Tonita's heels without so much as a backward glance at Lucy.

'It's strange how it worked out.' The Reichenbach Falls murder team was conducting a conference call case review with the Bern *Krimalpolizei*.

Alain continued, 'We were looking at two different possible leads, the Polish connection and the English one, and in fact, they turned out to be one and the same.'

'I cannot believe in this day and age, people are still prepared to kill for a title,' Herr Schmutz added.

'No,' Sylvie agreed. 'It does seem a bit feudal.'

'It was probably the wealth connected with the Shilton estate that was Kamiński's object. If M. McDonaghue's claim is recognised, he stands to acquire not only property in Leicestershire and London, but investments and vineyards all over the world.'

'M. McDonaghue will probably do a better job of managing it than Kamiński. Just as well he's thrown in his Wall Street job.'

The procureur thought the discussion was getting too speculative and brought it back to the facts.

'So, Schmutz: are we absolutely sure Kamiński was a lone agent and that his run-in with the Swiss police in the mountains is an end to the matter?

'As sure as we can be. It took the Polish police hackers ages to break into his phone and computer but their analysis is that everything points to him being a lone agent. Sergei overheard Maria confessing about stealing the hairbrush from Lord Shilton so he could do the DNA test and remembered his former army officer boasting about being the illegitimate grandson of the same lord and tried to arrange a deal where they shared the booty, but once Kamiński had the information, Sergei was just in his way.'

Sylvie took over the narrative.

'So, knowing that Sergei was obsessed with Sherlock Holmes, he agreed to meet him at the Reichenbach Falls with the intention of getting rid of him and Maria but Maria couldn't go at the last minute and so he had to race over to Grondère to dispatch her too, having tortured her first to make sure no one else knew.'

She winced at the thought and Alain continued.

'The press leak made him realise that someone had seen him at Reichenbach and he came back to Switzerland to spy on the police investigation. He recognised Lucy and Poppy in a chance sighting at the 1 August celebrations and from then on, he had us all tracked. He actually moved in with the Braythwaites for a short time and used it as a spying headquarters; it turns out he was a distant cousin of the wife's. Lucy and Poppy were his priorities, because, as far as he knew, they were the only ones who could physically identify him as Sergei's murderer. He didn't know that Poppy hadn't seen him.'

Blonnay took over.

'We lose track of him after he moved out of the Braythwaites but we know he came back here to deal with Lucy and Poppy. We think his plan was to make Lucy have an "accidental" tumble down the old *bisse* waterfall and that's where he met with a bit of resistance.' He smiled at Alain. 'Mlle Wilson somehow knew he was no ordinary hiker and took evasive action – and a helicopter ride. This is pure speculation, but we think he also tampered with Capitaine Dupertuis' parachute.

'Frustrated, he first had to go back to England to make sure Lord Shilton died before his wedding day and didn't father a legitimate heir.'

'Was this all in his computer?'

'Not directly, but he had a calendar with the book launch and the wedding date highlighted. Straight after the "hunting accident", he returned to turn his surveillance on Capitaine Dupertuis and Sebastian. He knew from Sebastian's phone calls that he knew nothing and Capitaine Dupertuis had vanished – he fortunately never seems to have discovered that his mother lives in Grondère. Things started to grow even more worrying for him when Sebastian was evacuated, at which point he knew he had a rival with a prior claim for the title. His lucky break came when Sebastian called New York from the Lesteraarhorn and he knew he had them all in one place. The army found a camouflaged tent over the ridge from the refuge, it still contained his computer and surveillance equipment: he'd been staking out the refuge for days, knowing that sooner or later his quarry would be taken off the mountain by helicopter and he could down them all with one shot.'

'How close we came to disaster,' the procureur commented. 'I congratulate you Capitaine Dupertuis for your foresight in sending Inspectrice Jacquier with them. And you …' He turned to Sylvie who was looking a bit uncomfortable.

'I do not know how to thank you, Inspectrice. I doubt anyone else could have hit that target first shot in those circumstances. You really are a talented markswoman.'

Sylvie blushed. Poppy, it turned out, actually had filmed the entire event. Her film had been confiscated and destroyed but not before a large part of the higher echelons of the Swiss police had watched it several times over, accompanied by multitudinous high fives. Sylvie Jacquier had become a total legend. Alain and Blonnay were extremely proud of her and basked in their reflected share of her glory.

The team went for a celebratory drink and discussed their holiday plans.

'In the hope,' teased Blonnay, 'that Mlle Wilson can avoid witnessing any more murders for a week or two.'

'Did you check with Mum before you gave the dog away? Alain asked a little indignantly that evening.

'I checked with her *afterwards* and I can promise you, she was delighted.' Lucy laughed, 'You seem to be taking Słowik's defection harder than me.'

'I'm just surprised, I thought you two had formed quite a team.'

'A team, yes, but not a bond. Słowik never felt like she belonged with me. She's not a mountain dog and she'd have hated it here in winter. No, Poppy's right, she's an aristocratic dog. Maria would like that, you know, that her dog was with a real lady.'

'You're right.' He gave her a hug. 'She was a bit too refined for my little mountain goat.'

Lucy gave him a playful kick in the shins.

'Oh, and by the way, next time you bring me a dog, can you please make sure it can sniff out truffles?'

'There aren't any truffles here.'

'No, but Poppy knows where there are.'

'I bet she does.'

Lucy had to share with her friends a little of the story of where she and Poppy had been. Sally, having packed Lucy's bag, had known something serious was up and they had all worried about where she was. Reunited, her friends would not be fobbed off with a 'hiking trip' story.

Lucy told them about her and Poppy's stay in the Bernese Alps and explained what she could of the reasons. She told them she had witnessed the Reichenbach Falls murder and that the murderer had recognised her that night of 1 August, when Johnny had seen the man with cold eyes.

'When the police realised he was following me, they decided to hide me and Poppy. He followed us up there too but he met his death.'

She explained Maria's unhappy connection to Lord Shilton and the resulting happy consequence of his death for Sebastian and Tonita. They listened in absolute disbelief and, as she finished, she could already see the unanswered questions forming.

'Please don't ask me anymore,' she pleaded. 'I just can't tell you.'

They agreed not to plague her with questions.

'There is one thing I can tell you,' she added. 'In a moment of weakness, Alain promised to pay for us all to go heli-skiing when it was all over.'

They broke into whoops of glee: only Eddie had ever heli-skied before, and that was just because a free spot had opened up at the last moment when Danny was being filmed.

Once the excitement had died down, Tommy looked at her seriously.

'You must have been in mega-danger, Lucy, for him to make a promise like that.'

'Yes,' she said frankly. 'Poppy and I both were.'

'How obliging of the baddie to get himself shot and tumble off the mountain like that.'

'Yes,' she replied cagily. Tommy winked to show that he was going to let her off lightly.

'Just tell us you're safe now.'

'Yes,' she sighed gratefully. 'We're all safe now.'

When the Swiss newspapers reported the story, it was in a small paragraph, in the low-interest pages. A formal report had been filed by the police about their timely intervention in an attempted murder by an unknown climber. The number of bullets fired and resulting death were buried in multiple references to and lengthy extracts from the relevant pieces of legislation. A few days later, a joint statement was issued by the Bern *Kriminalpolizei* and the Valais *Police judiciaire* that evidence found amongst the climber's belongings identified beyond doubt Jakub Kamiński as the Reichenbach Falls and Grondère murderer and those cases were now closed. Once the Swiss press had established that this was an imported crime and that neither the perpetrator nor any of his victims had any connection with their nice, safe country, other than the impertinence of importing their disputes there, they quickly lost interest.

The British media, on the other hand, with the victim/villain being the claimant to the Shilton title, had a field day. The British police issued an equally brief statement that they had indeed been treating Lord Shilton's death as suspicious and had been working closely with the Polish and Swiss police to resolve the matter. Salacious speculations began to circulate as to what the heir apparent was doing climbing mountains in Switzerland instead of staying safe at home and supervising his legal claim. When they discovered the very photogenic Sebastian McDonaghue and the fact that he had been Jakub Kamiński's intended target, the British press attention switched focus overnight. The new pretender to the Shilton title was immediately a big favourite, his British, Australian and American links enabling the press in each country to claim him as their own. Totally enamoured with this young man and his aristocratic bearing, they even championed his cause.

'It's strange,' said Lucy to Poppy as they were re-watching the secret copy of the film of Jakub Kamiński's demise that Poppy had managed to copy and conceal before her camera was confiscated. 'The newspapers say the body fell deep into a crevasse and it was too dangerous for it probably ever to be recovered, but as I got out of the helicopter, I clearly heard the pilot on the radio saying he had got the coordinates and would come back with a team and recover the body later.'

Poppy looked at her sternly. 'Think about it, Lucy.' Lucy thought and then the penny dropped.

'I see. If the body was found, someone might want to bury it and that would draw a lot more attention to the bullet in its head.'

'Exactly. I bet old Jakub Whatshisname has been neatly disposed of in one of those industrial incinerators by now. But no one, including your cute detective, will ever admit it.'

'Really, it's a bit sinister, isn't it?'

'I won't be spending any sleepless nights worrying about Jakub Whatshisname not getting a Christian burial and neither should you. If *he* was still alive, *you* wouldn't be.'

'I guess but …'

'But what?'

'It's just that I don't understand: Switzerland has this image of being such a nice, harmless, neutral country, home to the UN, Red Cross and all that.'

'It is. But I suspect it suits Switzerland to let everyone think it's a quiet, harmless place: that doesn't mean that it will allow itself to be treated like the village idiot. When someone threatens it, isn't it good to know that Switzerland is as capable, if not more, as any other country, of protecting that nice, harmless neutral-ness?'

Lucy smiled.

'Yes, Poppy.'

'So, in fact, it's not that you didn't understand Switzerland, you underestimated it.'

Lucy laughed. She loved how Poppy always had a different slant on a topic.

'Shame for Mildred, though.'

'Yes, Jakub Whatshisname was a big chap – his bones would have kept the larder stocked for the whole winter.'

'Just don't let on to anyone you've got that film, or I'll be in trouble with Alain for not telling him.'

'No fear! This is our secret. Though I can't say I really want to see it again: it probably would be wiser to delete it.'

Lucy asked Alain what had happened to the body but he refused to be drawn on the topic.

'At least, tell me this,' she insisted. 'Has anyone asked about his body?'

'No,' he allowed. 'We're pretty sure he was working alone. That's why he had to get rid of Sergei. His whole strategy depended on secrecy. You blew that for him, by seeing him at Reichenbach. If it wasn't for you, he might have got away with it.'

'But you all knew Sebastian was the rightful illegitimate heir, wouldn't you have said something?'

'That is delving into the realms of invention and takes me out of my depth. I am a police officer, not Jules Verne.'

'Huh.'

'All I can tell you is that he seems to have no close friends or family and that the world is a better place without him. Thank God Sylvie was with you, she's the only officer in the department who could have made that shot.'

'Yes, thank God for her. Will she be decorated?'

Now it was his turn to smile.

'This is Switzerland. We don't have an honours system and Sylvie already has all the shooting decorations. She might get the Alpine Decoration, but that's it.'

'So, nothing, not a promotion, or pay rise?'

'She and Blonnay are both already on the fast track career path. However, Sylvie may suddenly discover she is sent on an exchange visit to the Australian police accompanied by an unexpectedly large holiday allowance to compensate for the time she spent on the Lesteraarhorn.'

'Oh, well that's something.'

'Or should I say, to compensate for the time she spent on the Lesteraarhorn, unable to participate in your evening drinking sessions.'

'Ah.'

'Yes. Ah.'

'I never drank wines like those in my life.'

'Well, please don't develop a taste for it. My budget cannot compete with M. McDonaghue's private wine cellar.'

'I'm not interested in your wine-buying budget,' she smiled. 'As long as there's no limit on kisses!'

Carla Sturridge sat in her prison cell and yelled with rage. Furious, she stomped back and forth, gripping the week-old English newspaper, that someone had carefully made sure she received. She ranted, snarled and wailed. The prison warders, the kind providers of the paper, watched and listened on with delight.

The newspaper contained an article detailing how Sebastian McDonaghue was the first case where a descendant from an illegitimate branch of an aristocratic family in the UK had been recognised as the legitimate heir to a vacant title. It was a ground-breaking decision and the press was having a field day with the potential implications for the landed gentry, imagining all sorts of wonderful scenarios where the working classes would be ousting occupants from stately homes up and down the country. The Queen herself, they claimed, should be concerned, as there were people who could trace their lineage directly back to William the Conqueror. The television programme *Who do you think you are?* had already featured such examples. This was all, of course, total media provocation: the decision had clearly stated that it was based on the fact that there were no other claimants and that the 'illegitimacy' only went back one generation and could be proved genetically, but the media wasn't going to let such trivial details get in the way of their fun.

The photo accompanying the article was the final humiliation for Carla. It was the engagement photo of her son, the future Lord Shilton and his beautiful fiancée, the talented and successful jewellery designer, Tonita Shalott. If prison had not been sufficient to put Carla in her place, this final frustration was. If those interfering Swiss detectives hadn't wrecked her plans, she would now be enjoying the elevated status afforded to the mother of a titled son and Tonita wouldn't have got her claws into him; Carla would have made sure of that. Her dream of becoming a true member of the upper classes had been snatched away and she was sure it was the fault of her ancient rival, Poppy Smythe, and that conniving little Lucy Wilson. Her rage was something to behold.

A few days later, Carla received a letter from her son's lawyer, Maître Aulnay, informing her that she had now received all the help and support that her son was prepared to provide. He considered that he had fulfilled all remaining obligations to her and his sister and she should now consider their relationship at an end. He instructed her never to contact him again or expect him to contact her. She had deprived him of the father he loved, something for which he could never forgive her and the thought of any further communication with her was unthinkable.

Her son had, in short, voluntarily orphaned himself.

In the same prison, in another cell, in another rage, another woman was also reading the newspaper. As if it wasn't already bad enough that the awful cousin who had insisted on inviting himself to stay had turned out not to be the future lord he had promised but the Grondère murderer, entitling her to another visit from those arrogant Swiss police officers, now Laeticia Braythwaite was reading an article in French about the unexpected discovery of a new singing talent following the surprising concert of *West Side Story* in the ski resort of Grondère. Jodie Scott's rendition of *I Feel Pretty* had gone viral, with over 80,000 YouTube hits at the last count. Her beautiful and pure vocals conveying perfectly the youth and innocence of Maria had taken the music world by storm, she read. Apparently, Jodie had been offered a scholarship to the *Haute École de Musique de Lausanne* and a bright future was predicted for the young yoga teacher who the media had christened the Grondère Nightingale. BL sat on the edge of her bed and wept for what she still believed could and should have been hers. And then she stopped crying and started thinking. This prison was sorely deprived of cultural activities: it could do with a choir …

———————————

Charles Sidforth-Sykes looked sadly around at the luxury pad he had previously owned and then rented as his bad business decisions had gradually whittled away his capital. His final bad decision, to entrust the Braythwaites with what little of it remained, meant he could no longer even pay the rent. To avoid losing face in front of all his Grondère friends, he would have to return to the UK where at least the UK government would look after him better than he had managed to look after himself and better than the Swiss government would be prepared to.

He looked around to see if there were any paintings or sculptures he could sell but he already knew that the art dealers of Grondère had fooled him into paying vastly inflated prices for up and coming 'next sure thing' artists who had disappeared into obscurity and whose work was never likely to achieve the market values predicted, and not even the hefty prices he had paid.

His mood wasn't improved by the recent information that Sebastian and Tonita had recently formed a couple. It was just too bad of Tonita to have thrown herself at Sebastian like that. But then, she had always had a mercenary side to her, that's why she'd got engaged to Malcolm, even though he was so much older than her. No, she wouldn't have done for Charles after all: he'd had a lucky escape there.

As he shuffled around beginning to work out how to discreetly disappear from Grondère, his phone buzzed.

'Charles, old chap.'

'Humphrey.'

'You are not going to believe this.'

I will, Charles thought gloomily, unless you tell me that I won a lottery I didn't know I'd entered.

'You remember ten years ago, you gave me some dosh for my nephew's dodgy business start-up.'

'I do,' Charles said. He had often regretted throwing £20,000 after that openly acknowledged speculative project just for the sake of showing off. He could really have done with that money now. 'Some computer gaming thing, wasn't it?'

'Yes, jolly sporting of you at the time to throw your money into what we all thought was a dirty great black hole. Well, it turns out we were all wrong.'

Charles stopped breathing. He tried to sound casual but the possibility that he was about to be cast a lifeline was too strong to completely hide his eagerness.

'You don't mean we're actually going to get our money back, old chap?'

'And more,' laughed Humphrey. 'They've just signed a deal to sell the whole kit and caboodle to Sony. I calculate your share at £10 million.'

Charles nearly fainted. He had thought this sort of happy ending only happened in fiction.

'Charles, are you listening?'

'Oh yes, Humphrey. I'm listening.'

———————————

Lucy was given Lina's new phone number by Sylvie, who informed her that Lina would shortly be leaving Switzerland and so Lucy took the train down to Savigny to say goodbye.

'The Polish man the police shot? That was definitely him?'

'Yes, that was definitely him.'

Lina looked pensive.

'I need to know more. I know this is not very Christian of me but I need to know how that evil man got his punishment.'

Lucy was surprised at the vehemence in Lina's voice but then, she wondered, how would she feel if someone murdered Sally, or Poppy or one of the others? Wouldn't she also want some answers and a bit of revenge? She knew she was breaking Alain's trust but, at the same time, she was talking to the one living person she knew who truly loved and mourned Maria.

'Lina, this is between you and me only, you must promise?'

'I promise.'

Lucy gave her an abridged description of how the Lesteraarhorn drama had unfolded. When she had finished she added, 'What happened up there was unavoidable: it saved the lives of eight people and was a superb act of bravery and defence of life.'

Lina looked at her knowingly.

'Inspectrice Jacquier promised me she would bring Maria's killer to justice.'

'She kept her promise, but maybe not quite as she would have wished. We are all safe now but you must never speak of this to anyone, do you understand? Especially as you are going back to Poland. I will be in terrible trouble for telling you and we don't want any "friends" turning up. Please don't ask me anymore.'

Lina smiled grimly. 'That will do for me: I have heard what I needed to hear, thank you for your honesty. No one will hear a word from me.'

She added gaily, 'My old lady died.'

'Oh.' Lucy wasn't quite sure how to react in the face of such unconcealed delight at someone's demise. Maria saw her hesitation and laughed.

'She was 97. Eventually her heart stopped. I'm not sad, she was ready to go and so am I, back to Poland.'

'I'm happy for you.'

'Thanks. Her family thought she was going to outlive them all; she did outlive some of her children.'

'Did she have many?'

'Five but only two left. They were so grateful that I'd looked after her that they told me I could take as many of the hated porcelain figurines I liked, to remember her by. They said their mother cared more for porcelain than them and they never wanted to see them again.'

'But you didn't like them either.'

'Exactly! I took all the horrible shepherdesses that Maria coveted the most and took them straight to the antique dealer. Turns out Maria wasn't that dippy – they're all 18th century Meissen and stuff like that!'

'You sold them?'

'On the spot. The dealer contacted some collectors and paid me Fr20,000.'

'Crikey!'

'Yes, I'm off home to set up my own business and so, you see, I have something really wonderful to remember Maria by.'

Lucy laughed; she had no doubt that Lina was off to make her fortune.

'I wish you luck but I'm sure you don't need it.'

'No, I'm onto a winner – please tell Inspectrice Jacquier that I will be expecting her to join you in Warsaw for the opening of my *raclette* restaurant.'

'You're taking *raclette* to Poland!'

'Trust me, Poland is about to undergo a *raclette* revolution!'

Thirty

... if I were a bird I would fly about the earth seeking the successive autumns.
George Eliot, Letter to Miss Lewis

Lucy sat on the balcony looking down on Grondère. Sunrise was her favourite moment of the day and, as she often did, she had crept out of bed while Alain was still sleeping, made herself a cup of tea and snuggled up in a duvet in the cosy rocking chair Alain had put there for her. The hillsides below carried the fading russets and golds of the season. As the sun broke through the burgeoning clouds, it cast tints of orange on exposed rocks, contrasting starkly against the metallic blue sky.

Above the treeline, frost blanketed the empty pastures. In the woods behind the chalet, where Lucy had come so close to being Jakub Kamiński's third victim, the last red leaves clung to the dark branches of the trees and in the bare branches of the dogwood bushes, beneath the evergreens, pink berries hung like precious jewels in the darkness. A gold carpet of larch needles on the muddy forest floor deadened the forest sounds and rusty leaves spun in the air until they too fell to the ground, filling the hollows and forming mounds against the bases of trees and rocks. The transient plants in Lucy's little garden had died back but the shapes and silhouettes of the dwarf conifers and boulder features inspired by the Japanese Garden came into their own. They gave it a sculptural identity which was beautiful in its own right – just as she had planned. She felt quite smug when she looked at it and looked forward to seeing how it would bounce back in the spring.

The weeks she had spent in the Lesteraarhorn eyrie had deprived her of the early splendour of autumn, but not its final glory. On her return she had enjoyed a couple of weeks wandering in liberty, breathing in the beauty of the season and happily scrunching the akermast beneath her boots, safe in the knowledge there was no one lurking in the shadows watching her. The forest had been a patchwork of brightness: the golden spires of the larch trees, dark green parasols of the conifers and russet and brown pompoms of the deciduous broadleaves all intermingled. Entire hillsides were sheathed in bright red where the disc-shaped leaves of the blueberry bushes, long since stripped of their fruits, stubbornly clung on in a brazen scarlet display as if laughing at the foragers and saying 'we were here all the time'. Burnished shades of straw and bronze of the dying heathers, bracken and grasses shone in the gentle sunshine. Even the long autumn shadows contributed to the beauty, casting shades of purple and indigo on the flanks of the mountains. Autumn colours, she thought, have their own unique quality: spring colours are cheerful, those of summer gladden the heart but the colours of autumn, they glow – like the embers of a dying fire.

Most satisfyingly, Lucy had made it back in time to harvest the magical fruits from the blackthorn bushes lower down in the valley that she had been jealously eyeing throughout the summer. When she returned, their over-charged branches were bent under the weight of their fat, bitter, black fruits, and she had monitored the temperatures, hoping the birds wouldn't take them before the first frost. Early on the morning when she had detected the sparkling of that first frost she had collected several kilograms of the dusty sloes (and quite a few scratches) and raced home where she had prepared a stock of gin and sugar, pricked the berries and cracked a few of their kernels with a hammer to give the gin a more 'almondy' flavour, as the recipe advised. The brew was now steeping in the cool, dark room with all her other foraged treasures. Alain had told her she could leave her harvest of foraged goodies in the unused room she had purloined and that, in the spring, now that he was aware of her strange requirements, he would construct her a purpose-built larder.

Lucy had missed a trip with her friends to the biggest *désalpe* in the area but had returned just in time to see the Grondère *désalpe* with Tommy and Sally proudly bringing down their troop of black Herens cows for the first time together with Tommy's future partner, Christophe. Lucy and Poppy stood at the side of the road and applauded proudly as the herd went past, Poppy clicking like mad on her camera. Unlike the local women, who all wore sensible canvas trousers or jeans, Sally and Jodie had insisted on wearing traditional peasant dresses and Tommy and Eddie, farmers' hats: they fitted the tourist's idea of Grondèrians more than the genuine article. Sally and Jodie had made huge crowns of paper flowers for the cows and were adamant that theirs had been the most beautiful on the mountain. Poppy nudged Lucy as she noticed Christophe looking longingly in Jodie's direction. Lucy giggled.
'Another budding romance?'
'I don't know if it's reciprocal. Poor lad, he looks completely smitten.'
'He does, do you think she knows?'
'If she's noticed, she's not showing it.'
'I'm not saying anything.'
'No. Jodie will be moving in very different circles from now on. Singers, especially pretty ones, attract a lot of admirers.'

'Do you think we'll lose her?'

'Not while she's studying, but eventually I think it's inevitable: if she makes the big time, her work will take her all over the world.'

'Something tells me she'll always gravitate back to Grondère.'

'I know some opera singers; they're actually very normal, grounded people. It's often the people opera attracts who are a bit weird.'

'Really?'

'Trust me, you come along to an opera concert at the festival next year: it's another universe.'

They all joined the *désalpe* party in Pattier and Tommy made Lucy promise to join them for the *inalpe* the following spring, but before that, they had a whole winter of skiing adventures ahead of them. Cold winds rhymed with approaching snow and, like all skiers at that time of year, Lucy could feel an excitement building inside her, an itching to click boots into bindings, a yearning to stretch shoulders down the slopes and float over untracked powder. She wondered what skiing with Alain would be like. He had skied since he was able to walk and he seemed to love it as much as she did. She hoped he wouldn't be too good.

Lucy also came home to the news that Émilie had made it onto the Swiss ski team. Grondère was talking about little else: it was a huge triumph for a ski resort to produce a national skier and an opportunity for everyone to claim their share of reflected glory, not least the resort itself. Émilie's face was on posters in every shop window in the resort, and her sponsors were justifiably flagging their involvement. New sponsors were queuing up and she was in demand for magazine articles and television interviews.

'Do you think your relationship will survive all this celebrity stuff?' Tommy asked his friend bluntly.

'We talked about it,' Eddie replied. 'I told her she must live for the moment and I would understand if trying to maintain a relationship was too big a strain.'

'That was brave.'

'Not really. I don't want to feel like a hanger-on. It's not my style.'

'So?'

'She told me she didn't know how long her sporting career would last or if she'd have any success but she'd rather have someone genuine at her side and so, would I mind sticking around.'

'So what does that mean? She's going to be away such a lot.'

'We're just going to see how it goes. I'll join her as much as I can for the European events and we'll adapt.'

'It's going to be hard.'

'Yes, thank goodness you're doing one last season and Lucy's moving back in.'

Tommy felt a bit worried for Eddie and mentioned it to Poppy.

'I think that young lady has a firm head on her shoulders, she knows that there's a huge risk of injury and even if she makes it, she's never going to make a fortune: this is about following her dream. Anyway, the Swiss don't let their champions get big-headed. Eventually she'll have to come back down to earth and make a living – probably back here, taking over her parents' property business.'

'I guess, but she's going to start getting invited to all sorts of fancy functions, that other ski superstar landed up with a footballer: Eddie can't compete with that.'

'But Tommy, that's a chance everyone takes in a relationship. You can't just settle for someone that you think there's no risk of losing. And, I think that not only are you underestimating Émilie, you're seriously underestimating your friend.'

Tommy looked at her seriously with his big blue eyes.

'I just don't want him to get hurt. Losing Danny was bad enough.'

'I think you should stop worrying and leave them to sort out their own issues. You three and Sally should just concentrate on having a great last season together.'

'You're right,' he smiled. 'I have a good feeling about this coming season.'

'Me too. Let's hope Lucy can avoid being at any more murder scenes.'

'No one can be that unlucky!'

Lucy and Alain had spent the previous couple of days tidying and cleaning: it was time to close up their mountain refuge for the winter and they were determined to make sure there was not a scrap left lying to tempt any mice to turn their summer idyll into their winter quarters. Lucy was more than ready for her mid-mountain guide exam and Alain had taken the day off work so they could enjoy their last night in the little chalet by the old *bisse*.

Alain came out to join her on the balcony as she was starting on her second cup of tea.

'What a glorious morning.'

'Yes. It's a wrench to leave.'

'The chalet or me?'

'Oooh, that's a tough one, let me get back to you.'

Later that afternoon, Alain came home from collecting the post.

'What on earth is this?'

He handed her an odd-shaped bag.

Lucy squealed with delight as she pulled some straggly roots from their plastic wrapping.

'Brilliant! I didn't think they'd arrive in time! I'd better get them into a bucket of water quickly. I'll just have time to get them in the ground before we leave.'

'*Them* being?'

'They're bare root roses,' exclaimed Lucy, 'from Canada. They're specially bred to cope with harsh conditions. I ordered one red and white. Like in the fairy tale. You know?'

'No, I don't know.'

'A mother had a rose bush of each colour outside her bedroom window, and her daughters were called Snow White and Rose Red and they make friends with a bear and ... Oh it's just about trust and kindness prevailing over greed and cruelty.'

'You really are the strangest creature!' Alain pretended to look despairingly but he thought the story just about summed up his girlfriend. He was also secretly delighted that Lucy was beginning to act like it truly was her chalet too.

'Oh, and your half-naked body is plastered all over the railway stations of Switzerland. Mum said it looks great.'

'That's nice. Apparently I'm going to be plastered all over all the travel magazines in the world too,' she told him proudly. 'Ricky's really happy. He says I've made his reputation.'

'Hmm, I'm not sure how much it's done for yours.'

'Nonsense, nobody ever knows the name of the model. Anyway, I can promise you that being associated with a bit of nudity is a vast improvement on murder.'

'I'll bet.'

He grinned at the thought of Blonnay, who that morning had sent him a very complimentary text telling him Lucy looked like John William Waterhouse's *Mermaid* which he had seen recently in London when he had been over to see his new girlfriend, some history buff detective from Scotland Yard.

Blonnay must be in heaven, he thought, an English girlfriend who sounded as nerdy as him.

'Oh, Sebastian has already asked you and me to the wedding but, do you think Blonnay will get an invite? He's desperate to get inside Lunstag Hall and, apparently, the Lords Shilton get married in Leicester Cathedral: he's pretty eager to go there too, something about a hunchback king. Although I suppose he could organise his own visit now he's got this girlfriend in Scotland Yard.'

Lucy nodded.

'I should think he'll be on the guest list, but I'll ask Tonita anyway. She doesn't have much family and she loathes her father, so she'd probably be glad to have such a loyal supporter present.'

'He's been a fan of Tonita's ever since she introduced him to Lord Tennyson and Pre-Raphaelite art.'

'Leicester Cathedral, you say?'

'Yes.'

'Well that puts the other part of that premonition to rest. Tonita in the cathedral and me in danger in the forest.'

'Yes, I'm glad you don't think I'm totally weird.'

'There are lots of things we can't rationalise. That vision or whatever it was probably saved my life.'

'Yes, and the shadow over Grondère has also been dispelled.'

'You didn't tell me about that one.'

'No, it was more of a feeling than a premonition.'

A sound distracted him.

'What's that bird singing,' he asked, 'I haven't heard it before, it's really pretty.'

Lucy pricked up her ears 'I haven't heard it before either, but I know what it is from my birdsong CD. Isn't that wonderful?' She looked at him happily. 'It's a nightingale.'

'In French?'

'A *rossignol*. Remember, like the little bird Gluey Hughey gave me.'

'And like the name of the chalet.' Alain grinned widely.

'Which is?'

'*Le nid des rossignols.*'

'You're making that up.'

'No, I'm not. Go and look at the sign.'

She walked round to the front door where a newly carved sign bearing the name he had given her and an engraved picture of a nightingale had been nailed to the wall of the chalet.

'That wasn't there before. You just named your chalet.'

'*Our* chalet, and yes, I bumped into Gluey Hughey a week ago and asked him to make me the sign. He refused any payment and yesterday morning I just found it on the doorstep.'

'How sweet.'

'Very. But please don't invite him to move in.'

'Trust me, if Gluey Hughey wanted to move in, he'd already be here.'

Trying to remember something about a nightingale's nest, Lucy plunged the bare root roses into a bucket of water and then stripped off and immersed herself into the plunge pool. How strange to hear it in late autumn, nightingales belong to summer … ah, that was it: it was in that anthology of poetry.

'I've got it!' she shouted.

'What?'

'The Nightingale's Nest! It's a poem! Can't remember who wrote it, or many of the lines, just this one: *and her renown hath made me marvel that so famed a bird should have no better dress than russet brown.* It's just perfect for our little brown chalet that looks so ordinary from the outside and is so beautiful inside. I'll have to print it out and frame it.'

He smiled; he didn't really get what she was going on about but she had said *our* chalet.

It really was starting to get chilly: the first snows clothed the mountain peaks above and it was only a matter of time before the snow line descended to reach them. Lucy felt nostalgic to be leaving their idyllic mountain home but happy at the thought of the oncoming ski season and getting back onto the slopes.

'It's strange this "transhumancing" business,' she sighed. 'This "shifting" with the seasons. It means you're in a permanent combined state of nostalgia and anticipation.'

'Or just a permanent state of happiness,' he smiled. 'Happy with where you've been, and happy with where you're going. I'll be happy if you can just stay out of trouble for a while.'

They had decided that Lucy would return to the little chalet with Tommy, Eddie and Sally for the winter season. Alain would continue to rent his studio in Savigny and they would stay at Alain's mum's apartment at the weekends when the chalet ranks would be swelled by Jodie and Émilie. It wasn't an ideal arrangement but they couldn't think of a better solution in the interim; rental prices skyrocketed in the ski season and so renting their own place was out of the question. Lucy was happy at the thought of living with Tommy and Eddie again even if the chalet was likely to be rather overcrowded with Sally having moved in and Jodie planning on joining them whenever she had the chance. She sensed that their chapter was drawing to a close and so she wanted to make the most of what she suspected would be their last winter season together. But Alain, her beautiful man, she would miss seeing him every day and sharing her nights with him.

She felt the cold penetrate her bones and her teeth began chattering. It really was too cold for bathing now. She clambered out and Alain handed her a warm fluffy towel.

'Oh, wonderful, thanks.'

He rubbed her down and she wrapped herself in her bathrobe and sat at the bench where he had put out some champagne glasses.

'Our last night here, I thought we'd better drink the last bottle of Prosecco.'

'Mmm, good idea.'

He took out a small black ring box and Lucy's heart sank. Shit, she thought.

'Lucy, I know that you are not ready to get married. This ring is just to tell you that I love you and that I would be really happy if, when you are ready, you'd consider me.'

He *does* understand me, she thought, I really am the lucky one.

She nodded, tears in her eyes, and let him place the ring on her finger.

Through her blurred vision, she recognised Tonita's design from the top of the Lesteraarhorn.

'It's absolutely stunning and it fits perfectly,' she managed to croak.

'Tonita measured your finger. I asked her for something special and she said you would *get* this. I had to force her to let me buy it. It wasn't easy, apparently, it's a prototype. And then we had a long discussion about what to call it: she didn't like the term "commitment" ring, she thought I should call it a "plight" ring, in English, then we could take either the verb or the noun meaning depending on our mood.'

Lucy laughed.

'She is a funny thing. I take it you've looked up both meanings?'

Alain grinned, 'Oh yes, I wouldn't have told you if I didn't get the joke. "Promise" for the verb and "a tricky situation" for the noun.'

'Blonnay would love that!'

'He would, but bizarrely, I won't be telling him.'

She sat admiring it as Alain poured.

'That's the real reason I had to go to the post office,' he confessed. 'And to get this.'

He held up the bottle with a smug grin.

'That's not Prosecco, that's pink champagne! You bought that specially.'

'Well it's a Swiss copy, but a good one. I think we've earned it, don't you?'

'I don't know if I have earned anything, I just seem to attract trouble and then other people get me out of it.'

'Oh, I think you did pretty well for an amateur.'

'You think so? I'm flattered.'

'But, if we could get through the winter season without incident, that would make a pleasant change.'

'I'll go around with my ears shut and eyes closed, I promise.'

'That sounds like a recipe for falling off a cliff,' he smiled, kissing her gently.

And then, as the first ephemeral snowflakes fluttered down, he handed her a glass and said the only word that can end any self-respecting Swiss whodunnit.

'*Apéro?*'

At some point in life the world's beauty becomes enough.
You don't need to photograph, paint, or even remember
it. It is enough.

                                                    Toni Morrison

Acknowledgements

Thank you to my wonderful team of reviewers: Holly Adams, Moira Davison, Lindsay Reuss and Christine Small, for helping me to make this a better book.

Nicky Christie and Tanya Freeman, my eagle-eyed proofreaders, your skill and professionalism overwhelm me. Once again you have caught loads of 'howlers' and saved me from certain humiliation. One day I will find a way to thank you properly.

Kirstie Swinnerton – another beautiful cover! Thank you for the gift of your art and your patient ear.

My gratitude once again to Dr. Sophie-Louise Hyde and Kathryn Cockrill at the online creative literary platform Wordsmith HQ: always there when I need you. https://www.wordsmithhq.co.uk

Many thanks also to the lovely Alicja Strycharska who, in one of those wonderful, inexplicable moments of chance, appeared from nowhere and kindly checked my Polish name choices.

Suzie Vaill took me exploring the Pembrokeshire coast, you're magic Suzie and you're going in the sequel.

The time and guidance the Police cantonale valaisanne are prepared to give a self-published author to ensure she doesn't stray too far from the realms of possibility is staggering. Thank you and I hope you will forgive me for my highly improbable ending.

Talking of the improbable, I am told the episode of Tommy and the tractor is implausible and yet it is based on a very similar event recounted to me by Rob Wemyss over a beer in après-ski. Thanks for sharing your stories Rob.

And a very special shout out for Wayne Hills, Julienne Loppacher and Lindsay Reuss for sharing those wonderful 'research' days with me in the Bernese Alps. If anyone would like to replicate Lucy and Poppy's hike, I can strongly recommend www.schweizmobil.ch (stages 10 to 14 of the Via Alpina cover much of the same ground).

Finally, thank you to my adopted country Switzerland and the wonderful resort of Verbier and the people who live there whose lives, stories and personalities are a 'mountainous' source of material and inspiration.

Dotting the 'i's

To those alpinists among you, scratching your heads, you are right: the peak of *Lesteraarhorn* does not exist. The mountain refuge described in this book is loosely based on the Finsteraarhorn; I kept it fictional to be able to bend it to my story. Its name also echoes the English county which houses the country residence of the fictional Lord Shilton and my mother's true county of origin.

When I created Lord Shilton in *Death in Grondère* I did so as a small personal tribute to the former English goalkeeper. I did not realise that the name had real links to the Earls of Leicester or that there was a place called Earl Shilton in Leicestershire. When, during my research, I did discover the fact, I debated with myself whether I should move Lord Shilton's country house to another county but the coincidence seemed so remarkable and, since I had already set my heart on Leicestershire and planned my story around it, I changed a few names and stuck to my original plan, in the firm belief that the kind inhabitants of Leicestershire would not take umbrage.

Bird experts will realise that I have stretched the distribution of the golden oriole and nightingale beyond their recognised ranges. I am aware of my misdemeanour: it is one of the joys of writing fiction.